MW01487532

The HOME MAKER

JEWEL E. ANN

USA Today & Wall Street Journal
BESTSELLING AUTHOR

The Homemaker

The Chain of Lakes Series

Jewel E. Ann

This book is a work of fiction. Any resemblances to actual persons, living or dead, events, or locales are purely coincidental.

Copyright © 2025 by Jewel E. Ann

ISBN 978-1-955520-64-5

Paperback Edition

All rights reserved.

This book is a work of fiction and is created without use of AI technology. Any resemblances to actual persons, living or dead, events, or locales are purely coincidental.

Without in any way limiting the author's exclusive rights under copyright, any use of this publication to "train" generative artificial intelligence (AI) technologies to generate text is expressly prohibited. The author reserves all rights to license uses of this work for generative AI training and development of machine learning language models.

Cover Design: Boja99designs

Photo: © Anna Shields Photography

Formatting: Jenn Beach

To the Swifties

Playlist

"**Fortnight**" - Taylor Swift

"**Crazy**" - Patsy Cline, The Jordanaires

"**My Girl**" - The Temptations

"**Dream A Little Dream Of Me**" - The Mamas & The Papas

"**Old Time Rock & Roll**" - Bob Seger

"**I've Got A Crush On You**" - Ella Fitzgerald

"**Put Your Head On My Shoulder**" - Paul Anka

"**Its Bitsy Teenie Weenie Yellow Polka-Dot Bikini**" - Brian Hyland

"**How Sweet It Is (To Be Loved By You)**" - Marvin Gaye

"**Wonderful Tonight**" - Eric Clapton

"**How Did It End?**" - Taylor Swift

"**(I Love You) For Sentimental Reasons**" - Nat King Cole

"**Unbreak**" - Camylio

"**As the World Caves In**" - **Cover** - Chloe Edgecombe

"**Stubborn Love**" - The Lumineers

"**All I Have to Do Is Dream**" - The Everly Brothers

Chapter ONE

Alice

We're all here to play a part. Play it well.

"Do NOT SUCK my husband's dick. It's an old dick that doesn't need to be sucked, so let's just get that out in the open."

I nod with a genuine smile. Wealthy people are the most fascinating creatures with lavish requests and baffling assumptions. The duties of my new position include everything except a blow job.

Got it. That's not on my CV anyway.

Vera Morrison needs a "homemaker" for her husband. And I need a place to live since my rent just went up, and I lost my job as a personal assistant because my boss died. He was kind enough to add me to a "special list" before he passed.

In Minneapolis, the one percenters have a private

network where they share staff recommendations. Everything from drivers and groundskeepers to nannies and sex surrogates.

This position pays twice what I was making, and it includes a well-appointed, *rent-free* guesthouse that's nicer than any place I have ever lived.

"More tea?" Mrs. Morrison offers in a raspy tone like she's losing her voice or perhaps, very Demi Moore. She curls her long black hair behind one ear, exposing a large diamond hoop earring as we politely discuss the duties of the position.

We're surrounded by flawless white furniture in the glass ceiling sunroom that feels more like a cathedral than a place to discuss the age of anyone's dick.

"No, thank you." I clear my throat to hide my impending giggle. I didn't expect the blow job discussion, but it's the highlight of my day.

Last week, I met Mr. Morrison at my first interview. He isn't the guy who needs to pay anyone for sexual favors. If Vera refuses, he's a fifty-seven-year-old real estate developer turned day trader who works out every morning and lives in a fifteen million-dollar home in the Lake of the Isles, Minnesota, and there's a long list of women (and probably a few men) who would happily open wide.

"If you decide to entertain, please ask your guests to park on the street. And if we're not here, you're welcome to use the pool, but don't let anyone in our house."

"Of course. And I won't be entertaining anyone. Well, there's this guy I've been seeing. But it's just casual."

She eyes me with a twinkle of curiosity.

"Sex." I clarify with unwavering confidence. If she can

bring up blow jobs, surely I can mention casual sex. "We get together when he doesn't have his kids."

"Sounds like a lovely arrangement." She offers a wry grin before sipping her tea, maintaining perfect posture and an air of dignity. "This weekend, my daughter, Blair, and her fiancé are arriving from San Francisco. Their wedding is this fall, right before she opens her art studio in SoHo. She's a ceramic artist. Anyway, they'll be staying with us this summer. We have lots of details to iron out for the wedding." Vera sets her cup and saucer on the coffee table. "And come to think of it, if she asks about you, let's call your position something like 'house manager.' My daughter won't understand why her father wants a homemaker. She's a feminist and, much to her father's chagrin, very liberal."

I playfully tsk while shaking my head. I'm apolitical. Blissfully ignorant. Just trying to keep my own shit together. And I have no idea what the current definition of feminism is, but I'm sure someone who needs a wife *and* a homemaker might not embrace feminism.

However, I'm not sure changing my title will hide the obvious, which is I'm being hired to do things Vera doesn't care to do, or maybe she thinks they are beneath her.

Canning.

Gardening.

Ironing.

Polishing silverware that belonged to Mr. Morrison's grandmother.

I'm not *managing* anything.

"All you need to know is I'm the queen." She smirks. "And I don't allow any political discussion when my daughter and husband are in the same house."

I nod several times. That's an excellent rule.

3

"I'll get you a credit card, but for now, you can use mine to pick out some uniform options. Let me show you." Vera taps her phone screen and angles it toward me. She smells like a bold perfume, probably something with a French name in a fancy bottle.

Just when I assume my day can't get any better, she proves me wrong.

"I know what you're thinking," she says.

I'm certain she doesn't.

"But if this is what it takes to keep my husband happy, I think it's worth it."

I inspect the dresses. They're 1950s-style housedresses with buttons, collars, and cuffed short sleeves. The possibilities make me giddy.

"I have a white apron that his mom gave me when we got married, but I've never worn it. You can wear it over your dresses, and he'll be thrilled. Also, he has a"—she snaps her fingers—"what's the right word? Affinity. Yes, he's always had an affinity towards shoes that have ankle straps."

"Oh, wedge heels would look great with this kind of dress," I say.

Vera eyes me for a second before her grin swells. I'm exactly what she's looking for but never thought she'd find. "Wedge heels would be perfect."

Mr. Morrison doesn't have an affinity, he has a fetish, and his wife is being very accommodating. This is how rich people show their love.

When I met Mr. Morrison, he didn't come across as overly demanding or eccentric. Quite charming, actually. Just a nice guy with too much money and a wife who seems committed to fulfilling his needs as long as she doesn't have to do it personally.

"If you need time off, just ask," she says with a hint of desperation, as if my silence means I'm second-guessing everything.

Either this is a great job, and I'd be crazy not to take it, or something will happen and there will be the most obvious "hindsight" moment. But I need a job and a place to live. As long as I don't end up in a dark room, chained to a steel column and used for sex, this might be the best job ever.

"I'll go shopping for uh ... *uniforms* tomorrow."

Vera claps her hands together, rings clinking. "Are you serious? Yes!" She hugs me. "Thank you so much! We'll feel like family before the end of the summer. I promise. And Hunter is a little *quirky,* but totally trustworthy. Now, if you have time, let's go through everything." Vera stands, adjusting the shoulders of her red V-neck dress that fits over her subtle curves like a second skin.

"Now?" I stand too. "Uh, sure."

She loops her arm with mine like we're best friends.

The wife and the homemaker.

Chapter TWO

Alice

The world is filled with peculiar people.
Learn from them.

My first official day starts at five with meditation, followed by a three-mile run around the lake, shower, a protein shake with the meds that keep my brain from malfunctioning, and then I'm out the door. An illuminated path of textured stone pavers, thick green grass, and perfectly manicured hedges connects the guesthouse to the main house. I enter the six-digit code to the back door and step inside, exchanging my leather slip-on shoes for linen wedge pumps with an ankle strap. I wear my hair in a silky, straight ponytail with an elegant, thin headband in corn-flower blue that accents the auburn tresses.

Light eyeshadow and mascara.

A touch of color to my cheeks.

Red lips.

"Good morning, Mr. Morrison," I say, placing his black coffee on a porcelain saucer in front of him as he sits alone in the dining room overlooking the two-tiered fountain with Greek goddess statues in the courtyard.

"Good morning, Alice." He eyes my legs and strapped pumps, returning a slight grin of approval as he inspects the rest of me. "This feels like a dream."

I innocently shrug. "It's just a Thursday."

While he sips his coffee from the gold-rimmed teacup and scrolls through his phone, I finish pan searing his rare-cooked, grass-fed steak, top it with pickled feta, and serve it with a side of blackberries and strawberries from the garden.

"Tell me, Alice, are you up on politics?" he asks, unfolding his napkin onto one leg when I set the plate in front of him. He tips up his chin with a confidence that matches his ten-thousand-dollar Italian cashmere suit.

"Current?" I check to see if he needs his coffee refilled.

He chuckles, offering a flirty smile that's only outshined by the intensity of his blue eyes and thick, dark blond hair with streaks of silver. "Is there any other kind?"

"Historically speaking, yes." I press my lips together to hide my grin.

"Touché. Does that mean you're a history buff?" He nods to the chair beside him.

I hesitate to sit because I have dishes to wash and clothes to launder. But maybe discussing my knowledge of politics over coffee is part of the homemaker's job. When he uses his foot to slide the chair away from the table, I assume that keeping him company during breakfast *is* part of my job, so I sit.

"I'll share my steak with you. Have you eaten?" he asks, cutting into the rare New York strip.

"Thank you, but I've eaten."

"What were we talking about?" He furrows his brow while slowly chewing. "Oh yes," he mumbles, pressing his fist to his mouth while swallowing, "I asked if you're a history buff."

"No. I'm not." I rest my hands on my lap, smoothing the white apron.

"A shame," Hunter says, stabbing his fork into a berry. "But are you a democrat?"

I bat my eyelashes, embodying the role I've been hired to play. "What do you think?"

With a hearty chuckle, he shakes his head. "I don't know what to think about you, yet. What are your hobbies?"

I smile. "Quilting. Soap making. Beekeeping. But I love fishing and skeet shooting too."

He stops mid-chew. After a couple blinks, he swallows, sets his fork down, and adjusts himself. "Careful. I'm a married man. And it's a little early in the morning to get me so aroused. Did Vera tell you to say all of that?"

"Which part don't you believe? The soap making or beekeeping?"

Mr. Morrison's face lights up much like Vera's did when I jumped onboard with the fifties housedresses and ankle-strap shoes.

He slowly nods and adds a wink. "I knew I was going to like you, but you've exceeded all my expectations in less than five minutes."

Now, I'm the one beaming with satisfaction. His words are the equivalent of a standing ovation.

"Good morning, my love." Vera sweeps into the dining

room, wearing white leggings and a zip hoodie from a luxury brand of athleisure wear with her hair twisted into a bun. She stops at the back of his chair and leans forward, kissing his cheek. Then she eyes me. "You look lovely, Alice. Did my husband give you his nod of approval as well?"

I look at him.

Mischief steals his lips. "Alice was just telling me how brilliant and handsome I am."

As she fills her hydrogen water bottle from the glass carafe on the table, she glances up at me. "Alice, dear, you can't compliment Hunter. He's an addict. It's like giving bacon to a dog. Now he's going to chase you with his tongue out until you give him more compliments."

"Isn't it a bit early for you to be up, darling?" Mr. Morrison asks.

"I need to go over things with Alice for this weekend before I meet with my trainer at nine."

"When are the kids arriving?" he asks as they talk over me.

"They'll be here by noon on Saturday."

I slip out of my chair and disappear into the kitchen, where I place the dishes in the sink to wash by hand since they don't like dirty dishes in the dishwasher, which kind of defeats the purpose of having one, in my humble, lower-class opinion.

"Oh, Alice," Vera says, stepping into the kitchen for a green banana from the bunch on the counter, "there are gloves under the sink. You really should wear them. Washing dishes is terrible for your nails."

I don the pink latex gloves and make a mental note to keep my nails manicured.

"I'll see you lovely ladies later," Mr. Morrison says, sauntering into the kitchen and straightening his tie before kissing Vera on her cheek. "I love you," he whispers. "Thanks for breakfast, Alice." He winks at me.

I quickly look away after gawking at the unexpected tender moment between them.

Vera smacks him on the butt. "You're such a flirt. Behave so she doesn't quit."

"You're welcome, Mr. Morrison," I say with a confident smile.

As soon as he's out the door, Vera rolls her eyes. "He won't be gone long. He schedules two business meetings a week. The rest of the time he's either golfing or in his study glued to his computer until the stock market closes for the day. Anyway ..." She flicks her wrist and rattles off a long list of things that need to be done to prepare for Blair and her fiancé's arrival.

After I commit them to memory and return the last clean dish to its spot, Vera slides on her sunglasses and hooks her purse over her arm. "And please remember," she says just as I head toward their bedroom to make the bed and tidy up the bathroom and closet.

"Yes?" I turn.

"Your job title is house manager. And if Blair asks about your attire, please tell her it's your preference."

"Of course, Mrs. Morrison."

"Blair wouldn't understand a hired *homemaker* dressed like a housewife from 1950."

"House manager it is." I knew this job wouldn't disappoint.

Chapter THREE

Murphy

The heart has a flawless memory.
Plan accordingly.

I DON'T KNOW why Blair agreed to stay with her parents for the summer. She and her mom can plan the wedding via phone, text, and video chat. Not that I'm complaining about returning to Minnesota. It's my favorite place on Earth, but Blair and her dad constantly exchange barbs.

"Be nice," Blair says, blowing out a long breath before opening the car door.

"Are you talking to me?"

She opens one eye. "No. I'm giving myself a pep talk. You're fine. My parents love you because you're annoyingly agreeable." She grins and steps out of the white Mercedes SUV, adjusting her tight jeans and pink sleeveless blouse.

I open the back to retrieve our luggage. "You used to call my agreeability *endearing*. What happened?"

"Babe, I want you to agree with me, not with my father."

"I don't agree with your father. See? Look at me being perfectly agreeable with you." I set the suitcases on the ground and close the back.

"Staying out of my arguments with my father is the same as agreeing with him in his eyes. He thinks if you agree with me, you'd say as much. So feel free to *say as much*."

"And risk him kicking me out of his golfing foursome this summer?"

Blair leads the way to the front door, flipping her long, blond hair over her shoulder along with a scowl for me as her rhinestone flip-flops scuff against the pavers.

I laugh. My fiancée is fiery and sexy as hell, but around her dad, she's a nuclear warhead.

"Who's that?" She stops a few feet from the front door, slides her sunglasses down her nose, and glances to the right.

A woman in a yellow dress and white apron, armed with pruning shears, snips pink roses and deposits them into a small bucket. She sets the shears on the ground and squints at the clouds while adjusting her silky, auburn ponytail.

"How would I know?" I ask.

Blair drops her hand from her forehead and opens the door for me.

"Darling," Vera coos, opening her arms to Blair.

"Hi, Mother."

"How was the drive?" Vera asks.

I release the suitcases to hug her. "It was fine, thanks. Where's Hunter?"

Blair scowls at me for asking, and I smirk.

"He's in his study," Vera says. "Get unpacked and settled. I'll see if lunch is about ready."

"Who's the woman out front?" Blair asks, finger-combing her hair in the entry mirror. She added a few dark purple streaks before we left California just to piss off her father.

"Our house manager."

"A house manager?" Blair scoffs. "A maid?"

"No." Vera fiddles with her diamond ring. "Rayne still comes once a week to perform a deep clean. We hired someone to take care of more mundane tasks like preparing meals and gardening."

"I thought you did that." Blair wrinkles her nose.

"I did, but not very well. I'm not domesticated enough for your father's liking, so we thought hiring a house manager would ease the tension around here."

Vera isn't the nervous type, but she seems off. I don't know her well enough to pinpoint anything beyond just ... *off.* She won't look at Blair or me for more than a few seconds.

"Well, let's get unpacked," I say to Blair, carrying the suitcases toward the guest room on the main floor that used to be the primary suite until they converted most of the second floor to the new one. It doesn't have the lake view of the new space, but it's on the opposite side of the house, which means we won't spend the summer wondering if her parents hear us having sex.

"Do you think my mother's acting weird?" Blair asks, carrying a pile of clothes from her suitcase to the closet. "Do you think she's sick? Jesus, what if she has cancer but doesn't want to say anything until after the wedding? What if the house manager is actually the woman she's chosen to replace her after she dies?"

13

"What?" I laugh. "I think you're jumping to conclusions *way* too quickly. Maybe she wants to pacify him and his *needs* without sacrificing her free time by doing all the domestic things he expects."

Blair pokes her head around the corner. "You know as well as I do that my mother has always done what she wants, regardless of my father's opinion."

I shrug, unpacking my jeans. "You're right. Let's just say what we're both thinking."

"What's that?" Blair calls from the closet.

"Polygamy."

"Stop." She snorts.

"Sex therapist?"

"Murphy!" Blair continues to giggle.

"What's all the ruckus?" Vera asks, standing in the doorway.

"Sorry. Your daughter has a wild imagination."

Vera peeks her head around the corner into the closet. "Well, lunch is ready."

"We'll be right there," I say as she turns to leave the room.

"You're nothing but trouble, Murphy Paddon." Blair wraps her arms around my waist.

"That's why you love me." I kiss the top of her head.

She lifts her chin to kiss my neck. "I love you because I'm the best version of myself with you. Come on." She clutches my hand and leads me to the dining room.

"Kids," Hunter says while standing from his chair at the end of the oval dining room table. "Welcome home."

"Father," Blair replies in a begrudging tone before hugging him.

"Mr. Morrison," I hold out my hand.

After releasing Blair, he shakes it. "The engagement is still on, huh? I'm impressed, young man," he says as a jab to Blair because this is the third time she's been engaged, but she has yet to make it to the altar.

I'm either delusional or the most confident man alive for hoping the third time's a charm.

"It's a miracle that she puts up with me." I smile at my fiancée, earning bonus points for "taking her side."

"Tuesday, we meet with the wedding planner," Vera announces, sitting at the opposite end of the table as Hunter while I pull out Blair's chair for her.

"That looks amazing," Vera says when her house manager carries a tray of food to the table.

"Alice, this is our daughter, Blair, and her fiancé, Murphy. Kids, meet our homemaker," Hunter says.

Blair's head whips in his direction. "Homemaker?"

Vera clears her throat. "House manager."

"Dear, you're the only manager," Hunter responds with a side-eye, daring her to dispute it. "Your mom got her for me. An early birthday present. I think it went something like, 'If you want a homemaker, then perhaps I should hire you one.' So I said, 'Sounds good to me.'" Hunter shrugs with a triumphant grin.

Now I know why Vera was nervous about Blair questioning the new help.

"It's nice to meet you," Alice says, setting the tray onto the table.

I lift my head, getting a good look at her because not only is her name triggering, her voice is so familiar it makes the hair on the back of my neck stand up.

Jesus ...

"Chicken and wild rice lettuce wraps. I'll be right back with the rosemary sourdough rolls," she says.

"Your *homemaker* bakes bread?" Blair murmurs.

Just as Alice turns to walk toward the kitchen, our gazes meet, and her steps slow, but her smile doesn't falter, like something that Blair would carve and cook in a kiln.

I know her.

Chapter
FOUR

Alice

Sorrow doesn't care if you live. Do it anyway.

Eight Years Earlier ...

THE LISTING SAID to park in the street, watch for wild turkeys, and remove shoes before entering the house. We had turkeys in Wisconsin, but I've never had an encounter with one. Prior to exiting my car, I googled "are wild turkeys dangerous?" The results were inconclusive, so I scanned the area for large, feathered friends before braving the walk to the front door of the old, two-story house outside of downtown Minneapolis. After entering the code, the door opened to stairs on my left, the vacation rental entrance to my right. A hook below the entry mirror held the keys, and a note card with a smiley face reminding me to remove my shoes. I toed-off my sneakers and set them on the plastic tray before

17

unlocking the door that opened to a living room with a piano to my left, sofa, coffee table, and TV straight ahead. An impressive fig tree sat in the corner by the window.

The wood floor creaked when I walked up the two wide steps to the dining room, furnished with a table for eight and a modern brass fixture. Beyond that was a galley kitchen with avocado green cabinets and white-speckled countertops leading to French doors overlooking a patio. A short hallway to my left connected two bedrooms; in the middle, a bathroom featured a crisp white shower curtain that looked brand-new in contrast to the cracked white subway tiles and stained grout. The rental was old, but clean and cozy.

A note by a basket filled with a bottle of wine, fancy crackers, local honey, nuts and chocolate read:

> Welcome to Fig Cottage, Alice. Make yourself at home and enjoy your stay. Please message me if you have any questions or concerns. There's a folder on the coffee table with house rules and information about the area.
>
> Sincerely,
> Murphy

It exceeded my expectations, an old brick building with fresh renovations—a perfect curation of vintage and quality contemporary pieces. The scattered planters filled with pothos, snake plants, and colorful glass watering bulbs added to the homeyness. But mostly it felt different. Unreal. The perfect escape.

I had yet to see if I liked the feel of the mattress or if the shower had good water pressure, but I'd already decided I never wanted to leave. Two weeks wasn't long enough, but it's all I could spare before my family sent out the search party.

"When in Rome ..." I said with a huge grin while opening the bottle of wine. It was kind of Murphy the Super-host to leave the corkscrew next to the welcome basket. He was off to a good start. I could already see a glowing five-star review in his future.

A turntable sat on a stand below the TV next to a wood crate with vinyl albums. A sweet Lambrusco *and* Sinatra? This Murphy guy was quickly becoming my Lord and Savior of what I declared an alternate universe. Bad shit didn't happen in Fig Cottage because—

"Oh yesss ..." My thoughts sidetracked as I sighed before taking another sip of wine. What a perfect record collection. Louis Armstrong, "Dream A Little Dream Of Me."

Queen.

Norah Jones.

Paul Anka.

Olivia Newton-John.

Lionel Richie.

Superhost Murphy got laid on the regular. Of that, I felt certain. I giggled, suddenly considering the possibility that Murphy was a woman, not a man. That made more sense.

The wine.

Flawless taste in music.

And so many living plants in such a small space.

Murphy was definitely a woman, so we would become fast friends, and maybe I would never leave the alternate universe.

After selecting Paul Anka's 21 *Golden Hits*, I padded back into the kitchen for a little more wine. A black cat with white boots eyed me through the French doors.

"Well, hello, kitty." I opened the door and stepped onto the cedar deck with an L-shaped sectional, rattan chairs, a rectangular, gas fire table, and string lights. A few blooms on a lilac bush remained, offering a hint of sweet floral perfume. The perfect oasis.

I reclined on the sofa, pulling up my white sundress to give my legs some of the glorious late spring sun. Mr. Kitty jumped up next to me and purred the second I ran my hand down his back.

The back door to the detached garage opened, and a dark-haired guy in a blue Minnesota Twins T-shirt, cargo shorts, and white canvas sneakers closed it behind him then paused when he spied me.

I sat up, covering my legs, and smiled. "Hi."

"You must be Alice." He grinned so big, it made me wonder if I'd be charged extra for it.

"Um, yeah. I just arrived." I stared at my wine glass for a second. "Clearly, I've already made myself at home. Are you Murphy?"

"I am." He carried a brown paper grocery bag in one hand while making his way to the split stairs that led to the second level deck. "Welcome. Is everything to your liking? Do you have any questions? Anything you need?" His smile was just as handsome as the rest of him. It all matched his flawless taste in music.

"You're a guy."

He chuckled, and it was kind, maybe even a little shy. "Last I checked."

"Sorry." I laughed. "Everything about the rental is so

spot-on. Too perfect to have been chosen by ..." I pressed my lips together.

"A man?"

I returned a guilty shrug.

He scratched his neck. "I think that's a compliment. What do you think, Palmer?"

"Palmer?" I questioned.

He nodded. "The cat. His name is Arnold Palmer. But we're guys, so I call him Palmer, and he calls me Paddon."

"Palmer and Paddon?"

"Like Batman and Robin."

I giggled.

"He's Batman, of course." Murphy grinned.

"Obviously."

"Well, it's really nice to meet you, Alice. Don't hesitate to knock on my door, call, text, or whatever if you have any questions."

"I'll illuminate the Bat-Signal," I said before sipping my wine.

He shook his head while ascending the stairs.

"Do you have a cat door for Palmer?" I asked.

"No. He's not mine."

"What?" I said, but it was too late; the door closed behind him.

Chapter
FIVE

Alice

Life is improv. There is no dress rehearsal.

I'VE MENTALLY REHEARSED this day for years, just not in this setting. And now I wish I were invisible. But his unblinking, dark-eyed gaze screams recognition, burning beneath my skin, so I bolt into the kitchen and I allow myself a quick gasp. That's it, one breath in for closure. Then I exhale, releasing everything.

"Oh my god," I whisper, pressing my hand over my chest, my heart pounding against it.

He is the fiancé of the Morrisons' only child.

That's it.

I close my eyes and repeat this several times to stay focused.

Don't lose it, Alice.

I'm the hired homemaker. It's my job and the role I've

chosen to play. So I get back into character. Keeping my chin tucked, I straighten my apron, pin a smile to my face, and return to the dining room, despite my pounding heart making it impossible to breathe.

"If there is anything else I can get you, I'll be in the kitchen tidying up," I say, placing the basket of sliced sourdough bread in the center of the table with a shaky hand.

"Thank you, Alice," Mr. Morrison says with pride.

What is Murphy doing here? These people are gloriously fucked-up. Hunter loves the horrified expression on his daughter's face because—who hires a "homemaker?"

"What's going on?" Blair asks, as I crane my neck to listen while setting out the blackberry sorbet to soften.

"What do you mean?" Hunter asks.

"I mean her, the *homemaker.*"

"Sweetie, calm down. It's fine. Your father just likes to get you worked up. When we hired Alice, we teasingly called her a homemaker. It's all in good fun. She's very helpful."

Vera is my favorite character in this bizarre universe, playing both sides of the fence.

Hunter clears his throat. "We're giving her a job. Paying her well. And she gets to live rent-free in the guesthouse. I thought you'd be proud of us for helping those in need."

"Are you kidding me?" Blair's voice shakes. "She's an attractive white girl. How *in need* can she be?" She makes a valid point. "Mother has hired you a mistress."

"Blair Ashlee Morrison, I beg your pardon." Vera's voice slices through the room.

"Are you sure you want to sign up for this, Murphy? My daughter will never bake bread for you."

"I uh ... need to use the restroom," Murphy says.

The sound of his voice unearths memories that no pill can erase.

"Is everything all right, babe?" Blair asks. "Sorry. I'm not trying to start a fight with my father."

I peek my head around the corner as she touches his arm. Murphy gives her a shaky smile. "It's uh … fine," he mumbles.

I jerk my head back to hide, pressing my body to the wall as he passes the kitchen on the way to the bathroom. Then I refocus on the dessert. By the time I have the cups filled with two small scoops of sorbet and garnished with mint leaves, Murphy has returned to the dining room.

"Have you always been a homemaker, Alice?" Blair asks, when I gather the empty plates and replace them with glass cups of sorbet, hands still shaking because I feel *his* gaze on me.

"No, Miss Morrison," I say, clearing my throat. "But I hope your parents are happy with my performance thus far. They are a delight to work for," I say, meaning the word *performance* in the most literal sense.

Mr. and Mrs. Morrison sit up a little straighter, chins an inch higher. Flattery goes a long way in the world of padded bank accounts and over-inflated egos.

"You're doing a great job, Alice," Vera says. "Thank you. That will be all. When you're done in the kitchen, we won't require anything else today."

"What about dinner?" Hunter asks, lifting his spoon toward his mouth.

I try to keep my gaze on him, but I can tell from the corner of my eye that Blair's fiancé isn't touching his sorbet.

"I've made reservations," Vera replies.

"Who will turn down my bed?" Now Hunter's just

toying with his wife and daughter, trolling them for a reaction.

"Excuse me?" Blair takes the bait.

I slowly slink out of the room.

"Your mom has an obsession with throw blankets and decor pillows, so Alice makes a neat pile of everything and folds down the bedding, assuring it's smooth and tight, just how I like it."

"Are we still talking about the bedding?" Vera asks.

"Oh my god, Mother!"

Vera and Hunter laugh while I anxiously wait for everyone to finish their dessert so I can clean up and get the heck out of here.

An hour later, the kitchen is clean, sourdough starter fed, and meals planned for the next day. Mr. Morrison has a button that needs to be repaired on his favorite shirt, but I'll do that tomorrow, since Vera seems eager for me to leave.

"Do you remember me?"

I startle, glancing up as I remove my wedge pumps at the back door and exchange them for my leather slip-ons. My insides twist when I look at him. His shoulders seem broader, more muscular. The shadow of whiskers on his face is thicker. He's just *more* everything in the best possible way.

Murphy eyes me with a forlorn expression, pain etched into his forehead, hands in his front pockets. I pause for a moment. He's giving me a choice? My conscience chews on the agonizing decision for a few seconds.

I'm better now.

He's engaged to my boss's daughter.

What good can come from remembering?

I remove my apron and hang it on the brushed silver hook. "You look familiar, but I can't quite place you." It's a version of the truth, a stretch. But *truthfully*, I don't remember everything, like how it ended.

His brow tightens, as do my heartstrings.

"Remind me?" I say with a cruel casualness that's unplanned but feels necessary.

He won't remind me. Not in this house. Not while he's in love with another woman. *I hope.*

"You ..." He swallows hard.

My breath stays lodged in my throat, strangling my reaction to the anguish in his eyes and the deep lines of indecision on his face, but I feel the emotion, and it pains me because I never meant to hurt anyone. Until this very moment, I didn't know for sure that he was collateral damage.

Murphy forces a smile, and it feels like pure pity. "I don't think it was you after all. Sorry."

His manufactured response tugs and tears at the threads of my soul. This isn't how it was supposed to be. "I guess I must have a familiar face," I say.

This man could send me spiraling. I should resign and run. Nothing good can come from spending the summer this close to each other. My facade will break or his pity will diminish, leaving him with nothing but an uncontrolled need to demand answers.

"Well, I guess I'll see you around," I say.

Despite his effort to look unaffected, I don't miss his tiny flinch. "Yeah," he murmurs.

Under his watchful gaze, I exit the back door.

One breath. Two breaths.

One step. Two steps.

When I'm behind the hedges, I sprint to the guesthouse.

"Hey!"

I gasp, slapping a hand over my heart when Callen grabs my wrist before I reach the door.

"What's wrong?" he asks, eyes narrowed.

I shake my head a half dozen times. "Nothing," I say through labored breaths.

"Why were you running?" He chuckles, turning his baseball cap around for a kiss while walking me backward into the door.

He's here for sex. That's our relationship. Callen is divorced, and he has two kids and a demanding job. Sex is all he's looking for. And I'm emotionally empty most days, so sex works for me.

"How did you know I'd be done so early?" I ask as he kisses my neck.

"I didn't. I was going to make dinner and surprise you."

"Excuse me?" I push him away and grin. "*You* were going to make *me* dinner?"

"Yes. Occasionally, I can be thoughtful." He hooks his arm around my waist again and continues kissing my neck. "It's so fucked up that they make you wear this church dress. When you sent me that picture, I thought you were joking."

I giggle. "I like the dress. What's messed up is they hired some sought-after landscaping guru to give his thoughts on redoing the north side of the house. I saw the bill. They paid fifteen thousand dollars *just* for his opinion."

"Fucking rich people." He opens the door behind me, and we stumble into the single level house with hickory wood floors and modern furnishings, a smaller version of the main house.

I lose both shoes before we pass the sofa.

"Don't you want a tour first?" I mumble between kisses.

Callen partially unbuttons the front of my dress, kissing the swell of my breasts by the time we reach the hallway.

"Kitchen. Hall. Bedroom," he says. "Got it."

We make it two more steps before his jeans are unfastened, one more step before my underwear dangles around one ankle. And then he's inside me.

I toss his hat to the floor, rubbing a hand over his buzzed, blond hair before closing my eyes and clawing at his firm backside as he pins me to the wall.

Then ... I think of Murphy Paddon.

Callen Langston coaches lacrosse at the university, is obsessed with true crime podcasts, and knows a freakish amount of random information. He's fun and easy. I've never met his kids, but when I mention them, he beams with fatherly pride.

After dropping out of college my junior year, spending fourteen months in a mental hospital, and seven years working odd jobs to find inspiration, I've given up on love and a successful career. But I take great joy in other people's lives.

Some people are participants. Others, like me, are spectators.

"What was that about?" Callen asks as we put our clothes back on.

I exchange my dress for shorts and a tank top. "What was what all about?"

"Sex with you has been good, really good." His cheeks flush as he buttons his jeans. "But that was next-level."

I pull the tank top over my head. "I don't know. When you said you were here early to make me dinner, it just ..."

"Made you horny?" he chuckles.

"Something like that." I grab his shirt and kiss him.

"When are you going to Disney?" I pad my bare feet into the kitchen for an orange Olipop soda.

"Next week. Are you good with it?"

I pop the top of the can. "I think it's cool that you and your ex get along well enough to take the kids on vacation together."

"Lindee and Hawley."

I narrow my eyes. "Huh?"

"You never say my kids' names. My daughter is Lindee. She's five, and my son is Hawley. He's seven. You always refer to them just as *kids*."

"Thought we were keeping it casual." I sip my drink.

"Alice, do you not like kids?"

"I like them." I chuckle.

"If I were standing in line for something, I could easily strike up a conversation with a stranger, and it could lead to me revealing my kids' names and ages. I'm not asking you to meet them or be their godmother." Callen laughs, filling a glass with water.

"Lindee and Hawley are great names."

He sips his water then nods. "Thanks. They're great kids. Now, if you want to share something about your personal life, I'm happy to listen in a very casual way."

"Thanks." I smile.

"Thanks? That's it?"

29

"What do you want me to say? I told you I didn't finish college, and I've worked odd jobs for the past seven years."

"But you never said why you dropped out of school."

I sit on the barstool at the counter. "Why does anyone drop out of school?"

"Failing grades. Lack of interest or money. Life-changing event. Job offer that doesn't require a degree. There are a lot of reasons. What was yours?"

I drum my fingers on the side of the can. "A friend died, and I lost focus and desire to continue with school."

He eyes me for a beat before slowly shaking his head. "I'm sorry to hear about your friend."

"Thanks."

"See, that wasn't so hard."

"No. It wasn't. Do you want to tell me more about your kids?"

He sits on the stool beside me so my knees slide between his spread legs. "No. We'll take it slow. Names and ages are good for today."

I giggle. "Stop. Point made. I can handle it."

"Let's talk about your job. Aside from free rent, do you like it?"

"Yeah. So far. It's too early to say, but they're fascinating, and it's oddly satisfying."

"Fascinating? Satisfying?"

"Mmm. Yes. The wealthy live such different lives. They have time to worry about stupid shit like politics and if the hedges need to be trimmed one or two inches. And they have the luxury of fixing everything with money, including things that are less than perfect in their marriage. I feel like a missing link. The glue that could hold their marriage together. Like the opposite of the mistress that tears happy couples apart."

"That's weird."

I sip my orange drink then laugh. "I think the less Vera resents doing things she doesn't like to do, and the less Hunter resents her not doing what he thinks a wife should do, the less they fight. Boom! Happy marriage."

"Spoken like someone who has never been married."

"Spoken like someone who is no longer married. You haven't told me why your marriage ended."

He opens his mouth.

I shake my head. "Nope. I don't want to know. That's more than you'd tell a stranger in line."

"God I love your fear of commitment." Callen slides off the barstool and kisses my cheek. "Your eagerness to screw." He finishes his water and sets the glass in the sink. "And your complete lack of neediness. You're a fucking dream, Alice."

"I do my best."

My thoughts drift to Murphy. He must think I'm a fucking nightmare.

Chapter SIX

Murphy

It doesn't have to make sense now.
It will ... eventually.

"SERIOUSLY. What if she's dying, and she's decided to find her replacement now?" Blair asks, as we stretch on our side of the pickleball net while we wait for her parents to join us. "Murphy, are you listening to me?"

"Uh-huh," I mumble. My focus is shit. It's taken me years to move past the best and worst two weeks of my life.

And now, Alice is here, and she doesn't remember me. Maybe that's good, but my heart feels every scar she left behind.

"And what's with the housedress and apron? Hair in the perfect ponytail? Heels? Murphy, that woman wears heels to do housework. It's weird, like she's doing it to impress my father. I know my parents can be a little eccentric, but a *homemaker?* He needs therapy. Right? Murphy?"

"Huh?" I muster a convincing smile.

Blair frowns. "What is going on with you? You've been off today. Everyone is acting strange except me. Is there something in the water?" Blair steps in front of me, demanding my attention as I focus on the guesthouse.

"I don't think your mom is sick," I mumble, refocusing on the woman I'm going to marry instead of the woman who derailed my life and made me question said life's purpose.

"Ready to have your clocks cleaned by people twice your age?" Hunter asks as he and Vera take the court in matching white shorts and light green polos.

We laugh it off, but then her parents make us chase the plastic ball around the court for two hours, kicking our asses. After the women head inside to get showered for dinner. Hunter fetches two bottles of beer, and we sit by the pool.

"My daughter's pissed about Alice," he says.

I take a swig of my beer and shrug. "She thinks Vera is ill, and"— it hurts to say her name, but I do it anyway—"Alice is her replacement in training."

He barks a laugh. "That would be something. Vera's not terminally ill. Blair just doesn't understand our marriage. You kids are young, and you only see the first stage of love. Think of it like hot chocolate with marshmallows. It looks amazing when it's fresh and hot. It's really sweet. And you just can't stop licking and sucking on the marshmallows. Well, that's the early years of marriage. Then the marshmallows shrink. They're not the mouthful they used to be, not as firm, and the chocolate isn't as hot as it used to be. But then, you realize all it needs is thirty seconds in the microwave and a handful of new marshmallows, and suddenly you like your hot chocolate again. See what I mean?"

Nope. I have no clue how he came up with that analogy. Is Alice supposed to be a marshmallow? Was Vera once a marshmallow? Is she smaller and not as firm? I'm so damn confused. And I don't like the images in my head right now.

I squint against the sun. "Does your *house manager* wear a uniform? Or are her outfits her own choice?" Talking about Alice isn't easy, but we can't stay on the marshmallow topic any longer.

Hunter chuckles, leaning his head back and closing his eyes. "It was just a suggestion. Vera said Alice seemed excited about it. Besides, a lot of jobs have uniforms. It's not like I'm asking her to be a bunny in my mansion or wear shirts that show off her hooters."

This conversation is so far off the rails, it's making me nauseous.

"What do you know about her?"

"Alice?"

I nod.

"She's witty, which means she's probably smart. But I don't know a lot about her yet. I've tried to drag stuff out of her, but she works the conversation in the direction she wants it to go. I think she works *me*." He grins. "Maybe better than Vera. And I respect that. I like a woman who knows she wields power. Hell, Vera hiring me a homemaker was a queen move. And don't you dare tell Blair I said that, or I will deny it. I'm being manipulated. Vera likes her cushy life and can't be bothered with things like making dinner, ironing, or stroking my ego. Make no mistake about it; *I'm* the victim."

He finishes his beer as we stare at the pool and listen to

the birds and lawnmowers in the distance, the sweet aroma of fresh cut grass mixing with the breeze. "I have a few things to do before I shower. Can I get you another beer before I head inside?"

"I'm good, but thanks," I say.

After Hunter disappears into the house, I set my half-empty bottle of beer on the table next to my chair and stroll toward the guesthouse between the perfectly trimmed hedges. When a man exits, I stop and step aside out of view. Alice follows him to his gray truck on the street. She's no longer in "uniform." Instead, she's wearing shorts, a tight, white tank top, and flip-flops. Her ponytail is gone, hair messy and blowing in the breeze. *My* Alice had shorter, blond hair.

The guy turns his baseball cap backwards and stops at his truck to kiss her, palming her ass as she wraps her arms around him. After he pulls away from the curb, Alice turns, stopping when she sees me, lifting a hand in a polite beauty queen wave before disappearing around the corner.

How can she not remember?

Chapter SEVEN

Murphy

High expectations are a gift.
Someone believes in you.

Eight Years Earlier ...

MY WORK-FROM-HOME OFFICE consisted of a desk and computer facing a window overlooking the backyard. Alice Yates, my cat-loving renter, sat on the deck, sipping coffee while petting Arnold Palmer. She seemed to stare off into the distance at nothing at all, slowly bringing her mug to her lips for a sip. It took her nearly an hour to drink her coffee. I studied her like a gallery painting, mesmerized and consumed with curiosity.

Maybe it was her form of meditation, but she looked sad and lost. Even when the breeze blew her blond, bobbed hair into her face, she didn't push it away. Occasionally, she'd squint as if confused or focused on a problem.

I typed for ten or so minutes and took a break to see if she had moved. For someone doing nothing at all, she was incredibly distracting. As a rental owner, I tried to make myself as invisible as possible, but I felt an unusual urge to check on her again, just to see if she was okay.

I had no errands to run, but I grabbed my keys as though I did. She swung her gaze to me as I descended the back stairs and gave me a beauty queen wave with a smile that looked equal parts shy and mischievous.

"Good morning. Is everything meeting your expectations? Can I make any restaurant suggestions? Places to explore or shop?"

She corkscrewed her lips for a beat. "Seems a little risky."

"Oh?" I stepped onto the deck, fiddling with my keys. She made me nervous with one look. It was the first time any woman had rattled me with nothing more than a smile.

Her blue eyes gleamed with curiosity. Her subtle moves oozed confidence.

"I have you on such a high pedestal. One wrong suggestion could ruin everything. Pizza with an inaccurate cheese to crust ratio. Tacos with pre-made guacamole. A clothing store that's a chain."

I scratched the back of my head. "Can I uh ... ask what I did to be put on a high pedestal?"

She emptied the last drips of coffee into her mouth and rubbed her lips together. "Your vinyl record collection is flawless. Your fig tree is thriving. And the jar of local honey is chef's kiss."

"Well—"

"Don't." She held out a flat palm and cut me off. "Don't say anything like your girlfriend picked everything out. Or the vinyl records are throwaways that used to belong to your grandfather. I really like what's in my head right now. I *need* it. So just"—her nose wrinkled—"don't ruin it for me."

"You like," I pointed to the door, "my oldies collection?"

She nodded slowly. "My dad inherited his parents' collection, along with a wood console record player that was a turntable on one end and storage for vinyl records on the other end. My mom hated it because it was so big and ugly. The music was unlike anything I had ever heard before. The first time I listened to Brian Hyland's 'Itsy Bitsy Teenie Weenie Yellow Polka Dot Bikini' I was hooked. Like, who sings songs like that anymore?" She grinned. "No one."

I got down on one knee. "Will you marry me?"

Alice giggled. It was the perfect giggle. Innocent and sincere.

I stood, suddenly feeling like an imbecile. "It was, in fact, part of my grandfather's massive collection, but nothing in it is a throwaway. If you so much as scratch one album, you will lose your deposit."

"That's harsh."

I shrugged, sliding one hand into my back jeans pocket. "In all seriousness, if there is anything you need, please let me know."

She nodded toward the cornhole game in the yard. "What if I need someone to play cornhole with me?"

"Well," I glanced at my watch, "I have a quick errand to run. But when I get back, I'll play with you." I cleared my throat and shook my head. "That came out all wrong. I'll play cornhole with you. Damn," I pinched the bridge of my nose, "that might sound bad too."

"I don't expect you to do that. I'm sure you have things to do."

"Nothing pressing." That was a lie. I had a project due the next morning. And I had no errands to run. Yet, I told her I did because I didn't want to seem too anxious. So I would run my fake errands, then play cornhole with her while I fell further behind on meeting the deadline that I acted like I didn't have.

Good job, Murph. You're an idiot.

"Well, you know where I'll be." She jabbed a thumb toward the door. "Inside, listening to your grandpa's records and drinking wine."

"Wine after coffee?" Again, I looked at my watch for a dramatic effect. "It's not even ten."

"And this isn't my real life." She stood and sauntered to the door. "So the rules don't apply to me."

Alice was mysterious and ... trouble. But I was past due for a little trouble, so I drove around for forty-five minutes, stopping for a coffee before returning.

"Where is she, Palmer?" I asked, closing the garage door behind me.

He meowed.

I retrieved the bean bags from the sack and tossed a few, only hitting the hole once.

"Are you cheating?"

I turned toward Alice's voice.

"Practicing to get a leg up?" she asked, descending the stairs from the deck to the yard while slipping on big black sunglasses. Her toned legs in her sleek shorts were almost as distracting as her fitted white T-shirt that said "Bite Me" with a fishhook.

Done. Whatever bait she dangled in front of me, I was

already chasing.

"Be my guest. Practice as much as you want," I said, collecting the bags and handing her the red ones.

"Nah. I'm good. Let's just start." Alice tossed one bag in the hole. Followed by another, and another. The fourth bag stopped just shy of the hole. She frowned. "Maybe I should have taken a few warm-up shots."

I was screwed and should have stayed at my desk, pondering all the possible reasons she looked lost and lonely.

"I think I'm being hustled." I narrowed my eyes at her.

Her red lips curled, revealing her white teeth. "Oh, I'm taking pity on you by missing one on purpose."

"Christ," I mumbled, tossing the first bag, missing the board all together because she had me so rattled. The second bag made it onto the board, two feet from the hole. The third bag slid into the hole, and the fourth slid off the end.

"Getting it into the hole twenty-five percent of the time isn't bad." She pulled her glasses down her nose for a second while giving me a look, an ornery gleam in her eyes.

Was that a shot at my manhood?

"So tell me, Murphy," she collected her bags, "does Arnold Palmer's owner know you stole him?"

"I did no such thing." I tried not to roll my eyes when she hit the hole again. "My neighbor, Rosie, found the cat, and she asked if I wanted him. I said, 'Nope.' So she feeds him, and I think she even took him to the vet, but she won't let him in her house. She's nearly eighty and widowed but refuses to be 'an old cat lady.' He hangs out here, unless it's time to eat. And during the winter, I let him stay in my garage. He keeps the mice population in check."

"So he's basically your cat." Again, she only missed tossing one bag into the hole.

"He's absolutely not my cat. There's a robin's nest in that tree. The tree is mine, but the birds are not. Palmer is a neighborhood cat. Everyone knows him and likes him, but no one wants to invite him into their home."

"Huh. That's sad. Maybe he should sleep with me while I'm here."

"No pets in the rental." I shot her a stern look before tossing my bags.

"Oh, gotcha. Winky wink. *No* pets in the rental."

"What? No. What's with your 'winky wink?' No *winky wink*. No pets in the rental. Period. No exceptions."

"Cats are clean and curious. Excellent companions," she said.

Only two of my bags made it onto the board. "Are you kidding me?" The last bag I tossed pushed her fourth bag into the hole, but my bag stopped short of dropping.

"No. I'm serious. Cats are—"

"I'm talking about my stupid bag, not your incorrect facts about cats."

"What's incorrect?"

We gathered our bags.

"They are not excellent companions. Dogs are."

"That's your opinion. But it's a fact that they are clean and curious."

I used three of my bags, tossing them into the air to juggle. "Oh yeah? Well, I'm clean and curious. Does that mean you want me in your bed?"

Shit.

That sounded different in my head. There went my perfect host rating. Who would want to stay at my place after Alice's one-star rating with a review that stated how I asked if she wanted me in her bed?

"Sorry, Murphy. Once again, I can't risk letting you fall off that high pedestal."

She took a weed whacker to my manhood in the most subtle ways, and she did so with a smile. Of course, I wanted to know if she was really suggesting I might not be good in bed. But I couldn't ask her. After all, the customer was always right.

"You won," I said.

She beat me in less than five minutes.

Alice rested a hand on her hip and nodded slowly, inspecting the boards like a crime scene. "Sorry about that. I'll let you win next time."

I lifted my eyebrows. "Are you serious? You'll *let* me win? That makes me feel great." I laughed.

Corkscrewing her lips, she repeated her slow nod. "Again, I'm sorry."

"Alice Yates." I held out my hand. "It's been a pleasure. But you are so far out of my league, I will most certainly fall off that pedestal. Again, if you need anything, let me know. Otherwise, enjoy your stay, and please leave a review if you have time—on the rental, not my cornhole skills."

She lifted her sunglasses onto her head and eyed me from head to toe, grinning like a fool while shaking my hand. "I didn't take you for a quitter. Granted, that's just me judging you based on your handsome smile, thick dark hair, and height. I didn't think it was possible to be over six feet tall and be a quitter."

"And the hits just keep coming." I pressed a hand to my chest and stumbled backward.

"Let me make you dinner to make up for the loss."

"I shouldn't. But thank you."

"Girlfriend?"

I shook my head.

"Wife?"

"No. I just can't risk anything going wrong and you leaving me a bad review."

Her grin swelled. "I'm an excellent cook."

I chuckled, heading toward the stairs. "Alice, I have no doubt that you're excellent at literally everything. Enjoy your stay."

Chapter EIGHT

Alice

Life is a journey.
But don't forget it's still a circle.

SUNDAY MORNING, I tend to the garden on my hands and knees, picking vegetables for the day's meals. At the sound of laughter, I glance over my shoulder.

Blair and Murphy have returned from a run, and they're stretching by the back door. He says something, and she throws her head back in laughter. Then she pulls the tie from her hair, letting her thick, sweaty tresses fall down her perfectly tanned back. She's the blonde I used to dream of being before tiring from my roots growing out.

Murphy opens the back door, and Blair lifts her leg. He squats in front of her to remove her shoes. She lovingly runs her hands through his hair, her enormous diamond catching the sun's rays like God himself is winking at her for finding the perfect man.

I have no good reason to hate her, but it's going to be a long summer, and I'm afraid I'll do it anyway.

After I finish in the garden, I set the basket of veggies aside and run back to my place to wash up and slip on a light blue dress with a white collar and buttons.

Minutes later, I'm in their kitchen with my strappy pumps and white apron, cleaning the vegetables while the breakfast casserole cooks in the oven.

"Good morning, Alice," Mr. Morrison says, his voice deep and husky. Manly, like his pungent spice cologne.

"Good morning," I say, scrubbing the vegetables from the garden. "A breakfast casserole is in the oven. Can I get you coffee?"

"Is there red meat in the casserole?" he asks, pulling a glass bottle of water from the fridge.

"Turkey sausage, per Mrs. Morrison's request."

"I'll take my usual, Alice. Thanks." He saunters out of the kitchen.

I sigh, shutting off the water and drying my hands before pulling a steak wrapped in butcher paper from the fridge. As soon as I have it seasoned and in the hot cast-iron skillet to sear, I serve Mr. Morrison his coffee.

"Murphy!" Blair squeals playfully from the other side of the house.

Mr. Morrison rolls his eyes, lifting his cup of coffee to his lips as I set a fork and steak knife on a cloth napkin next to his saucer. "How would you feel about staying in the main house this summer so we can kick those two out into the guesthouse?"

"Oooh ... a promotion already?"

He shakes his head. "I'm kidding. Sort of."

I return a polite grin before heading back to the kitchen to turn the steak. After it's flipped, I trim the flowers I cut from the bed on the south side of the house and arrange them into a vase for the dining room table, anything to keep from thinking about Murphy playfully doing god knows what to his future wife.

"Oh, wow. You work on Sundays?" Blair asks, tightening the sash on her white robe, towel wrapped around her head.

"Good morning. And yes, I work on Sundays. Can I get you coffee?"

"I'll make it. You don't know how I like it." She reaches for a mug.

"Splash of soy milk, dash of cinnamon." I smile, wiping my hands on a towel.

Blair's perfectly sculpted eyebrows lift a fraction. "My mom prepared you."

"Yes, Miss Morrison."

"Please," she rolls her eyes and shakes her head, "don't call me Miss Morrison. My name is Blair. I'll be a Paddon soon. And I can get my own coffee." She pours the coffee into her cup and retrieves the soy milk from the fridge, so I transfer Hunter's steak to the lower oven and check on the casserole in the top oven.

"So you cook, garden, and arrange flowers?" Blair asks, plucking the jar of cinnamon from the hidden spice rack. "What else do you do for my inept father?"

"I'm going to mend a button on his shirt after breakfast. And while everyone is eating, I'll make the beds and water the houseplants. Then I'll—"

"That's enough." Blair laughs while shaking her head and recapping the cinnamon. "Never mind. I don't want to know. It's all too weird." She sips her coffee. "My mother used to mend my dad's shirts." She eyes me. "But she didn't do it wearing a dress and heels. I thought my mother was sick, but it's clearly just my father who is unwell." She heads into the dining room before I can respond.

I finish the arrangement and pivot to take it to the dining room just as Murphy steps into the kitchen with chaotic wet hair, navy shorts, and a white polo shirt.

Despite my breath catching, I find a quick smile. "Good morning, Mr. Paddon."

He pauses, opening the cabinet door to the glasses. "How do you know my last name?"

I don't miss the hope in his eyes.

"Miss Morrison said she'll be a Paddon soon."

He presses his lips together after a few seconds and nods while retrieving a glass.

"Can I get you coffee?"

"Um, sure. Thanks. I like it—"

"Black," I say, taking two steps and stopping with a hard swallow.

"How do you know that?"

"Mrs. Morrison told me."

She did not.

"It's strange that she knows that," he says.

"Not really. She's observant and resourceful." I continue to the dining room.

After everyone finishes breakfast, the kitchen is clean, beds are made, and I've mended the missing button, I head outside to check the stock of towels by the pool and raise the sun umbrellas.

When I turn the corner, Murphy glances up from his book. He's in a lounger by himself.

"Did you get left behind?"

He rests the open book face down on his chest and slides his aviator sunglasses to the tip of his nose. "Blair and Vera went shopping. And Hunter took one of his cars for a joyride."

I open the towel bin. "And you didn't get invited on his joyride?"

"He invited me, but I passed because he smokes cigars on his joyrides, and even in a convertible, I end up eating half the smoke."

I crank up the sun umbrella over one of the tables. "Is there anything I can get you? A drink? Music? Sunscreen?"

"Hunter has a turntable in his study with an impressive vinyl collection," he says.

I blink several times before nodding. "I'm aware. But I don't think he'd want me bringing it out here by the pool for you."

Murphy deflates because I don't take the bait.

I lace my fingers behind my back. "Anything else?"

"Do you play pickleball?"

I glance toward the court. "I have played. I'm not that good."

"No?" He cocks his head to the side. "You seem like the type of person who is good at a lot of things."

"Why do you say that?" I squint against the sun, using my hand on my forehead as a visor.

"You cook, clean, sew, garden, arrange flowers. And make the perfect steak. Need I say more? Is there anything you can't do?"

"Plenty."

He stares at me as if I'll change my answer. When I

don't, he pushes his glasses back up his nose. "Are you originally from Minnesota?"

"Wisconsin."

"What brought you to Minneapolis?"

My facade is precarious at best. *He* brought me to Minneapolis.

"Urban amenities."

He shifts his attention to the water and the lone orange pool float in the middle. "Are you married?"

"Why? Do you need advice before you say your vows?"

The corner of his mouth twitches. "Do you have advice before I take my vows?"

"My mom would say, don't think you can change her. Blair will change, because people do. But she'll become who she needs to be, not who you want her to be."

"I shouldn't expect her to be a homemaker if that's not who she is now?"

I smile and pick up a few dead flower petals before they blow into the pool. "Exactly," I say with a tiny laugh while walking away.

"You didn't answer my question," he calls.

I stop without turning.

"Are you married?"

I continue walking.

Chapter NINE

Alice

Humans are not that complex.
We're all in search of pleasure.

Eight Years Earlier ...

NOTHING WAS off the table in the imaginary world I'd created.

Wine for breakfast.

Chocolate for lunch.

Three o'clock naps.

Sex with strangers.

It wasn't like the world would end—because it already had.

I pan seared a ribeye at nine in the evening with tongs in my right hand, an open bottle of wine in my left, and Ella Fitzgerald singing "I've Got A Crush On You." While I twirled in a circle, something moved outside. Through the French doors, my gaze locked with Murphy's as he picked up Palmer on his way from the garage to his stairs under the soft glow of the string lights.

I set my wine on the counter and opened the door. "Hungry?"

He stroked the cat's back several times before setting him on the ground. "It's late."

I wrinkled my nose. "Is the music too loud?"

"No. I'm implying I've already had dinner."

I snapped the tongs at him. "I'm not asking if you've had dinner. I'm asking if you're hungry."

"I'm good."

"Of course you're good, but I make a mean steak that's better than good."

Murphy offered a shy grin as he tucked his chin and rubbed the back of his neck. Did I make him nervous?

"I need to—" he began.

"Wash your hair?"

He glanced up with a goofy grin.

"Just come inside while you think up a better excuse than that." I waved toward the door. "I need to flip and baste my perfect steak." As I turned the sizzling steak, Murphy stepped inside, closing the door behind him, but he didn't go any farther.

"Remove your shoes. House rules," I said. "Unless you're not staying because you need to wash your hair. And I would totally understand because you have great hair. It's thick and the perfect amount of messy." I sipped my wine from the bottle. "I've been a blonde for two years. It was fun for a while, but the upkeep is exhausting."

"What's your natural color?" he asked, toeing off his sneakers.

"Murphy, you never ask a lady about her natural hair color." I narrowed my eyes at him before setting the bottle on the counter beside the stove.

"It smells amazing in here," he said, taking a few steps toward me then leaning his shoulder against the fridge.

I basted the steak with a spoon. "Butter, fresh garlic, and rosemary."

He nodded, narrowing his eyes. "Are you married?"

I shut off the stove and transferred the steak to a cutting board. "Are you asking me this because I can cook? You think only wives can cook?"

"I think wives wear wedding bands on their left ring fingers."

I looked at my hand and the emerald-cut diamond eternity band. "Oh, I found it." I sliced the ribeye against the grain in half-inch strips. "Hope you like your steak medium-well."

"That diamond band is quite the find."

"I don't have steak sauce, but you won't need it. This baby can stand on its own." I grinned, cutting the perfect bite and holding it toward his mouth.

Murphy retracted his head a few inches, eyeing my offering. "I don't want to eat your dinner."

"This isn't my dinner." I moved the bite until it touched his lips.

He opened his mouth and took it.

"Perfect, huh?" I grinned as he slowly chewed.

"It kind of is," he mumbled, reaching past me to tear a paper towel from the roll to blot his lips.

"Wine?" I offered him the bottle.

"What's going on? It's a Wednesday. This *isn't* your dinner. You're offering me wine from the bottle you've been drinking from. And you have a 'found' diamond wedding band on your finger."

I stared at him while picking up a strip of steak, bringing it close to my lips. "Are you a germaphobe? It's cool if you are."

"Are you married? It's cool if you are," he said, sliding his hands into his back jeans pockets.

I grinned before taking a swig of wine. Then I moved the band from my left hand to my right. "Better? And who says a diamond band has to be a wedding band?"

Murphy's gaze remained on the ring, so I removed it and opened the cabinet, taking a wine glass out and setting the ring in the empty spot. After wiping my germs from the bottle, I filled his glass halfway. He stared at it, then shifted his focus to the cabinet where I left the ring.

"It's sweet that you care," I said, handing him the glass.

He accepted it and brought it to his lips. "What do you mean?"

I took another bite of steak and shrugged a shoulder while chewing. "You're not the guy who has sex with another man's wife."

He choked, setting the glass on the counter while holding a fist to his mouth as he coughed. "W-Who said," he coughed again, "anything about sex?"

"I know ... I know." I rubbed my forehead. "It's risky with you so high on that pedestal. But despite your pitiful performance at cornhole, I think you *have* to be good in bed."

His cheeks filled with a blush. "How much wine have you had?"

I made a pitiful attempt at hiding my grin, which should

have been the answer to his question. "Tonight? Today? Or like ever?"

Murphy blinked with no discernible change in his expression, so I handed him the plate of steak and spun in the opposite direction, padding my way toward his collection of records.

"Are your hands clean?" he asked.

I smirked, wiping them on the front of my frayed denim shorts. "They are now." I swapped out Ella for The Mamas and Papas, "Dream A Little Dream Of Me."

Murphy plucked a strip of steak from the plate before setting it on the dining room table and descending the two steps into the living room.

"Do you happen to have an open slot on your dance card tonight?" I asked.

He shook his head, licking his buttery fingers. "Gentlemen don't have dance cards. Women wear them around their wrists or attached to their formal gowns. So it is I who should ask you if your dance card is full."

I flipped my wrist, looking at my imaginary dance card. "Nope. It's empty because I step on toes. No one wants to dance with me."

Murphy tried to suppress his grin while studying me. I didn't want to be figured out, I just wanted him to dance with me.

He bent one arm behind his back while bowing and offering me his other hand. "May I have this dance?"

With my thumbs tucked into the front pockets of my shorts, I twisted my lips to the side for a few seconds. "I suppose." I rested my hand in his, and he jerked me into his body, making me gasp as one hand rested confidently on my lower back while his other clasped with mine a few inches from my face.

He led. I followed. Well, I tried.

"You are truly an awful dancer, Alice Yates."

My two left feet didn't keep him from swinging me around the living room, dodging the coffee table and sofa. As the song ended, I risked a quick glance up at him. His hazel eyes ensnared me.

The wine.

The music.

The embrace of a stranger with great hair and a killer smile.

It was the best escape.

The next song on the track brought us out of the moment, and whatever was or wasn't about to happen, because the song was just flat-out weird.

I released his hand and covered my mouth to muffle my laughter. "What is this?"

He chuckled, stepping past me to turn off the music and slide the record back into its sleeve. "Who taught you to cook?"

"YouTube," I said.

He looked over his shoulder. "Seriously?"

I nodded.

"Well, thanks for sharing your dinner with me."

I shook my head. "I told you. It's not my dinner."

"You just what? Get a hankering for a steak at nine o'clock at night?"

"Something like that. You should take the rest with you. Crack some eggs in the morning. Put a little cream in your coffee." I grabbed the plate and handed it to him. "Just return the plate or I'll get fined."

"I like my coffee black."

I hesitated before returning a slow nod. "Okay. I'll remember that."

He scraped his teeth along his bottom lip. "I uh ... thought we were going to have sex."

My eyes widened. "Oh. Well, I mean—"

A shit-eating grin engulfed his face as he brushed past me toward the back door. "Good night, Alice."

Chapter TEN

Murphy

*If we are what we eat, make every plate beautiful, every
bite vibrant with flavor and color.*

WEEKS FLOAT by in an endless loop of monotony. Blair and
Vera spend an ungodly amount of time planning a wedding
that I've been told will be "simple and intimate." When I
offer to help, they chuckle like the idea is ridiculous.

I get work done on my computer at the desk in our
bedroom on the days I'm not golfing with Hunter. The
"homemaker" haunts me because I can't look at her as a
stranger in a dress and white apron. Instead, every time I see
Alice, I look for a spark of recognition, and I swallow all the
unanswered questions that race to the tip of my tongue.
When we make brief eye contact, she offers the same
perfected smile before asking if she can get me anything.

"Vera?" Hunter calls with agitation to his voice. "Vera!"

I poke my head out of the bedroom just as he stomps toward the front door.

"Are the women not back yet?" he asks me in a grumble.

"Not yet. Something wrong?"

"I'm speaking at a charity auction, and I can't get this fucking bow tie to look right."

"Mr. Morrison?"

Our attention shifts to Alice as she saunters toward him with ease and confidence. "Let me," she says, reaching for his bow tie.

He relaxes in tiny increments because that's the effect she has on everyone, except me. I want to shake her and demand she remember me, tell me what happened so I can get rid of this guilt.

"Did Vera teach you how to do this?" Hunter asks.

Her delicate, steady hands work the tie. "Vera told me I should know how to tie all your ties. But YouTube taught me." She smirks, shifting her gaze to his face for a moment, like she adores him as much as he adores her. Fuck, maybe Vera *is* dying, and Alice will be the replacement. That makes me nauseous.

"Do you want to go to this auction with me?" Hunter lifts a suggestive eyebrow.

"Not particularly." Alice gives him a big, cheesy smile while refocusing on his tie.

"Oh, come on. Vera never goes to auction dinners with me. Besides, all our friends know she hired me a homemaker. I'm the envy of the neighborhood and everyone in our social circle." He glances back at me. "Murphy, you'll understand after twenty-plus years of marriage."

"There," Alice says, taking a step back to admire her work.

Hunter turns toward the entry mirror. "Not bad."

"Thank you." She smiles, bending into a playful curtsy.

"There will be a band. Do you like to dance?" Hunter looks at her reflection in the mirror.

"Yes, by myself, with the shades drawn."

He laughs. "Then we'd be in trouble. Vera is the dancer, so I let her lead. Blair loves to dance, too. What about you, Murphy?" He turns away from the mirror. "Can you dance?"

I look to Alice for any sort of recognition, but she offers nothing more than a soft smile while waiting for my response like she doesn't know the answer. And once again it hits me —she doesn't. God, this is torture.

"I'm okay," I say just as my phone vibrates on the desk, so I retreat to check my message. "Blair just messaged me," I say. "She and Vera are going to dinner with friends. Vera wants me to go to the auction with you." I step outside of the bedroom with my phone. "I can lead when we dance."

Alice snorts.

"Or you can go by yourself," I say, "and I can get some more work done."

Hunter nods. "Alice can make you dinner."

"I can make my dinner." When I look at her, she averts her gaze. Did I offend her?

"Looks like you have the night off, Alice." Hunter struts up the stairs.

"I'll finish organizing your study before I go," she says.

"You're a gem, thank you."

She smooths her hands down the front of her apron. A stranger before me. But all I see are the familiar things. The blue eyes. Turned-up nose. Bow-shaped lips. Delicate fingers with trimmed nails. A mole on her neck that I've kissed countless times. The three-inch scar on her right arm that I've traced with the pad of my finger.

"Would you have gone with him had he pushed you on it?" I ask.

"Of course."

I slip my phone into my pocket. "Really? Do you *like* this job?"

Alice folds her hands in front of her, fingers relaxed. "It's the best job I've ever had."

I rub my chin and nod several times to hide my reaction. What happened to her that *this* is the best job she's ever had?

"That's interesting. Why do you say that?"

Her brow wrinkles.

"I'm just curious. That's all."

"Well, Mr. and Mrs. Morrison are very kind to me. And they're entertaining. I like their dynamic, this house and its location, and I have a wide variety of tasks, so it's never boring."

"And who doesn't love to wear a dress and apron every day?" I chuckle.

"Well, sometimes I think life was probably better seventy years ago. Less noise. A simpler life. Great music. And yeah," she glances down, "women brushing their hair fifty times before bed and needing no excuse to look cute and feminine in a pre-yoga-pants era is appealing to me, even if it's weird to you or your fiancée."

I'm a dick.

Eight years ago, she imploded before my eyes, leaving me in the rubble. What I would have given to see her in absolutely any dress, doing any job.

"What do you do for a living?" she asks before I have a chance to apologize for my comment.

"I'm a freelance technical writer. Basically, I write—"

"You write support documents for technical and complex information. Instruction manuals."

"Uh, yeah. How did you know that?"

She squints for a second. "I don't know. I must have come across someone who had the same profession."

I bite my tongue, thinking *me*. You came across me.

"Okay. I'm out of here. Last chance for one of you to join me," Hunter says, parading down the stairs.

"Have a lovely time, Mr. Morrison. I'm off to finish your study," Alice says.

I jab my thumb behind me. "You know where I'll be."

"Yeah, yeah," he mumbles on his way to the back door.

It clicks shut, and a few minutes later, I hear the rumble of his red 1967 Corvette coupe pulling onto the street. I force myself to work for another twenty minutes before breaking for dinner. Taking the long way to the kitchen, I peek into Hunter's study. Alice has all of his books in neat piles on the floor, while she stands on the sliding ladder to dust the shelves. Her wedge heels are next to his desk, and Billie Holiday is singing "I'll Be Seeing You" on Hunter's upscale turntable.

When Blair introduced me to her parents, I was instantly drawn to his vinyl collection and his fifteen-thousand-dollar turntable. She said her dad never let her touch his collection and didn't understand why I cared about something so old. How would she feel about the homemaker playing his records?

I leave Alice to her work and make myself dinner. While I smash avocado with lime, garlic, salt, and cilantro, I hear footsteps behind me and turn. Alice has her shoes back on.

"You don't have to wear those for me," I say.

61

"I thought I smelled something burning," she says, ignoring my shoe comment.

"A little cheese ran out of my quesadilla." I nod toward the griddle. "Don't worry. I'll clean it up."

"I would have made you dinner." She pulls a plate from the cabinet.

"You're not my homemaker. I've got this."

"I'm *the* homemaker. And you live in this home for now, so I'm your ..."

I chuckle. "Maker?"

Alice returns a half grin. "Yes. Where are your tomatoes?"

"I don't need any. This will work."

"Of course you need tomatoes. Be right back."

"Alice—"

She's out the door before I can finish my protest. A few minutes later, she returns with the perfect orange and yellow heirloom tomato. After a quick rinse, she sets it on the butcher block cutting board and dices it.

"Don't you have a study to finish organizing?"

"I'm about done. It's been a three-day project." She checks on my quesadilla and transfers it to the cutting board, where she uses her chef's knife to cut it into four wedges. Then she steals the bowl of guacamole from me and mixes in the fresh cut tomatoes.

I step aside because I know she gets into a zone while cooking. It's hard to hide my grin when she chops red onion to add to the guacamole. Then she arranges the quesadilla on the plate and transfers the guacamole to a smaller dish that fits nicely in the middle of the plate.

"What can I get you to drink?" she asks, taking the plate

to the dining room table where she sets it on a placemat and arranges utensils on a cloth napkin next to it.

I hold up my bottle of beer when she turns to face me. "Got my own drink like a big boy. And I will not use any of that silverware. I'll eat it with my hands, lick my greasy fingers, and wipe them on my jeans if I need a napkin."

God I wish I could read her mind. How does she not remember the best (and worst) two weeks of my life? A fortnight that ended abruptly, a scar that I've carried ever since.

"I'm going to finish up in the study. If you need anything, let me know."

"I need you to eat dinner with me. I was going to take it to the bedroom and eat it at my desk while working, but now you have everything neatly arranged at this big table. So I need company."

"I really should finish in the study."

I sit at the table. "Hunter says you're an excellent listener, way more attentive than Vera. Sit. I have some grievances to air about this upcoming wedding. Do I have home-maker-client confidentiality privileges with you?" I dip the quesadilla into the guacamole.

Alice studies me for a few seconds before smoothing her hand down the front of her apron and pulling out the chair next to me, sitting with her legs crossed. I remember so many things about those fucking incredible legs, but I wish I didn't.

She clears her throat, and my eyes lift. There's an awkward breath as we share a silent acknowledgment that I was staring at her legs.

"Blair told me I could have lots of input on this wedding." I dive into conversation as I hand Alice a wedge of my quesadilla.

She shakes her head, so I set it on the table in front of

her, which makes her frown while picking up the wedge and eyeing the grease it left behind.

"I was told I could pick out whatever cake flavor I wanted for the groom's cake. Makes sense, right?" I mumble over a bite of food.

Alice offers a one-shouldered shrug with a tiny nod. Then she steals the knife to spread guacamole over the top of her quesadilla. I keep my grin in check.

"So I said chocolate cake, and Blair and Vera rolled their eyes at me. The baker suggested red velvet cake, and that seemed to please Blair and her mom, but I don't want red velvet cake. I want regular chocolate. Then they suggested a filling if I wanted chocolate. They said orange, cherry, or raspberry pair well with chocolate cake. Nope. I just want plain chocolate cake with chocolate frosting."

Alice finishes chewing and licks her lips. "So what cake are you getting?"

"Rum cake."

She presses her fingers to her lips to muffle her laughter. Then she reaches for my beer.

I don't stop her, but before the bottle touches her lips, she freezes, and her smile dies as she slowly sets the beer back on the table.

"Sorry," she mumbles, swallowing hard. "I'd better get back to work."

I don't argue because even if she doesn't remember me, her body has muscle memory of how we were together.

Chapter
ELEVEN

Alice

Sex is an underrated icebreaker.
Don't be a prude.

Eight Years Earlier ...

WITH MY LEGS tucked into my shirt, knees to my chest, I grinned before taking a sip of my steamy coffee. Had I really propositioned Murphy for sex?

Palmer jumped up next to me on the outdoor sectional and purred the second I touched him. My gaze climbed the back side of the building just as Murphy opened the shades. He smiled, and I returned a beauty queen wave.

I liked my escape, and I never wanted to leave.

No job.

No responsibilities.

No one hovering over me, making sure I didn't slit my wrists.

A few seconds later, Murphy descended the back stairs with a coffee mug in one hand and something indistinguishable in his other. "Good morning," he said.

"What are you eating?" I asked.

"A quesadilla."

I wrinkled my nose. "For breakfast? With coffee?"

"Correct."

"Why is it so limp?"

"What do you mean?" He stepped onto the deck.

"They're supposed to be crisp on the outside. Grilled to perfection with a side of guacamole."

"I throw cheese on a tortilla, fold it in half, and nuke it. But enough about me. How'd you sleep after all that wine and red meat?"

"Like a baby. You?"

He yawned. "Not so great."

"That's too bad. Why not?"

"A lot on my mind?" He sat next to me on the sectional.

"Sex?"

He smirked before sipping his coffee, then he shook his head. "Wow. I thought it was just the wine and music. Twilight-induced bravery. But you're going there this morning. Just throwing it out there before I'm properly caffeinated."

"You've said on multiple occasions to let you know if I need anything. I don't want this to come across as a threat, but when I leave my review, I'll have no choice but to mention your lack of responsiveness to my requests."

Murphy chuckled before shoving the rest of his

quesadilla into his mouth and chewing slowly. Then he cleared his throat. "Just like that, huh?"

"Just like what?" I stroked Palmer's back.

He wiped his hands on his jeans. "You've been here four days, and you're ready to have sex with me?"

I narrowed my eyes. "Have you ever met a woman at a bar and taken her home only to say, 'Nice knowing ya,' the next morning? I believe there is a name for that ..." I twisted my lips.

"A one-night stand?"

I snapped my fingers. "Bingo."

He wiped the corners of his mouth with the back of his hand. "Are you sure you're not married?"

"Positive." I drank my coffee, enjoying Murphy's real-time contemplation.

"Fine." He stood. "Let me brush my teeth."

My lips parted, eyes unblinking as he climbed the stairs with the same unhurried pace as he'd descended them, like sex with me was something to mark off a to-do list.

On the off chance that he was serious, I ran inside and brushed my teeth, too, combed my hair, shaved my legs at the bathroom sink, and rolled on deodorant. Then I stared at my reflection in the mirror. Was I really going to have sex with a virtual stranger? I glanced down, tracing the scar on my arm.

"I have a haircut in an hour," Murphy called from the other room. "Are we doing this or not?"

My heart pounded, but before I let any sort of reason steal my bravery (my recklessness), I opened the bathroom door. Murphy was by my bed, checking the glass watering bulb to the plant on the nightstand. When our gazes locked, I shrugged off my nightshirt, leaving me in just my black underwear as I took three steps and wrapped my arms around his neck.

He pulled back a fraction when I tried to kiss him. I narrowed my eyes, and he grinned.

"Hi," he whispered.

It was simple, yet emotionally jarring. I almost chickened out. *Almost.*

I don't know what I expected. After all, Murphy seemed like a gentleman who cared about my marital status, and he had flawless taste in music and a knack for keeping houseplants alive. Adding those things together led me to expect a hot romp in the sheets with a little cuddle time afterward.

Nope.

Murphy ditched his shirt then backed me into the desk opposite the bed, peeled my underwear down my legs, and released himself from his jeans, all the while fervently kissing me.

"Oh god ..." I threw back my head and gasped, gripping his arm with one hand and the edge of the desk with my other as he drove into me.

It was all very à la carte. No foreplay, and I presumed it wouldn't end with desktop cuddling. Just sex.

It was *exactly* what I needed, as if Murphy knew the circumstances that brought me to the Lake of the Isles for two weeks. We screwed like someone injected something into our veins that made us lose our minds, and everything that had haunted me just disappeared for a few minutes.

Our gazes locked, and he grinned which made me mirror his response. It was that "holy shit, we're really doing this" grin. Then he kissed me again, and we hummed at the same time like, "holy shit, this feels *so* good."

He ducked his head and drew my nipple into his mouth.

When he tugged it with his teeth, I climaxed. He fused his mouth to mine, swallowing my cry while he pumped into me harder, then orgasmed with a low, sexy groan vibrating his chest. When it was over, we clung to each other, breathless and utterly satisfied beyond all expectations. At least, that's what I planned on writing in his five-star review.

For the record, I had never gone home with a stranger from a bar for a one-night stand. It was all feigned confidence on my part. But more than that, I had never experienced such an uncontrollable pull toward another human.

Murphy fisted the back of my hair and kissed me again, his tongue sweeping the inside of my mouth. Then he kissed his way down my neck while simultaneously tucking himself back into his briefs and zipping his jeans. I opened my eyes when he froze and peered over my shoulder.

He reached behind me and ran his finger along the chipped drywall where the desk had rammed against it.

"I'm not paying for that," I said.

He couldn't hide his grin as I hopped off the desk and grabbed my underwear and nightshirt before sauntering to the bathroom. "Looks like you'll get to your haircut on time. Five stars for efficiency, Murphy Paddon."

As soon as I closed the door, I covered my mouth and cried my fucking eyes out.

Chapter
TWELVE

Alice

There are two kinds of people:
grumpy people and those who nap.

"ENOUGH WITH THE FLOWERS," Blair grumbles, traipsing into the kitchen before breakfast. She tightens her robe sash. "I'm here for the summer. I'm a goddamn artist. There's no reason for you to arrange flowers every morning. There's no reason for you to do most of the things you do, but certainly not this." She slides the vase away from me.

"Okay then." I give her a tight smile.

"I stripped our bed, so why don't you throw the sheets in the washer if you're looking for something useful to do."

"Yes, ma'am."

"*Blair*. Please stop the ma'am shit."

I bite my tongue and take a few steps toward her bedroom.

"Alice?" Blair sighs. "I'm ... ugh! I'm so sorry. I'm PMSing, miserably on the verge of starting my period. And literally everything is irritating me. Planning this wedding is stressful. I just want to move to New York. And I'm sure you don't care about my problems, but I'm really sorry for snapping at you. I was out of line."

Is she *apologizing* to me? I'd rather she not. It's easier for me to deal with my feelings for Murphy if I don't relate to his fiancée.

"It's fine. Planning a wedding isn't all it's cracked up to be."

"Oh, have you been married?"

"No," I murmur, continuing to her bedroom, stopping at the doorway because Murphy is on the phone, pacing the room.

He smiles, holds up a finger and mouths, "One second."

I point to the pile of sheets on the floor and quickly gather them before he's off the call and we're forced to make small talk.

"Okay, that sounds like the best plan. Thank you, Rob. I'll call you later." He ends his call. "Good morning."

Too late.

"Morning." I focus on gathering the sheets instead of looking at his bright smile.

"Give me a sec. I need to shake them out because I think Blair, in her impatient mood, gathered up my wallet that I tossed onto the bed."

I slowly release the sheets and step aside just as Murphy steps in the same direction, then we do it in the other direction.

Risking a glance up at him, I return a nervous smile.

"I guess you can dance after all." He smirks.

I step to the side to put space between us, but bump into the desk. It hits the wall, and I cringe, inspecting for any damage.

"Sorry, that was my fault," he says. "And don't worry. If it dented the wall, it won't be the first time I've had to do a little wall repair from a desk."

Is that a reference? Why would he? He doesn't know I remember him.

There *is* a little dent from where the desk hit the wall. "Dammit," I whisper.

"Hey, I'm serious. It's okay," Murphy says, shaking out the sheets. "Ah, there's my wallet."

I run my finger along the dent.

"It's barely noticeable," he murmurs over my shoulder.

When I turn, Murphy is so close our noses nearly touch. I feel pinned to the desk while craning my head back to create space between us.

His gaze sweeps across my face. "Have you ever had déjà vu?" he whispers.

It's not déjà vu, and he knows it.

"You feel like you've lost your wallet in the sheets before, but you haven't?"

His lips corkscrew. "Sort of. But it wasn't a wallet I lost."

"Murphy?" Blair calls.

He takes a giant step backward and draws in a sharp breath.

"Be patient with her," I say. "She's on the verge of getting her happily ever after, but sometimes that can be stressful."

His lips part, but he just as quickly clamps his jaw shut and nods several times. "Coming," he hollers.

I gather the sheets again.

"Are you happy?" he asks as I step toward the doorway.

I pause for a second without a backward glance. "Of course," I murmur and continue toward the laundry room. "Alice, can you come in here for a second?" Hunter requests as I pass his study.

"Yes, sir." I quickly toss the sheets onto the laundry room floor and return to his luxurious two-story study lined on three sides with bookshelves and modern wood stairs with a metal railing to the second-story catwalk. Magnificent arched windows behind his desk illuminate the grand space. A sweet and spicy smoke aroma lingers despite the cracked window. Vera doesn't let him smoke cigars in the house, but he clearly does it anyway.

"How do you feel about reading books?" he asks, removing his readers.

"Um, fine. I guess. Why?"

Soft jazz plays on his turntable.

"I want you to read to me." He lumbers from his desk chair and loosens his red tie, then he scans the neatly organized bookshelves while unbuttoning the top two buttons of his white dress shirt. He selects a book from the bottom shelf. "Have you read *Three Men in a Boat?*"

"I have not," I say, then press my lips together to hide my grin. This job just keeps getting better.

"It's a soothing story. Would you mind?" He hands me the book, then he slides a tufted brown leather chair close to the matching sofa. "Have a seat. What can I get you to drink? Scotch? Wine?" He adds ice to a glass, ice that I filled earlier. But now he's serving me?

"Just water," I say. "Thank you."

He sets the ice water by the table lamp and reclines on the sofa, ankles crossed, hands folded on his chest, eyes closed.

After a few seconds of silence, he peeks open one eye. "Just a few chapters. Then I have work to do."

Does he really? I continue to suppress my giggle.

Crossing my legs, I clear my throat and begin reading. By the end of the first chapter, I think he's asleep, but since I don't know for sure, I keep going for two more chapters. At the end of chapter three, I wait. Is he going to wake up? Am I supposed to wake him?

"Mr. Morrison?" I whisper.

He doesn't move.

I set the book aside and lean forward, resting my hand on his arm. "Mr. Morrison?"

His eyes pop open, and he sits up, stretching his arms over his head on a big yawn. "You have a calming voice. What do you think of the story so far?"

I think no one would believe me if I told them I got paid a hundred dollars an hour to read to a silver fox.

"It's entertaining." I offer a smile.

"I can't get Vera to read it. Maybe when we're done, you can convince her." He stands, tucking in his shirt.

So this will be a regular thing? Hunter Morrison is a peculiar man, and I'm here for all his rich man's indulgences.

"Is there anything else I can do for you?" I ask, returning the book to its spot on the shelf.

"You could slip this registration in the glove compartment of my Ferrari and put the new tag on the plate." He slides a folded piece of paper across his desk. "Grab the keys by the door. They're the ones with the Ferrari logo."

I nod. "Okay."

"And, Alice?"

"Yes?"

"Do you by any chance make bar soap?"

Sometimes I think there's a hidden camera, and this is all a joke. In fact, I make a quick inspection of the corners of the room. He continues to challenge my composure. A giggle tries to work its way up my chest, but I swallow it back down and clear my throat. "Um ... not yet."

"If you do, avoid vanilla. I'm not a fan."

I nod slowly.

"Thank you, Alice. Best nap of my life."

"You're welcome."

I first toss the sheets into the washing machine, then I find the Ferrari keys and head down to the basement, where there's a two-lane bowling alley, a second kitchen, and a theater room, along with two more bedrooms. Then I pull on the maple bookshelf to expose the hidden door to the underground garage, which doubles as a panic room. The ramp at the far end leads to the driveway. It opens, seemingly out of nowhere, straight to the main street. There are no words to describe the Morrisons' lavish home.

After a few steps toward the car, I hear someone behind me and glance over my shoulder at Blair and Murphy holding hands.

"Are those my dad's car keys?" Blair asks, nodding toward the key chain around my finger.

"Yes. He asked me to do something for him." I continue toward the Ferrari.

"He's not letting you drive his car, is he?"

I close my eyes and remember she has PMS brain and can't be held responsible for her bitchiness.

Again, I stop. This time, I turn toward her.

"It doesn't matter, come on," Murphy says, pulling her toward their white SUV.

She wriggles out of his grip. "It does matter. He won't let

anyone drive his Ferrari. Not me. Not my mom. So if he's letting you drive it, then there must be a reason."

"Such as?" I don't know why I feel the need to play her game. I *just* defended her to Murphy, and this is the thanks I get?

"My parents have been happily married for thirty years. Don't mess with that."

"I'm not. I think I make both of them happier than they were before me." I wink.

Murphy bites his lips to hide his amusement.

"What is that supposed to mean?" Blair scoffs.

I hold up the registration. "I'm just putting this in the glove compartment, not going for a joyride."

She deflates, dropping her gaze in embarrassment.

"Just say you're sorry, and let's go," Murphy says.

"You don't have to apologize. My dad cheated on my mom." I pivot and continue toward the garage. "I'm not the woman who sleeps with another woman's husband."

At least, that's not the plan.

Chapter
THIRTEEN

Murphy

*If you're going to lie,
make it the best story ever told.*

Eight Years Earlier ...

DID I fuck another man's wife? I hoped not.

I wasn't a one-night-stand novice, but having sex with someone who was paying money to rent my place felt different. Alice felt different.

She was spontaneous and fun. Flirty and confident. But mostly, she was an enigma. Sometimes I wanted to figure her out, but other times I just wanted to revel in the wonder and curiosity she provoked. There was a certain level of satisfaction that came from not knowing everything about her, like staring at presents under the Christmas tree and having no clue what was inside them.

Why the diamond ring?

Why was she in Minneapolis for two weeks by herself with no obvious purpose?

Wine in the morning.

Steak as a late-night snack.

Offering to have sex with a man she just met.

My brain was shit. I had deadlines and no concentration. Sleep distracted me because I knew she was just below me, and I couldn't stop wondering if she was awake, too, thinking about me.

The next morning, I stared at her through my window while the cursor on my computer blinked like a virtual tap on my shoulder.

Hello? Remember me? Your job?

The problem with Alice, and there were many, was the inexplicable feeling of familiarity I felt around her. More than déjà vu. More than instant attraction.

She sipped her coffee and curled her blond hair behind her ear, and then, out of the blue, but also with disturbingly accurate intention, she looked straight at me.

I hurled my body away from the window so quickly, the chair tipped over.

"Shit," I grumbled, rubbing the back of my head before wrestling with the overturned chair to find my feet again. Why was I acting like a twelve-year-old with a crush?

Just as my heart rate returned to normal, she knocked on my door, sending it into a frenzy again. I scrubbed my hands over my face. "Get it together," I said before stepping out of my office to open the door.

"Nice haircut." She winked.

My dick stirred unnecessarily. It was confused. We (my dick and I) weren't used to girls winking at us. Flirty smiles, lip biting, blushing ... sure. But a wink felt like a bold move. Only confident people winked. We (my dick and I) wondered if Alice was confident that the three of us would have sex again.

"Thanks." I dragged a hand through my hair.

"What are you doing today?" She sipped her coffee while keeping her eyes trained on me.

"Working. Why?"

"So not riding your bike?"

"Uh ..."

"I assume the bike hanging in the garage is yours."

I nodded.

"Mind if I borrow it?"

"I ... uh ... yeah." I nodded again like a bobblehead doll.

"I'll have to lower the seat for you."

"Is that too much trouble?"

"Nope. Just give me a minute."

"No hurry. I'm going to make a smoothie and get dressed. Have you had breakfast?"

"I have."

"Cool. Just let me know when it's ready."

Like a child playing hide and seek, I closed the door and counted to one hundred to give her time to go inside before I headed to the garage to lower the bike seat and check the tires. Then I knocked on her door twice and stepped inside.

"It's ready," I called.

"Oh, that was fast," she hollered.

I slipped off my shoes and poked my head around the other side of the galley kitchen. Alice was brushing her teeth. She spat and dabbed her mouth with the towel.

"I thought it might be a good idea to get it ready now so I can focus on work the rest of the day."

She frowned, shutting off the bathroom light. "I'm a distraction. I'm sorry."

"No. Don't apologize. I'm happy to do it."

Alice stepped into the bedroom and returned a few seconds later with a pair of socks. "Well, thank you." She sat at the dining room table to put them on.

"What is your job? Something with wood, I'm guessing, since you don't keep your car in the garage, just some interesting tools and lots of wood."

"I like woodturning. My dad taught me. But I have a day job as a freelance technical writer."

"What does that entail?" She glanced up and squinted while pulling on her socks.

"Technical writing or woodturning?"

Alice chuckled. "Both."

"I write support documents for technical and complex information like instruction manuals. As for the woodturning, that's just cutting and shaping wood using a lathe and different tools. A lathe is a machine that spins the wood so the shapes I create are symmetrical."

"Huh. That's interesting. *You're* interesting."

I pinned back my shoulders, chest out because I enjoyed being interesting in her eyes.

Alice curled her hair behind her ears then rested her hands on her legs. "We had sex."

I tried to control my grin while rubbing the back of my neck. "Yeah."

She bit her bottom lip for a second. "It was fun. Thanks."

My shit-eating grin took on a life of its own because this woman never disappointed. "Happy to do it," I said.

Her cheeks pinked. "I checked the listing, and it wasn't under the amenities, so I may have overstepped."

"You think I should add it under amenities?"

Alice stood. "Nah. I like to feel special." She sauntered to the back door, but I didn't move because I just wanted to watch her. Alice Yates was the epitome of special. Her gait was smooth, as if she were floating. Mesmerizing in every way.

"Coming?" she asked, eyeing me while squatting to put on her tennis shoes.

I nodded. "Was it just a one-afternoon stand, or is kissing allowed, like an amenity, of course?"

She grinned, keeping her head bowed while tying her shoes.

"I'm letting you borrow my bike. I'll let you borrow my lips too. It's just something to consider."

"Would that complicate things?" she asked, standing straight.

I twisted my lips. "Not on my end. I'm not needy or an addict. I've fostered dogs. When it's time for them to go, I'm good."

She wrinkled her nose. "Are you comparing me to a dog?"

"No. Well, it depends. How do you feel about dogs?"

Alice brought a finger to her lips. "I don't want to say. Palmer might hear us." She opened the door and led the way to the garage.

"I don't want to be predictable and ask what you do for a living, but—"

"Good," she opened the garage door. "Because I don't do anything."

"Independently wealthy?"

She turned after I stepped into the garage. "Filthy rich. Old money, of course. In fact, I think my great-great grandmother was a queen. Never worked a day in my life."

"Geesh." I scratched the back of my head. "I wish I'd known that. We would have done it in the bed instead of nailing your royal ass to the desk."

Alice snorted, covering her mouth, eyes wide.

"So, Princess Alice, since you don't have a job, do you have any talents I should know about?" I plucked my helmet from the hook and tightened the strap.

She lifted a shoulder. "Oh, you know ... nothing much. I'm good at synchronized or *artistic* swimming. I stole a turtle when I was eight. And in high school, I played Hermia in *A Midsummer Night's Dream*."

I raised an eyebrow at her as she tipped her chin up, grin brimming with confidence. Was she toying with me? "Are we playing two truths and a lie?" I asked, fitting the helmet on her head, then checking the strap and removing it to tighten it a bit more.

"Do two of my talents sound like lies?"

I laughed. "Maybe. Although, I'm not sure stealing turtles is considered a talent. Did you get caught?"

"No. That's why it's a talent." She tipped her chin up for me to fasten the helmet.

I latched it, then patted the top twice. "I've never seen or read *A Midsummer Night's Dream*, so I don't know if Hermia is a good part."

"Yes." She headed into the alley where I had the bike next to my car, and she lifted her leg over the bar. "Hermia was a courageous woman in love with Lysander, but her father wanted her to marry Demetrius. She basically had to fight the patriarchy, then deal with the man of her dreams being given a love potion that made him fall in love with her friend. It was such a beautiful mess."

"I'm not a fan of Shakespeare."

"Well, you're just saying that because you never met the guy, and you probably skipped all Shakespeare's stories in favor of google search summaries."

She pegged me correctly, but I wasn't going down that easily.

"No one who has attended school in the twenty-first century has read anything but summaries of Shakespeare, or Dickens for that matter. It's basically the entire purpose of the internet."

She rolled her eyes.

"Need me to adjust the seat?" I held the bike while she sat on it, feet pressed to the pedals.

"Nope. Feels pretty good." She slid off the seat and slipped on her sunglasses.

"Cool. Well, enjoy your ride."

"Thanks." She grabbed my shirt and pulled me to her while wearing a grin.

"Ouch," I said when she tried to kiss me because the helmet's sun visor hit my forehead.

"Oh, sorry." She snorted.

I rubbed my forehead.

She giggled. "I was going to kiss you."

"Yeah, I caught that."

Alice unlatched her helmet and hung it from the handle-bar. Then she lifted onto her toes and grabbed the back of my neck so she could kiss my forehead where the visor hit it. But I didn't need my boo-boo kissed; I needed to taste the inside of her mouth, so I did just that.

"Hi," I whispered over her lips, then kissed her. And

before I knew it, the bike fell on its side as I pulled her to my body.

She kissed me back with just as much fervor. Everything about Alice was unexpected and exciting. And I felt about her the way she felt about wine for breakfast: when in Rome ...

"In ..." She broke the kiss and panted while I kissed down her neck. "Inside."

There was no need to ask me twice. I carried her into the garage and pushed the button for the door to close. She released her arms and legs from me, sliding to her feet, and turned toward the door to the backyard. I kissed her neck and snaked my hand down the front of her shorts, pressing my chest to her back.

Her breath caught, then she moaned, "Oh god, Murphy," pressing her hands to the door.

I peeled her leggings and underwear down her legs, removing one of her shoes to free that leg. My patience vanished, hands just as eager to touch her as they were to unfasten my jeans. Gripping her beautiful ass, I spread her open and thrust inside of her.

"Murphy," she chanted my name, arching her back and grinding into me while her fingernails scraped along the door.

It was sexy, spontaneous, and a little unhinged. I liked Alice's unreal life just as much as my hands liked the feel of her breasts and taut nipples as I shoved her sports bra up her chest to release them.

When it was over, I hugged her back to my chest to keep her upright as her knees wobbled. "My god that was good," I said between labored breaths.

"So good ..." she mumbled with a long exhale.

I tucked myself back into my underwear before helping her get her leggings back on.

"For the record," she said, turning toward me and adjusting her sports bra to cover her breasts again, "I meant *inside* the house."

I glanced up, zipping my jeans. "Oh, no shit? Dang. Sorry, I got that wrong."

"Are you really?" She narrowed her eyes.

I smirked. Some misunderstandings felt like fate.

"Well, you've ruined our status. Now what?" she asked, messing with her hair.

"What do you mean?" I untied her shoe and handed it to her.

She shoved her foot into it. "It's no longer a one-afternoon stand. It's a two-afternoons stand. And I'm not sure that's a thing, but maybe we can make it a thing just while I'm here."

I nodded slowly, twisting my lips to the side while doing some quick thinking. "If you can have wine with breakfast, we can have an afternoon delight."

Laughter bubbled from her chest. "Isn't that a song?"

"I believe so."

She briefly glanced to the side before studying me as if I would say I was just kidding. But I wasn't.

"You want me to be your regular afternoon delight?"

I chuckled, ducking my head to kiss her lips, then along her jaw to her ear. "No. I want to be your afternoon delight."

She giggled, but I wasn't sure if it was what I said or if her neck was ticklish.

"No mornings or evenings. Correct?"

"Correct," I said without really thinking about it, but I smiled before trapping her ear between my teeth.

"No pining. No touching. No flirting." She playfully shoved me. "No biting my ear outside of the sex window."

"The sex window? Are you making rules, Alice?"

"Yes. Rules keep expectations in check. It's sex. Fun. Unattached. You can't fall in love with me. And I won't fall in love with you. Just. Sex."

I opened the garage door, set my bike upright, and checked to make sure the gears were okay. "No-strings-attached sex. You're basically describing every man's dream. Are you still going for a ride, or have you had enough between your legs for one day?"

She rolled her lips together to hide her grin, and we stared at each other for a few minutes. Who were we kidding? The chemistry was undeniable. Every look was flirtatious. I wasn't going to fall in love with her, but I loved that she was staying in my rental.

"How does one get into synchronized swimming?" I asked, instead of suggesting we have sex again, which was exactly what I wanted to do.

Alice opened the back garage door and headed toward the deck. "Well, I don't know how everyone gets into it, but my friend begged me to take lessons with her, so that's how I got into it."

"I bet you can hold your breath for a long time."

"I bet you're right." She disappeared into the house.

A few minutes later, she returned with a bottle of water as I pulled a few weeds near the fence.

"Will you feel inadequate if I still go for that bike ride?"

I laughed, shaking my head while brushing the dirt from my hands. "I don't know what to say. You've got me fumbling my words all over the damn place." And she did. Women rarely intimidated me because there was a push and pull.

Emotions and egos at stake. No one liked being rejected or dumped, but Alice was immune to all of that. She acted as if she had nothing to lose, and I tried to feel the same way, but it felt foreign to me.

"Don't worry. You still have a five-star review coming your way," she said, sauntering toward the garage, once again proving my point.

Chapter
FOURTEEN

Murphy

Silence is underrated.
It's also open to interpretation

"SHE'S PRETTY, don't you think?" Blair asks, as we relax by the pool on this ninety-degree afternoon on July first.

"Who?"

"Alice."

I keep my eyes closed. "I don't know. Why?"

"What do you mean you don't know? You're not blind. It's not a trap. I'm just making a statement. She's pretty. Why would my mom hire someone so pretty to be my dad's ..."

"Homemaker?" I grin.

"Stop." She smacks my arm, but not without laughing. "Before we ran errands, I walked past my dad's study, and guess what they were doing?"

"Discussing what cut of steak he wants for dinner? Fireworks for the Fourth?"

"No. She was reading to him. I kid you not; he was reclined on his leather sofa, eyes closed, and she was in the chair next to him, reading a book like a bedtime story. How messed up is that?"

"What book?"

"Murphy, what does that matter? That's not the point. He's a grown man having a book read to him like a child."

"Well, maybe your mom won't read to him."

"Murphy!"

I laugh. "Okay. Okay. Yeah, it's weird. But what are you going to do about it?"

"Why can't you just agree with me without making a case for him?"

"I do agree with you."

"But I want you to agree with me *and* do something about it."

"What am *I* supposed to do?"

"Say something to him. Maybe shame him a little. Like one man to another, tell him how messed up it is that he has a woman close to his daughter's age reading him a book."

"Babe, I'm not having that conversation with him."

"Ugh! You're useless." She stands.

"Blair."

She grumbles, stomping into the house.

I shake my head and remove my sunglasses, then I jump into the pool to escape her irrational anger. She's stressed, and there's only so much I can do about it. Perhaps, just staying out of her way while she works through it is the best option.

The air from my lungs escapes into tiny little bubbles

before my face as I sink to the bottom of the pool, where everything is peaceful. I think about Alice and how long she had to hold her breath as a synchronized swimmer. How long can I hold my breath? Until we're in New York, and I no longer have to see Alice every day? Until I'm married?

I relax my body and count.

After a minute and twenty-six seconds, there's a pinch on my arm, a hand gripping it, pulling me to the surface.

Ribbons of long, dark hair.

A blue dress.

White apron.

Legs frog kicking.

I pull away, and Alice whips her head around as we breach the surface at the shallow end.

"I'm fine," I say, shaking the water from my hair.

Alice's blue eyes pierce me, red lips parted, satin head-band clinging to her drenched ponytail as she pants.

"I'm fine," I repeat.

Drops of water cling to her long lashes as she returns a blank stare like she's not hearing me or even seeing me. Then her nostrils flair and, without a word, she turns, arms limp at her sides as she climbs the corner steps and grabs a towel from the bin.

"Alice." I follow her, snagging my towel from the chair.

She quickly grabs her shoes and hurries toward the guesthouse.

"Alice!" I don't run, but I take bigger strides to catch up to her. "I'm sorry. I didn't mean to scare you."

She shakes her head and mumbles with a shaky voice, "It's ... uh, it's fine."

"It's not fine. You're soaking wet, and it's my fault." I follow her to the slider door at the side of the guesthouse.

With her back to me, she unbuttons her dress and lets it fall to her feet. It's wrong to look at her, but it's so familiar, not eight years ago familiar, more like eight seconds. She opens the door and takes one step inside, wearing just a white bra and underwear.

My chest constricts. She's no longer for my eyes, my hands, my fucking heart, but that's just my brain searching for a little self-preservation. That spark, the invisible *thing* that was always between us, is still here. Her lack of acknowledging it doesn't make it less true; it just makes the pain cut a little deeper because what was so right is now so wrong.

"Do you remember me?" I ask.

She stops.

I'm afraid of either answer.

Never mind. As she takes another step into the house and closes the door, I realize I'm most afraid of not knowing.

I run my fingers through my hair. "Shit."

"How many kids do you want? Is it weird that we haven't discussed this?" Blair asks as we get dressed to go to dinner with her parents.

I button my shirt. "We've discussed kids."

"Yes, but not how many we should have or when we want to start our family. I'm thinking two, preferably close together so we can just go all in with the parenting phase of our life. And we're not getting any younger, so I say we try within the next year. What do you think?" She applies lip gloss in the full-length mirror.

"I'm thirty-two, and you're twenty-seven. I wouldn't call that old. I think we should take it one day at a time."

She traces the edge of her lower lip. "What's up with your mood?"

"My mood?" I slide my wallet into my pocket.

"You've been dying to just elope, skip the big wedding, and start our future as soon as possible. But now that I want to discuss our future, you seem hesitant, like you're putting on the brakes. If you don't want to start a family right away, we don't have to. I'm just saying I don't want to miss our window. I'll blink and be in perimenopause. Did you know Elise Rayburn, who lived next to us in San Francisco, is already in perimenopause, and she's only thirty-five?"

I nod slowly.

"Murphy, what is your deal?" She turns toward me, capping her lip gloss. "Are you worried I'm going to break off our engagement or leave you at the altar?"

"Should I be?" I narrow my eyes at her.

Blair flicks her wrist, waving me off. "Stop. You let my dad get into your head too much. Before long, you'll be asking me to read to you before bed." She smirks, sliding her feet into her heels.

"Fine. I want five kids. Three boys first, then two girls," I say.

Blair coughs, smacking her hand over her chest. "W-what?" Her eyes widen as she chuckles.

I shake my head. "I'm kidding, just testing you."

She straightens my tie. "What kind of test is that?"

"Okay, not a test, just a bad joke. Sorry."

She offers her cheek, and I kiss it.

It's a nice cheek.

She's a nice woman.
Our life will be ... nice.

Chapter FIFTEEN

Alice

Moms don't see their children's flaws.
They see opportunities for growth

"Hey," I say, calling my mom while staring out the window at the sunset over the lake. People and their dogs still milling around the grass and making a final effort to get 10K steps in for the day.

"Hi. How's my girl?" Mom asks.

I put her on speaker and sigh. "I've been better."

"Oh? What's wrong?"

For the first time since seeing Murphy again, I get tears in my eyes. "Nothing," I murmur.

"Doesn't sound like nothing. Don't keep it inside. You should know that by now."

Again, I sigh. Everything about Murphy right now is one

big sigh. "The guy I was with eight years ago at the vacation rental, before I went to the facility ..."

"The one who called us?" Mom asks.

"Yes."

"What about him?"

"He's the future son-in-law of the couple I'm working for. He and his fiancée are living with her parents for the summer." I push back my emotions.

"Oh. That's a small world. Does he remember you?"

"Yeah." I bite my thumbnail, watching the Morrisons leave for dinner.

"Did you thank him for calling us?"

"Not exactly. Do you remember when I said I didn't know if I'd ever be ready to share things I discussed in therapy?"

"I do. And I haven't pressured you, have I?"

"No. I'm just bringing it up because I want to tell you something."

"Alice, sweetie, you can tell me anything."

I turn away from the window and sit in the recliner, tucking my feet under me. "I was romantically involved with him."

"With who? The guy who called us?"

"Yes."

"The one who's getting married?" she asks, as if it's ridiculous.

"Yes."

"Alice, you were—"

"I know, Mom," I whisper. This hurts. The secrets. The lies. The hearts that were broken. So many wrongs that can never be righted. "It's unimaginable," I continue, "maybe even unforgivable, that I did that so soon after ..." I still hate saying the words, so I don't. "I just needed an escape. I needed to pretend that it didn't happen, that my life was different. So I painted a new reality for two weeks. It wasn't planned. It just happened. And I didn't feel dead inside. And that felt *so* good."

"You were in denial."

I nod to myself. "Yes," I whisper.

"Alice, I don't know what to say."

"You don't have to say anything. I feel your disappointment. Who does what I did?"

"Oh, no, sweetie. That's not it. I'm not disappointed in you. I'm heartbroken for you and disappointed in myself. A mother should know when her child is struggling and unwell. And I just ..."

"You were grieving too."

She doesn't respond.

"It was in the past. I moved on. But now he's here."

"What does this guy and his fiancée think of you working for her parents?"

"I don't know what he thinks because I haven't let him know that I remember him."

"What? Why on earth not?"

"Because he's engaged. And I really like this job. Not to mention the free rent and great pay. So I don't want to lose it or make things awkward. And what if he hasn't told Blair, his fiancée, about me? Also, I still don't remember the details of that night, so all I have is what you've told me. What would I say? 'Hi! Remember me, the woman who lost her mind from PTSD and ended up in a mental hospital?'"

"I can't believe you never told me about your relationship with him."

I wrinkle my nose. "What do you mean? Why is that so surprising? I was ashamed of what I had done to everyone."

"You didn't do anything."

"I left!" I sigh, rubbing my temples. "I left," my tone softens. "Escaped when everyone else had to deal with reality. I didn't let anyone be there for me, and I wasn't there for anyone else."

"Alice, it was awful. No one blamed you for leaving. We knew you'd come back."

I grunt a laugh. "I came back in pieces."

"And your pieces have been put back together."

"And I'm working near the one person who could unglue every single one of them."

"Alice, what are you talking about? So you had sex with a stranger because you weren't yourself. That was eight years ago. It's not like you fell in love with him."

I don't respond.

"Alice?"

"Huh?"

"You *didn't* fall in love with him, did you?"

Chapter
SIXTEEN

Alice

Reality is what we make it,
so make it unforgettable.

Eight Years Earlier ...

"STOP!" I squealed as Murphy chased me through the living room, around the sofa, up the two stairs to the dining room, and around the table in only his black underwear and white crew socks.

I wore his Vikings T-shirt, and I may have suggested the Packers were a superior team.

"Take it back, or I'm going to peel that shirt off you and lock you out of my place," he threatened.

We froze on opposite sides of the table in a standoff. He faked in one direction, but I reacted just as quickly as

Marvin Gaye sang "How Sweet It Is (To Be Loved By You)" from the turntable.

"This place is mine for another five days," I said, legs wide, body rigid and alert, ready to bolt in either direction.

Per our agreement, we spent every afternoon having sex. Once the sun set, we were platonic friends who ate dinner together and took leisurely walks around the lake. Then we retired by ten each night in our own beds.

Nothing felt real with Murphy. Reality was overrated.

We were silly and playful one minute, and physically ravenous the next. The sex was in a whole other league.

He liked my cooking.

I enjoyed watching him shape a boring piece of wood into something beautiful.

But mostly, we enjoyed the simplicity of each day. There was a perfect balance of work (he worked), play (sex), time alone, and deep conversations as friends. Our mutual love for older music spurred long talks about how times had changed, the shifting of priorities, and the age of the internet and online dating compared to how our parents and grandparents met. We imagined what the world would be like in thirty years.

"Don't say I didn't warn you," he said, faking a right around the table, but then he jumped over it, taking the runner and wood bowl in the middle with him.

"Ahh!" I screamed, then giggled as he trapped me in his arms, kissing my neck while I squirmed.

When his lips hovered over mine, I surrendered and waited.

Say it.

"Hi," he whispered before capturing my lips in a deep kiss. Then he took me prisoner, pinning my back to the top of the table, shoving down the front of his underwear and lifting the ugly Vikings shirt while settling between my legs.

"Yes ..." I closed my eyes for a second when he buried himself inside of me. God, it was heaven.

Oldies playing on vinyl.

Chicken in the oven and the aroma of rosemary and thyme in the air.

And the cringy yet laughable realization that we did not shut the blinds. It wasn't the first time that Rosie didn't have to pay for porn while she washed dishes. When I turned my head, she gave me a smile that said, "Get it, girl."

"Best. Renter. Ever." Murphy sighed, collapsing on top of me after we surpassed our orgasm quota for the day.

"In your review, I will say you exceeded my expectations as a host. Filled all my needs and did so with enthusiasm."

He laughed. "What will I say about you?"

"Don't tell me. I want it to be a surprise."

"A surprise it is." He stood, pulling his underwear back into place, as I hopped off the table and headed straight into the bathroom.

"Disinfect the table before dinner," I hollered.

"On it."

After using the bathroom, I grabbed a shirt from the bedroom along with leggings.

"Found my Packers shirt. I knew I brought it," I said, handing Murphy his Vikings shirt after he returned the all-purpose cleaner to its spot under the sink.

"You look much better in purple." He smirked, pulling the shirt over his head.

I laughed. "Put your pants on."

He looked down. "Earlier you thought it was sexy."

"Yes. There was something kinda sexy about you in

underwear and those socks, but the shirt just ruins it, and I'm not only referring to the pitiful team mascot on the front."

"Have you seen the movie *Risky Business* with Tom Cruise? It's an older movie. And there's a scene where he lip-syncs to "Old Time Rock and Roll" while dancing in his white socks, underwear, and a shirt."

"I have not seen that." I laughed.

"Oh, let me show you. I have that vinyl." He sauntered into the living room, and a few seconds later, "Old Time Rock and Roll" played. He grabbed the TV remote to use as a microphone. When the song started, he ran and slid in his socks along the wood floor.

I giggled.

He danced and lip-synced, jumping on the sofa, then playing air guitar on the coffee table.

When I bent over in laughter, he tossed the remote aside and bear-hugged me. "See, it's totally sexy."

"Oh my gosh," I said, catching my breath and wrapping my arms around his neck. "I love you."

Those three words came out so innocently and automatically that I didn't catch it at first, but then Murphy's smile faltered just a fraction.

I shook my head a half dozen times. "No. I didn't mean that like it sounded. I love that you just did that. You have no idea how much I've needed that kind of laughter."

Murphy studied me, rubbing his lips together and nodding. "Yeah. Of course. That's what I thought you meant." He released me and took a step backward while clearing his throat. "I'll put my pants on."

My cheeks ached from forcing a smile and holding it for so long. When he disappeared into the bedroom, I covered my face and blew out a long breath.

Stupid.

"Everything good?" He returned too quickly, forcing me to make a fast recovery.

"Uh-huh." I pinned a fake smile on my face.

"Don't sweat it," he said, padding into the kitchen where he turned on the oven light for a peek at the chicken. "There are a lot of things I love about you, too, like this amazing dinner you've prepared."

I *loved* the way he prioritized making me feel at ease. I *loved* chasing every improbable moment, holding on to it like trying to catch water in my hands. Everything slipped away. An unavoidable law of nature.

"Hypothetically," he cleared his throat, "if I didn't believe you have royalty in your bloodline, and therefore had a real job, what would that real job be?" he asked, leaning his backside against the counter while I pulled the tossed salad from the fridge along with a bottle of dressing.

Murphy wanted into my life, my real life. And while I didn't blame him for it, I also couldn't allow it.

"Hmm, hypothetically, I'd act in local theater productions."

"That's a cool hypothetical job."

"It is. The pay is shit, but passion is priceless."

He hummed. "Yes, it is."

When he gave me a look that I wasn't emotionally ready to handle, I changed the subject. "Where do you get your wood?"

"Good question. I'm glad you asked. Your fabulous tits give me pretty good wood, but sometimes I get it just from seeing your flirty smile."

"Shut up." I laughed.

He uncorked a bottle of wine. "I get wood from trails, the

local dump, clean-up from storms, orchards, back roads, demolition sites."

"I know the other day you said you display some of your work at local galleries, but it's so good, you could open your own. Have you ever thought about that?" I pulled the chicken from the oven.

"Nah. It's just a hobby. If I tried to make it a full-time business, I'd start to resent it. Putting pressure on your creative side to be your everything is the quickest way to squash inspiration."

I tried not to look at Murphy Paddon as the most interesting person I had ever met because it felt like the ultimate betrayal to my past, but every day I liked him more and more.

After dinner, we took our usual stroll around the lake, but this time, Murphy reached for my hand to hold it.

"Nope." I pulled it away from him, keeping my gaze in front of us at the ducks along the edge of the lake and a turtle chilling on a floating log. "I have no self-control around you. It's no longer afternoon, so no more *delight*."

"Alice, do you know how much power you just gave me by saying that? Knowing that you can't control yourself around me is too much. There's no way I won't take advantage of that. So this is me apologizing now for what's to come."

I nodded toward the group of four young women jogging toward us in the opposite direction. "Let's find you a wife, one who can cook, so you won't spend your life malnourished from eating microwaved quesadillas. What's your type? Tall and thin? Beautifully curvy? Long hair? Short hair? Do you want kids? A wife who stays home or an equal breadwinner? How many kids do you want?"

"How many kids do *you* want?" he asked.

"Oh, that's easy. I want five. Three boys first, then two girls."

Murphy shot me a sidelong glance with a huge grin. "I'm not sure what to follow-up with first. That it's rare to hear anyone want five kids anymore. Or your preference for three boys and two girls and in that order."

"Do you have siblings?" I asked.

"A sister two years younger."

"Well, I'm an only child. But my experience with big families is that they are fun. Perhaps chaotic at times, but fun. And older brothers looking out for younger sisters just melts my heart."

He smirked. "I can speak from experience. There's a lot of tormenting before the instinct to protect kicks in."

"But you protect her now, right?"

"I don't see her often. She just completed her associate degree as a vet tech and moved to Idaho to work for a livestock vet. Our parents aren't thrilled."

"Why?"

"Because she only moved there to get away from here."

"Is she not on good terms with your parents?"

"My dad had bypass surgery last year. He's fine now. But Ophelia thinks he's going to have another heart attack and die, and she doesn't want to be here when it happens. But it's not like it's going to prevent it from happening. She can run, but she can't really hide."

I swallowed hard. He wasn't talking about me. Besides, I wasn't hiding. I was just taking a break from reality.

"I love the name Ophelia. And I bet she meets a rugged cowboy out west."

Murphy laughed. "Ya think?"

"I do."

"Is that what you're looking for? A rugged cowboy who keeps you barefoot and pregnant on his big ranch?"

I twisted my lips. "Milking cows and goats? Collecting eggs? Baking bread? Sure. That would work."

"Synchronized swimming in a big pond?"

I giggled. "Exactly."

"And you'd have plenty of turtles, so there wouldn't be any need to steal them."

I grinned, elbowing his arm.

It was all a wonderful dream.

Chapter
SEVENTEEN

Murphy

*The past can never be changed,
but we can change how we look at it.*

IF I'M HONEST, Alice was my first love. I'd had girlfriends, and we threw around that four letter word with the same carelessness as any other word. But Alice was different.

Every day mattered. She lived without reservation. When we were together, there was nothing to chase. No dreams. No tomorrows. Every moment with her felt like the reason for existing, like I'd figured out the meaning of life.

In a blink, she was ripped away from me, and I spent years recovering from a fortnight.

I've moved on, but there's still an invisible string attached to her. And now she's here, and I can't break that string. Every time she looks at me, that string gets tighter and stronger, and I fear I'll break before it does.

"Do either of you know anyone in New York?" Vera asks as the four of us drink around the rectangular fire pit table on the patio overlooking the pool after dinner. "Or will you have to make new friends?"

"Cam and Sage are in Brooklyn. They'll be at our wedding, and they're getting married two weeks after us, so we'll be back from our honeymoon in time to attend their wedding. It's in Buffalo because that's where most of Sage's family lives," Blair says with her feet propped on my leg.

"Do I know Cam and Sage?" Hunter asks.

"No." Blair shakes her head. "But Mom met Sage when we took the girls' trip to London last summer."

"I'm going to use the restroom. Excuse me," I say, lifting her feet from my legs and resting them on the love seat. "Can I get anyone anything while I'm inside?"

"We're good, but thanks," Hunter answers for everyone since the women don't seem to hear me.

After I take a piss and head toward the back of the house, I hear something from the open window in the kitchen. Alice is in the yard between the main house and the guesthouse, playing cornhole by herself with a canned beverage in one hand. The boards are dimly lit by the LED path lights next to the hedges.

I exit through the front door so Blair and her parents don't see me walk to the side of house. "Who's winning?" I ask.

Alice jumps, turning toward me.

"Sorry. I didn't mean to startle you."

She returns a shy smile, curling her hair behind one ear. It's wavy like she let it air-dry. One of her shorts pockets is frayed and ripped, and she's barefoot. She's never looked so beautiful. And why that thought just popped into my mind is not only disturbing, but frustrating. I love Blair. *She* is beautiful. Alice is nothing but a door that never got closed, and these feelings are nothing more than a distracting draft of air, blowing my common sense around like a scattered pile of papers.

"Currently, I'm in the lead, but it's a close game." The corner of her mouth twitches.

I grin, sliding my hands into my back pockets. "Are either of you any good?"

She sips her orange Olipop soda before bobbing her head. "We're okay."

"There are a lot of bags in the hole. Looks like one of you is more than okay."

"Just a lucky night."

I nod. "I've wanted to apologize again for the pool incident. Or perhaps I should thank you. Had I been drowning, you would have saved my life."

"It's fine. Forgotten. Don't worry about it." She retrieves the red bags, tucking a couple under her arm since she only has one hand to use.

"I can probably play a quick game with you before anyone sends out the search party for me." I pluck the blue bags off the ground.

She eyes me for a few seconds before nodding, but I don't miss her tiny grin. And I wonder if it's any sort of recognition or a familiar feeling, or if she's just happy to have someone to beat.

"You can go first," she says.

I ready myself to toss the bag. "Years ago, I owned a vacation rental. A guest challenged me to a game of cornhole, and she kicked my butt in a matter of minutes. I haven't played since then." I toss the bag and hit the board, but nowhere near the hole.

"Bruised ego? Is that why you haven't played again?" she asks, tossing the red bag right into the hole.

"Maybe." I take my turn and miss the board.

Alice gets ready to pitch her next bag.

"But mostly it's because I've tried to forget that time in my life," I say two seconds before she tosses it and misses the entire board by at least three feet.

And I know, right now, without a doubt—she remembers me.

She sips her drink, trying to look unaffected, but her other hand balls into a fist, and she cracks several knuckles.

There's not enough alcohol on the premises to numb the pain in my chest. I thought it hurt when she didn't recognize me. But this ... it's fucking torture.

She clears her throat after I chuck my next bag. "So you sold your vacation rental?"

"Yeah. My dad worked so hard to recover from a heart attack only to have an aneurysm take his life in a blink. He'd helped me convert the building into two separate living spaces, and we used to turn wood in the garage together." I shrugged after she tossed her next bag and made it on the board again, but not in the hole. "The place held too many memories of my dad and ... someone else. I needed a fresh start."

Alice doesn't say a word or look at me as we toss our last two bags.

"Do you still turn wood?" she asks as we collect our bags.

"No."

She brushes her auburn hair out of her face when the

breeze tangles it. "But you're marrying an artist. Does she encourage you to do it again?"

I shake my head, eyeing the hole only to throw the bag way past the board. "She doesn't know I ever did it."

"What?" She squints at me, mouth agape. "Why not?"

"Like I said. A fresh start." I'm not sure anything feels fresh about my new life since Alice is here.

"Does a fresh start mean your past doesn't exist?" she asks.

"I don't know. What do you think?"

Alice shifts her attention from me to the board. "I'm asking you. What I think doesn't matter."

"But what if it does?"

She returns a nervous laugh before sipping her drink. After she swallows, she wipes her mouth with the back of her hand. "It shouldn't. I'm just the homemaker. A virtual stranger."

I take a step closer, and she seems to hold her breath as I reach for her face to brush a few hairs away from it, but then I stop and return my hand to my side. It hurts to look at her like a stranger. My mind might know how to play tricks, but my heart is incapable of such games. "You're the most familiar stranger I've ever met. And eventually, I'm going to figure out why you feel so familiar."

It's reminiscent of when my mom used to catch me or my sister in a lie, and she'd give us every opportunity to confess before calling us out.

Alice presses her lips together, and I can't tell in the dim light, but it looks like she has tears in her eyes.

"Well, I should get back to—"

"Your fiancée," she whispers.

"Yeah," I murmur, dropping my head and staring at her

bare feet as she curls her toes into the grass. For a breath, I close my eyes and go back eight years.

"Murphy, do you walk barefoot in the grass? You should. This is the softest spot, right here by the fence."

"Alice, that's where Palmer pees the most."

"Yuck! Why didn't you tell me before now?"

A tiny grin finds my lips as I remember her running to the spigot to wash her feet. Palmer peed in the sand, but she didn't know that.

When I look at her, Alice assesses me with her sad blue eyes and takes a step closer.

Fearing what her proximity might do to me, I retreat and find a genuine smile. "Good night, Alice."

"Good night, Mr. Paddon."

Chapter
EIGHTEEN

Murphy

Sex is a distraction. It's okay to get distracted.

Eight Years Earlier ...

"Mr. Paddon, are we role-playing this afternoon?" Alice asked, glancing up from her wine and game of solitaire on the dining room table as I stepped into her kitchen wearing a black suit and tie just before lunch. The inviting sweet smell of freshly baked cookies enveloped me.

"Do you like to role-play?" I lifted an eyebrow, possibilities swirling through my dirty mind.

Alice had part of her shoulder-length hair pulled into a messy ponytail, lips twisted into a naughty grin as she counted three more cards and turned them over. "What kind of question is that? You know I'm an amateur actress."

"A hypothetical actress."

Without looking up from her game, she smirked. "Yes, Mr. Paddon. So if you're not here for role-playing, then who died?"

"My grandfather."

She jerked her head up. "Jesus, Murphy, I was kidding. Please tell me you are too."

I adjusted my tie because I hated wearing a suit. "Sadly, I'm not. If it makes you feel better, he died a week before you got here. But my uncle has been in Germany on business, and this was the earliest he could return."

"I'm so sorry. I can't believe you're just now mentioning it. We've solved every single world problem on our walks, but you didn't think to share that piece of information? Was he the vinyl record grandfather?" She jabbed her thumb over her shoulder toward the turntable.

"Yeah. And I guess I didn't want you feeling sorry for me."

"Well," she stood and padded her bare feet toward me to wrap her arms around my neck, "I *am* sorry."

"Thank you." I rested my hands on her waist as she released me. "You know what makes funerals more bearable?"

"Wine?"

I chuckled. "A plus-one."

She crinkled her nose. "A date?"

I nodded.

"No." She turned and headed back to the dining room table. "A plus-one for a funeral is a terrible idea. Who wants to meet a complete stranger when they're at their worst? Funerals should be private events. No outsiders."

"He had a ton of friends. It's a big funeral. You won't stand out as an outsider."

"Maybe. But I don't do funerals," she said, refocusing on her game.

"You make it sound like a pastime. No one 'does' funerals. They're about as much fun as a colonoscopy."

"Exactly. And you wouldn't invite me to hold your hand while they stuck a scope up your ass, right?"

"I mean ... I might. But that's not a fair comparison."

"Murphy, it's your comparison, not mine."

She was right. It was a weird and stupid idea.

"Well, then I'll see you later."

"Again, I'm sorry for your loss." She shot me one last glance and frowned.

"Thanks." I turned toward the door, then stopped. "I mean ... you've been to a funeral, right?"

She deposited another card in a row.

"Alice?"

"Do you mind if I use your bike again?"

She heard me. Right?

"Of course you can use my bike."

"Thank you."

I opened my mouth to say more about the funeral, and just as quickly, I clamped my jaw shut. Part of me felt close, maybe even connected, to Alice. After all, we'd been intimate. She gave me her body. What more could she have given?

A lot.

She, by plan, gave me nothing disguised as everything. And I didn't know if I could or should ask for more. I had a feeling that what I loved most about her wasn't real.

❧

After the funeral, burial, and luncheon, I returned home with great intentions of asking Alice a few personal questions that didn't start with "hypothetically." However, when I stepped into the backyard, loosening my tie, my desire to dig up her dark secrets died because she was face down on the outdoor sectional, sunning herself in just her undergarments—her bra unhooked to prevent a tan line.

She turned her head toward me. "Hi," she said, instead of asking me about the funeral.

"Are you wearing sunscreen?"

"Sure." She closed her eyes and smirked.

"Who put it on your back?" I slowly walked up the patio stairs, unbuttoning the top two buttons of my dress shirt.

"Palmer, of course."

I chuckled. "Did you go for a bike ride?" I moved her glass of water and sat on the ceramic side table.

"Mm-hm."

She seemed relaxed, maybe even receptive to answer some questions. But my dick had a different case to make. I glanced around as if I could tell if any neighbors were peering at us from their second-story windows.

"My parents invited me to dinner at their house tonight since we have a lot of family in town." I ghosted my fingertips up the back of her leg. "Would you like to come with me?" My finger teased along her underwear while I bent forward to kiss her shoulder.

"You can't touch me like this while talking about your parents."

I kissed her cheek, and she grinned.

"Maybe we can revisit this conversation in a half hour," I whispered before kissing her ear, inhaling subtle hints of floral in her hair.

"A half hour?" She peeked open one eye. "Are we trying something new? A half hour seems a little slow for our pace."

"New indeed." I kissed her shoulder again. "Just hear me out. I was thinking we could try a bed. I realize that seems unconventional, and we love things like desks, tables, walls, and the back of the sofa so much better, but I'm in the mood to venture into uncharted territory with you. What do you say?"

"Aren't you sad about your grandpa?"

"He lived a good life. I'll miss him. But I'm sad that you're leaving next week, and I'm going to get so much work done and hate every minute."

"Is that your way of saying I'm an excellent distraction?"

I kissed her nose. "It's my way of saying, don't go."

She slowly sat up, holding her bra to her chest. "I wish we were real."

I shook my head. "What does that mean? Is this about the diamond ring? Have I been screwing another man's wife?"

Alice stood, stepping past me toward the house. "I'm not married. Never have been." She opened the door. "Never will be. But ..." With a flirty glance over her shoulder, she let her bra drop to her feet. "I'll be in bed. Bring your list of fantasies, and I'll see what I can do to start checking them off." She winked.

Chapter
NINETEEN

Alice

You're never too old to play.
Stay young at heart.

"YOU EVER BEEN MARRIED, ALICE?" Hunter asks as he pours me a glass of water before his afternoon story-slash-nap time.

I've come to enjoy our midday ritual. It's hard to explain, but our time together feels intimate in a way that's not physical or any sort of cheating. Maybe it's like therapy, like we have an unspoken agreement that what's said during our time in his study will never leave this room.

"I have not," I say.

"Can I give you some sage advice?" He sets the water on the end table.

"Sure." I use my finger as a bookmark and rest the book on my lap.

"Skip the big wedding. Go to the courthouse if you want to make it legal or have a minister or priest marry you midweek with a witness if necessary, but skip the theatrics. Save your money. If your parents are paying, ask them to give you the money instead and invest it."

"Spoken like a true romantic, Mr. Morrison."

He settles on the sofa. "Just trust me. It's not worth it."

"Well, I don't think I would have taken this job had I planned on getting married."

"Because I'm your sugar daddy?"

Laughter bubbles up my chest. Despite his "fetishes" or rich-guy eccentricities, Hunter Morrison is a kind soul.

He peeks open one eye and glances at me with a smirk. "Don't deny it. You're grossly overcompensated, yet somehow worth every penny. Go figure."

"Thank you. I'll take that as a compliment."

"You should." He chuckles. "By the way, the hand soap you made for my bathroom is amazing. It's robust and masculine. What's the scent?"

"Vanilla."

He barks a laugh.

"Cedar and citrus," I say with an unavoidable grin because I bought the handmade soap from a local store where they cut and sell it by the ounce. He doesn't need to know all of my secrets. "Is it weird that my favorite character in this story is the dog?" I ask, returning my attention to the book.

"Montmorency is a hoot," he says. "But you gotta love the camaraderie between the men."

"For sure," I say, opening the book and reading to him. By the end of a chapter, Hunter appears to be asleep.

However, before I utter the first word of the next chapter, he says, "You're a beautiful young woman with a calming disposition. Why don't you have dreams of getting married?"

I pause, waiting for him to open his eyes or move another part of his body, but he doesn't.

"Um," I clear my throat. "Why would you ask me that after giving me *sage advice* not to get married?"

"My advice was to forgo a big wedding. But now I'm curious why you don't want to get married." His chuckle triggers a little cough, so he fists his hand at his mouth.

"Water?" I ask.

Keeping his eyes closed, he shakes his head and relaxes his folded hands back onto his chest. "I know it's none of my business. What can I say? My nosey wife has rubbed off on me."

"I'm just unlucky in love. That's all."

"So is my daughter, but it hasn't stopped her from trying. I'm not sure poor Murphy will get an official 'I do' out of her. But perhaps the third time's a charm."

"Why did she break off her other engagements, if you don't mind me asking?"

"She's commitment phobic. Indecisive. Her mother calls her a 'free bird.' And that's great. I support that, but then just admit that you won't make a good lifelong partner. You know?"

I nod slowly. "Do you think Murphy's the one? Or will she back out?"

"He's a great guy. But, just between us, he's not the one either. I don't think 'the one' for her exists."

"Maybe he's the exception."

"I doubt it. He can't love her like she needs to be loved."

I rest the open book face down on my lap. "What do you mean?"

"My daughter is like me, even though she'll never admit it. And I'm needy as fuck."

I roll my lips between my teeth to suppress my laughter. Hunter's self-examination is not only shocking but refreshing.

"Of course, I tell everyone else she's like Vera, but it's a lie. That girl is neurotic as hell. *Free bird* my ass. And Murphy doesn't give a shit if she's pissed at him for something stupid. He's not a groveler or a people pleaser."

"Opposites attract. Maybe he's exactly what she needs."

"Oh," Hunter peeks at me, "she absolutely needs a man like him. But give it time, and what she wants will trump what she needs."

"What does she want?"

"Someone who worships her. Spoon-feeds her ego."

"Is that my job? To worship you and spoon-feed your ego?"

His chest bounces with laughter. "Vera would kill me if I asked you to get on your knees for any sort of worship, so just read to me and tell me I'm handsome."

In the most unromantic way, I love Hunter Morrison.

Despite the dick-sucking clause in my contract, Vera, Hunter, and I are a threesome. As with any good threesome, there are power struggles and alliances. I'm not sure where my loyalty lies. It depends on the day.

After story time, I iron Vera's air-dry-only jeans. She's not immune to enjoying the perks of a homemaker, and perfectly pressed denim is one of them.

"There you are," she says, stepping into the laundry room with an inflated smile. "I have a favor."

"Mrs. Morrison, I work for you. You can call it a duty or a task." I glance up from the ironing board.

"Very well," she flicks her wrist, "I have a task for you. Will you bake something and deliver it to Rupert Rawlings? He lives in the two-story next door." She points in that direction.

"Sure. Anything specific you want me to bake?"

"Something wholesome, like an apple pie."

I laugh a little.

"Hunter and Rupert are very competitive. And it's Rupert's birthday. He's just barely younger than Hunter. Both men are proud of their financial portfolios and their full heads of hair."

I unplug the iron. "Do you want me to sing to Rupert?"

She snorts, shaking her head. Then she narrows her eyes. "Would you?"

"Of course. I love that they're competitors and friends."

"Oh, no. They're not friends." Vera fiddles with her rings. "Rupert wanted this house, and Hunter outbid him the same day Rupert's dad died, and he was too preoccupied to bid higher. So Rupert knocked on the door of the house he lives in now, offered the owners, who were not planning on selling, a price they couldn't refuse. And he did it all just so he could be our neighbor and torment Hunter. If Hunter buys a car, Rupert one-ups him with the same car that's worth just a little more. When Hunter used to jog around the lake, Rupert followed him just to make Hunter run faster until he was ready to vomit by the time he got home. So now Hunter only runs inside on the treadmill."

"Then why are you having me bake a pie for his birthday? I draw the line at poisoning anyone."

Vera follows me upstairs to her bedroom, where I put her jeans in the luxurious walk-in closet filled with hanging tags on unworn clothes, gobs of sparkling jewels and real gold necklaces and bracelets, shelves of red-bottomed shoes, and complete with a crystal chandelier hanging in the middle.

"This isn't about those two men. It's about me. And it's about you."

"Me?" I close the drawer and raise my eyebrows.

"Hunter wanted a homemaker, so I hired you. But he's treating you like his mother, who, yes, was a homemaker. However, putting my husband down for a nap in the afternoon by reading him a book is going too far. Not on your part. You're just doing what is asked of you. But he needs a little reality check. So that's why I want you to take a pie to Rupert for his birthday. After all, a homemaker would absolutely do something kind like that for a neighbor. Right?"

She's asking me? I'm just playing this role for fun, money, and a lack of anything better to do with my life. And I like story time, but I won't tell her that.

"I mean," I shrug, "sure. So you're trying to make Mr. Morrison mad? Jealous?"

"I'm just trying to pull his head out of his ass. He's getting lazy. I have to lube myself for sex and be on top every time. It's getting ridiculous."

The threesome was figurative. Still, I snicker.

"Sorry." Vera sighs, sitting in the cream velvet chair at the end of the closet island. "I miss really good sex. I miss sex that never makes it to the bed. Have you ever had that? The feeling of being desired and just ... ravaged." She briefly closes her eyes. "There's nothing like it."

I fold my hands in front of me as if we're discussing the dinner menu.

"Blair says sex with Murphy is out of this world. I want out-of-this-world sex. Instead, I have a sexy, silver fox husband who doesn't offer out-of-this-world sex anymore. It's definitely *in this world*. It's like ... Iowa sex."

I snort.

"I'm serious, Alice." She grins. "Don't settle for that kind of sex. I honestly thought hiring you would get him a little ..." She taps her pointy, manicured nail on her front teeth. "Riled up. Inspired. Horny."

I twist my lips and nod.

"Not for you. Like when you watch a steamy movie, and then you have great sex."

She's not saying the word "porn," but that's what she's implying.

"I should be sexier?"

She bites the inside of her cheek and slowly shakes her head. "You're plenty sexy. We need to figure out something else. What book are you reading to him?"

"*Three Men in a Boat.*"

"Oh, for the love of god. How is that supposed to inspire anything in the bedroom? You need to read him something where the hero bites the heroine's bare ass before really giving it to her. You know?"

I return a contemplative nod. How did I get so lucky? And what is wrong with me that I, in fact, feel lucky to have landed this "role?"

"If I'm going to deliver this pie to Rupert today, I should make sure I have all the ingredients in case I need to run to the store. But I'll give your request some thought for when we're ready to start another book."

"Thanks, and sorry. I needed to vent. I'll save it for my therapist next time."

"No. It's fine. I'm a good listener. It's just getting late."

"Of course." She stands, tossing her hair over her shoulders. "I'll tell Hunter I'm in the mood for a drive, so he won't know you're making a pie that's not for him. Then we will have dinner reservations later, so you can call it for the day after you deliver the pie."

"Sounds good." I head to the kitchen while she turns toward his study at the bottom of the stairs.

After I make the pie, smooth my ponytail, reapply red lipstick, and unbutton the top three buttons of my dress to show a little cleavage, I exit through the door to the terrace, nearly running into Murphy coming into the house.

"Whoa!" He jumps aside to avoid a pie collision. "Sorry. I was looking at my phone."

I ease my death grip on the pie. "It's fine."

"Where are you going with that pie? It smells amazing."

"Sorry. It's for Rupert Rawlings."

"You're kidding."

"It's his birthday." I offer an exaggerated smile.

"Hunter can't stand that guy."

"I'm aware."

Murphy narrows his eyes. "So, what are you doing?"

"I'm being neighborly as a good homemaker would be."

"Did Vera put you up to this?"

I blink without responding.

"This is beneath you. Don't let them put you in the middle of their fucked-up issues."

"I'm a big girl. I knew what I was getting into when I accepted the job."

His gaze drops several inches. "You missed a few buttons."

I keep my chin up. "I didn't."

"You look like you're offering more than pie for his birthday."

"I'm glad you approve."

"I don't fucking approve," he snaps, and quickly recovers with a long sigh and a headshake. "That was out of line," he stutters. "I'm sorry."

"Bad day?"

Murphy rubs his temples. "I have a headache."

"Anything I can do?"

He drops his hands and stares at me. "You can give me a piece of that pie."

"I can't deliver a birthday pie with a piece missing."

He crosses his arms. "You just said 'anything.' Did you not mean it?"

"Where's Blair? Oh, and I'll wash the dishes as soon as I get back. I don't want to wait any longer to deliver the pie."

"Blair's getting a massage. It's just the two of us and that pie. And I want a piece."

After a brief standoff, I lift the edge of the foil and pinch off a tiny *piece* of the crust. Then I lift it to Murphy's mouth. He doesn't look at my hand. It's as if our gazes are glued. He grabs my wrist and wraps his lips around the tips of my two fingers.

Holy shit.

I can't breathe.

My skin tingles and my nipples harden beneath my bra. I hate his perfect life and the woman who will be his perfect wife. I don't want him having out-of-this-world sex with her.

I looked for him. He's the entire reason I'm in Lake of the Isles.

And now he's here, but it's too late.

Too late to rectify the past.

Too late to have a future.

Too late to want him this much.

As his grip keeps his lips pressed to my fingers, I swallow hard.

"Smart ass," he says, releasing my wrist before shouldering past me without looking back.

I brush my hand over my dress, pushing my nipples back into hiding before continuing toward Rupert Rawlings' house.

After ringing the doorbell twice with no answer, I turn to head back home, then the door opens.

"Can I help you?"

I turn and smile. "Mr. Rawlings?"

"Yes."

Indeed, he has a full head of salt-and-pepper hair. Symmetrical face. Charming smile. Rupert is effortlessly cool like George Clooney.

I go into character as if the curtains just opened on the stage, and the spotlight is on me. Confidence is just good acting.

"Happy birthday to you ..." I sing each line with a wide smile. I don't go full-on Marilyn Monroe "happy birthday, Mr. President," but I do my best to make Vera proud. And from the look on Rupert's face, he's pleased with my performance.

"This is from the Morrisons." I hand him the pie. "I'm Alice, Mr. Morrison's homemaker. I hope you like it."

Rupert shifts, posture straightening, gaze sweeping head

to toe. "Yes. I heard he had a *homemaker*." His tone implies more than homemaker.

I keep smiling, letting his dirty imagination run wild.

He nods at my chest. "Does Vera let you walk around the house like that?"

I keep my shoulders back, chest out. "I'm not allowed to suck Mr. Morrison's dick. That's the only house rule." I give him the full show, batting my eyelashes.

"Well, damn, young lady. One sec ..." He holds up a finger before setting the pie on a credenza and jogging up the curved grand stairway behind him, shoes tapping on the marble. A few seconds later, he returns and hands me a black business card with a number but no name. "Call me. Whatever that schmuck is paying you, I'll pay double."

I smile, trapping the card between two fingers and seductively sliding it into my bra. "I'll think about it. Hope you blow out all of your candles." I pivot and skip down the stairs to the sidewalk.

"I'm telling Hunter you spanked me in my birthday suit."

I bite my lower lip and giggle.

Chapter
TWENTY

Murphy

Doing the right thing can be wrong.
You're going to fuck things up. That's life.

"WHAT ARE YOU DOING?" Alice asks as I wash the dishes.

"What does it look like?"

"It looks like you're doing my job." She buttons her dress as I glance over at her.

I guess I don't get cleavage for doing the dishes.

"You gave me a piece of pie. The least I can do is clean up."

"Go to your room. I've got this." She nudges me aside and dons the pink latex gloves while I dry my hands.

"But, Mom, it's not my bedtime yet."

Alice keeps her chin tucked to hide her grin. "You're trying to get me fired. Then I'll have to work for Rupert Rawlings for twice the money."

"You're kidding. He offered you a job?"

She takes over washing the dishes. "Don't act so surprised. I'm a rare commodity. Not a lot of women my age, or any age for that matter, would do what I do."

I take the glass bowl from her and dry it. We've washed a lot of dishes together.

Flirty glances.

Playful nudges.

Stolen kisses that led to losing our clothes.

I doubt that will happen tonight.

"No one else does dishes?"

Alice elbows me. I guess *we are* playfully nudging tonight.

"Oh, you must be talking about the sexy fifties dresses. Or do you mean reading stories to old men while they nap?"

She eyes me, and I get to check "flirty glance" off the list. That just leaves stolen kisses and losing our clothes. My mind doesn't care that I have a fiancée, but I wish it did because it *needs* to get really fucking serious about these unresolved feelings.

"Does Blair know you're this obnoxious with other women who you don't know that well?"

"I feel like I know you." I inspect her while drying the measuring cup, looking for a hint of recognition. Eventually, she'll crack. "Do you feel like you know me?"

She shrugs a shoulder, keeping her gaze on the sink of sudsy water. "I feel like I know guys like you."

"Guys like me? Dang. And here I thought I was an original. Please elaborate on what you mean by guys like me."

"Homemakers are peacemakers. I'm not here to critique you. I'm here to make you feel at home."

"In that case, stop what you're doing. When I lived at

home, my mom worked nights, and my dad fell asleep in his recliner by seven. So the dinner dishes didn't get washed until the following morning because my sister and I snuck out of the house as soon as our dad's eyes closed. And you'll need to empty most of the clothes onto the floor by the washing machine. The fridge is entirely too organized. And don't get me started on the perfectly made beds with no chip crumbs in them."

"Sounds like a normal house." She shoots me a quick smile.

Everything hurts inside. What if I put an end to this charade? Tell her I know she knows me. Then what?

Will she tell me everything?

Will it change anything?

Standing this close to her, just the two of us, it feels like we're cleaning up after dinner in the little rental, like I could kiss her and it would feel normal, maybe even expected.

"What was your childhood home like?" I ask.

"My dad did all the cooking because he was a stay-at-home dad. That's where my love of cooking started. Later I consumed every YouTube video I could find that would refine my cooking skills. And I had to wash the dishes every night. No waiting until morning at my house."

"So your dad stayed home. What did your mom do?" I don't know if she's telling me the truth. This is all new information.

"She's a biomedical engineer."

"So you've taken after your dad. A homemaker."

Alice laughs. "I get paid, he didn't. That's one reason they're divorced now." She hands me the last dish.

"I'm sorry to hear that."

"Actually," she drains the water and pauses, "I took after my mom."

"What do you mean?"

"I went to college to be a civil engineer, but after my third year, I dropped out."

The Alice I knew didn't go to college. Who's the liar? Old Alice or new Alice?

"Why did you drop out?"

She dries her hands. "My friend died, and I lost focus. The only reason I was studying engineering was because my mom supported it and my friend was studying it as well."

I pause. Did her friend really die? When? Was it the same friend who convinced her to be a synchronized swimmer? "I'm sorry," I murmur.

After hanging the towel to dry, she puts away the clean dishes. "Stop apologizing for the miserable things in my life. Look at me now. I'm living the dream."

"Dream bigger." I laugh.

She closes the cabinet and leans against it. "Are you living your dream?"

Nightmare is more like it.

"What do you think?" I ask with a little laugh, as if the answer is obvious.

"I think you're just along for the ride in someone else's dream."

"Is that not what you're doing?"

Her gaze slips along with her smile, and she stares at the floor between us.

"Can I tell you a secret?" I ask.

Alice returns her attention to me.

"I met a woman eight—"

"Ugh! Traffic is insane," Blair interrupts, tossing her keys onto the counter and dropping her bag on the floor before draping her arms around me.

I hug her waist as she practically hangs from my neck like she's too tired to stand on her own.

Alice and I stare at each other. I was going to tell her. Did Blair just save me from making an epic mistake?

"I need a shower before dinner. Want to join me?" Blair kisses my neck.

"Thanks for your help," Alice murmurs, untying her apron and pivoting to walk to the back door.

Blair shoots a quick glance in her direction before turning back to me. "What did you help her do?"

"The dishes," I murmur, with my gaze still glued to the cabinet as if Alice were still there.

Blair's nose wrinkles. "Why?"

I shrug. "Seemed like the nice thing to do."

"Babe, that's her job. She doesn't help you do your job."

I peel her hands from my neck. "What does it matter?"

"It's just weird." Blair pinches my chin, forcing me to look at her. "Did you hear me? I asked if you want to shower with me."

"I already showered."

She frowns. "Hello? I'm basically asking if you want to have sex. Is that a no?"

"Your parents should be back soon."

"Murphy, they know we have sex." She takes my hand and leads me toward the bathroom. "I'm feeling generous, if you know what I mean."

Chapter
TWENTY-ONE

Alice

You'll never fall in love if you don't jump.

Eight Years Earlier ...

"I LOVE YOUR WOOD," I said.

Murphy smirked behind his shield, glancing up from his wood-turning lathe. The garage was sticky despite the whirling fan hanging in the corner, and the air smelled musty from the scraps of walnut.

Nothing felt as cathartic as watching him create something beautiful from a simple piece of wood, not even sex. And that said a lot because Murphy Paddon knew his way around a woman's body.

"Did you build this rocker?" I asked, rocking in said wooden rocker with Palmer on my lap.

"My dad did," he replied, as ribbons of wood shavings dropped to the floor.

"So your dad's better with wood than you are?"

Murphy turned off the lathe and stepped back before lifting his face shield. Then he looked at his watch. "We're late for afternoon delight. No wonder you're infatuated with wood talk."

I rolled my eyes. "I'm joking. Keep working. I've got Palmer to keep me company."

"Yeah, but he's a pussy. You need a real man."

I giggled. "I want to watch you work. But I also want that other thing you're talking about. Also, I'm hungry. I should start dinner now. Or what do you think about going out?"

He pressed the button, and the garage door closed. Then he tugged on his belt to unbuckle it. "The thing with wood is you need to be confident but gentle. You have to know when to go deep and when to have a light touch."

Palmer jumped off my lap as Murphy stepped in front of me, unzipping his jeans.

"Stop!" I laughed, standing and grabbing his wrists to prevent him from going any further. "Keep working, or let's go somewhere."

He narrowed his eyes, sighed, and zipped his jeans. "Where do you want to go?"

"I heard you have some hidden falls around here. Let's go to lunch, then to the falls. After that, we'll grab groceries."

His thumb traced the scar on my arm. He did it a lot. "Where did you get this?" he finally asks. "It looks like a recent scar. Red and raised."

I swallowed hard. "I was swimming in the river and snagged it on a branch."

Murphy nodded and continued to study me. "Can you give me ten minutes before we go?"

I smiled, delighted that the scar conversation was over. "Of course."

"Good." He kissed my neck and unbuttoned my jeans.

"What are you doing?" I grinned, sliding my fingers into his hair.

"Don't worry about it. We'll be done in less than ten minutes." And before he kissed my lips, he grinned and whispered, "Hi."

There were three important things I learned about Murphy Paddon that day. One: He knew where to get the best Banh Mi sandwich in Minnesota. Two: He carried snacks for the squirrels in his pockets. Three: He organized the cart returns in the grocery store parking lot.

Food connoisseur.

Animal lover.

Perfectionist.

"Not cool," I said, resting a hand on my flipped-out hip when he nested the carts in a perfect line.

"What's not cool? Helping the store out?" He laughed.

"Those employees probably fight over who gets to bring in the carts because it means they get outside in the sun and fresh air for a while. But now you've done half their job, which means less time outside."

"Get your sexy ass in the car and stop pestering me about my stellar manners."

I stood at the end of the cart return checking my nails as if his command meant nothing.

"I bet you were spanked a lot as a child," he said, after pushing the last cart into the others.

"Why would you say that?" I glanced up just as he grabbed my arm and the back sides of my legs.

"Murphy!" I squealed when he hoisted me over his shoulder.

"Because," he swatted my ass, "you can be too sassy for your own good."

"Put me down! This is embarrassing."

He continued toward his Explorer and placed me on my feet at the front passenger door. I scowled while straightening my shirt and righting my shorts. When I opened my mouth to give him another round of "sass," he grabbed my face and kissed me.

No "hi." No warning. Just his tongue sliding past my lips. I moaned as it scraped along the roof of my mouth. The warm door met my back as his body pressed against mine. My heart ached knowing our time was ending. And then it ached even more as memories of why it had to end seeped through the walls I'd built around the wreckage.

Our kiss slowed, and his lips brushed along my cheek as his hands threaded through my hair, tugging at the roots. "I don't want you to go," he whispered.

I knew that. And I didn't want to leave Minneapolis, the quaint little apartment, Palmer the resident cat, or the woodturner with a killer smile and equally sublime dance moves. Reality was overrated. But the only way to escape it forever was to leave the world behind. Since I chose life, I couldn't stay with Murphy, but I hated to go. And the realm between what was real and what was not wasn't strong enough to contain my grief.

"You can't ask me to stay," I said in an equally agonizing whisper. "And you can't love me."

Murphy paused. "I'm not asking you to stay. I'm just asking that you never fucking forget that I don't want you to go."

I wasn't sure if the heart could grieve two things at once. What if I had to let go of one to let go of the other? I blinked back the tears brimming in my burning eyes, and I wrapped my arms around his neck to hug him as hard as possible. He held me just as tightly. And I don't know how long we stood in the parking lot like this. It felt like an infinite moment, and I knew those arms were the only things holding me together.

After a silent, melancholy drive back to his place, we put away the groceries, and I pulled out a skillet to start dinner.

"It's my place," he said.

I glanced over at him. He had his shoulder resting against the fridge, arms crossed over his chest, face pensive.

"What?"

"This is my place," he said in a chiding tone.

I laughed nervously, drizzling oil into the pan. "I'm aware."

"I make the rules here. They're in the binder on the coffee table."

"I'm aware of that too." I capped the oil and risked another glance at him.

The muscles in his jaw flexed. "So if I say you're not allowed to cook for me and then just leave, you have to obey."

Again, I managed a tiny, nervous laugh as my insides twisted. "Is that so?"

"Yes. And you can't befriend Palmer and just leave."

"Mur—"

"And you can't step all over my toes while I teach you to dance and then just leave." His face turned red as his volume escalated.

I had no more nervous laughs to offer, just trepidation gripping my chest.

"You can't let me touch you and kiss you and"—he swallowed hard—"be inside of you and just. Fucking. Leave!" His hands balled into fists.

The already shattered pieces of my heart turned to dust. The nauseating whoosh of blood echoed in my ears. I wasn't scared of him. I was scared of all the feelings pouring out of him in waves so big I knew they would suffocate me.

In the next blink, several tears slid down my face. "I told you—"

"I know what you told me!" He stabbed his fingers through his hair. "I know. I *know* what you told me. But that was then, and this is now. And I'm all too aware that we haven't known each other for a full two weeks yet, but I don't care, Alice. Some things in life you don't have to figure out. You just know. And I know," he jabbed a finger into his chest, "that you didn't come here for a two-week fling.

"I know it's killing you too. And I don't know if you're married, if you have two kids and a dog waiting for you. I don't know if you're terminally ill, or just really fucking lost in life, but I want to. I want to know everything about you because you didn't give me a chance *not* to fall in love with you. Instead, you made up this stupid rule that I am not allowed to have feelings. And it was cute at first, but then you just ... FUCK!" He turned his back to me, hands laced behind his neck, head bowed as he huffed.

I wiped more tears as the oil in the skillet smoked. So I

quickly pushed it off the burner. "Ouch!" I recoiled my hand after the metal burned it.

Murphy whipped around and shut off the burner before turning on the water and guiding my hand underneath the stream. I didn't look at the burn mark; I stared at the scar a few inches above it on my forearm.

Everything good in life left a mark.

I swallowed past the lump in my throat, waiting for Murphy to say something, but he didn't. Instead, he retrieved a first aid kit from the linen closet, applied burn cream, and wrapped my hand as I sat on a dining room chair. Then, without breaking the silence, he stood, leaned forward and kissed my cheek, letting his lips linger while I closed my eyes.

I didn't open them until after the thud of his feet faded and the back door clicked shut behind him.

Chapter
TWENTY-TWO

Alice

Commitment is messy. Keep it simple.

I CAN'T BREAK the fourth wall, but I want to.

Murphy knows I remember him. But the second one of us acknowledges it, the illusion will be shattered. There will be questions and consequences. So why did he almost do it?

I have a good life. Good enough.

And so does he.

In the fall, he will marry Blair and move to New York. I will stay here and put most of my paycheck into savings so I can buy a house in Edina.

Single and alone.

During the holidays, Mr. and Mrs. Murphy Paddon will come home to visit. Perhaps they will bring their children, and I can be the nanny while the adults go to dinner and sit in a private box at the theater to watch *The Nutcracker*.

Maybe Vera will die, and Hunter will make me his secret lover.

As I serve breakfast to Blair, Murphy, and their children, I'll overhear one of their kids saying he heard Grandpa Morrison making noises the previous night. Murphy will discreetly mumble to Blair, "*Sounds like your dad found someone to suck his old, gray balls.*"

Blair will gasp and slap his arm, but not before snorting. She'll say, "*Stop! That's gross. Can you imagine who would be desperate enough to sleep with my old dad?*"

"Do you have something you'd like to tell me?" Hunter asks, bringing me out of my ridiculous hallucination as I refill his coffee.

What is wrong with me? Why does my mind wander so far out of reality?

It's just him and Murphy for an early breakfast. They have a tee time in an hour, and Blair and Vera are still in bed. Murphy eyes me, glancing up from his plate of steak that Hunter has him eating every morning, too. He shamed him with something about "real men" being carnivores. But I like to believe that Murphy eats steak because I'm the one cooking it.

"Sorry. Was there something I was supposed to do for you?" I press my lips together and squint at Hunter.

"Yes. You're supposed to work for me. But I got a text from my neighbor saying you baked him a pie for his birthday and spanked him in his birthday suit."

Murphy snickers, pressing a fist to his mouth while coughing.

I shrug. "I was told by the powers that be that a good homemaker bakes pies for neighbors. But the spanking him in his birthday suit was on my own time." I shoot him a toothy grin. "Not on the clock."

Hunter scowls at Murphy when he won't stop laughing.

"Did he try to steal you?" Hunter asks.

I nod.

"How much?"

"Double what you're paying me."

"Christ." Hunter shakes his head. "Before you pack your bags and cross the line into enemy territory, just know that he won't be paying you to cook him breakfast and do his laundry. He'll make you wear a bikini while you apply hemorrhoid cream to his ass. I might be 'needy' according to the missus, but Rupert Rawlings is nothing but a blend of vanilla-flavored meal replacement sludge and dick enhancement drugs. Now," he takes one last sip of his coffee and stands, "if you'll excuse me, I need to smother my wife with a pillow and brush my teeth so we don't miss our tee time."

After offering a tight smile, I return to the kitchen.

"How does it feel to be the trophy for which two old guys are fighting over?" Murphy asks, bringing his dirty dishes to the kitchen.

"Just something to check off my bucket list."

"Is that so? If that's the case, I'd love to hear the rest of your bucket list."

I take the dishes from Murphy. "Thanks. But you have to stop doing my job."

"I'm just helping out. Do you want to know what else I like to do?"

"The dishes?" I turn my back and run water in the sink.

"When I go to the store, I like to organize the carts in the cart return so they're in neat rows."

I close my eyes for a second before adding soap to the

water. He's pushing *so* hard. That fourth wall will not last until the end of summer.

"That's nice of you."

"I think so too. But I once knew this woman who—"

"Do you think she's going to make it this time?" I ask, cutting him off.

"Who? What are you talking about?"

I scrub the plate with the sponge. "Blair. Do you think she's going to make it down the aisle and say yes to you?"

There's a long pause. In fact, I'm not sure he's still in the room, so I glance over my shoulder. Murphy's expression dies. He looks lost.

I turn back toward the sink. "It must be agonizing," I say. "Loving someone with your whole heart, planning for a future, yet living with such uncertainty. Because you do, right? You love her with your *whole* heart?"

"Let's go, Murphy," Hunter calls from the back door.

My spine straightens and I hold my breath hostage when Murphy steps closer, so close the heat from his body singes my skin, so close that the mix of eucalyptus and sweet birch from his body wash fills my next breath.

"Thanks for breakfast," he whispers in my ear, his face brushing my hair, and I feel it everywhere.

"Have you been to Disney?" Callen asks as we lie tangled under a chenille throw on the leather sofa at sunset.

"I have. Why?"

"Just curious."

"Did you tell your wife you want to bring your girlfriend

next time?" I tease his ribs while resting my head on his hairy chest.

"*Ex-wife.* And no, I didn't tell her that because I didn't know I had a girlfriend. Are you applying for the position? Think you can handle being a homemaker *and* a girlfriend?"

I giggle. "You're right. I'm not your girlfriend, just your lover."

He kisses the top of my head. "I just worry that you had a terrible childhood, and I don't want to flaunt my trips in front of you."

"Then you should have left your Mickey ears at home."

"Shut the fuck up." He laughs. "I didn't bring Mickey ears."

"But you have a pair, right?"

"No. But I have a cool lightsaber that makes noises."

I grin. "Did your kids have a fun time?"

"The best."

"And you and your *ex* got along just fine?"

"We did."

"Did you have vacation sex after the kids were asleep?"

"What?" He grabs my arms to lift me off his chest so he can see my face.

I sit up between his spread legs, pulling the blanket to my chest as I roll my eyes. "I'm kidding. Or not. It doesn't matter, Callen. I don't care if you did. I'm *not* your girlfriend."

"Well, for the record, I do happen to care if you're screwing some other guy, so maybe we should have a talk. We don't have to be serious, but I prefer we be monogamous. Despite what you think, I'm a coach, not a player."

"Cute," I say, giving him a fake smile while standing. I

drop the blanket and pull my black sundress over my head before padding to the bathroom.

When I return, he's dressed and sitting on the edge of the sofa with his elbows on his knees and his head resting in his hands.

I stare at him for a few seconds before climbing over the sofa and hugging his back. "Callen, will you go steady with me?" I kiss his neck.

"Don't. You make me sound insecure. And I don't want this." He shakes his head. "Or at least, I didn't want this. Fuck, I don't know. You're giving me exactly what I thought I wanted, and now I'm acting like a goddamn pussy about it."

I laugh before trapping his earlobe between my teeth.

"Let's stick to lover or mistress," he says.

"Mistress?" I crane my neck to look at him. "Can I be your mistress if you're not married?"

He twists his lips to the side. "I think so. Basically, you're my secret girlfriend. We sneak around and have sex. It feels naughty."

"So we've decided to continue doing exactly what we have been doing?"

Callen returns a guilty smile. "Something like that."

"Wanna go for a swim?"

He angles toward me, pulling me onto his lap. "Is that allowed?"

"They've gone to dinner and then a show. So they won't be home until at least eleven, if not midnight. I'm allowed to use the pool."

"Skinny dipping?" He lifts an eyebrow.

"I'm going to say no since there are several two-story houses with views of the pool."

"And you're opposed to public indecency?"

I think of Rosie watching Murphy and me having sex on the dining room table through the faux wood Venetian blinds.

"No," I say. "But since my job is tied to it, I think we should play it safe and wear suits."

"I don't have a suit."

"You can wear your briefs. That's sufficient." I slide off his lap and offer my hand. "Come on, lover."

Chapter
TWENTY-THREE

Murphy

If you can't be happy with what you have,
be happy for those who have what you want.

"I can't believe we missed the show," Blair says.

Vera glances back at us as Hunter pulls his Rolls Royce into the underground garage. "I'm sorry. I thought I purchased tickets for tonight."

"It's fine," he says. "We'll go next month on the actual date."

"I have menopause brain. That has to be why I messed up the date," Vera says with a long sigh.

"We can go for a swim." Blair squeezes my leg. "Or sit in the hot tub."

"You two have at it. I'm tired. The stress of messing up the show date just makes me want to crawl into bed." Vera yawns.

We head upstairs to change into our suits, and just as we step onto the veranda overlooking the pool, Blair grabs my wrist, nodding in front of us at the pool.

"Alice?" Blair squints.

The couple in the pool whip around in our direction. Alice wrings out her hair and the guy standing behind her slicks his back.

"Oh. Hey. I could have sworn Vera said everyone would be out for the evening. I'm sorry if I messed that up. We'll get out."

"No. You're right. We were supposed to see a show, but my mom mixed up the dates. Sorry to ruin your fun." Blair shuffles in her flip-flops toward one of the chairs and drapes our towels over the back of it.

"It's no problem," Alice says.

The guy behind her clears his throat. "Um ..."

Alice looks back at him and he gives her a wide-eyed look. Her nose wrinkles.

"It's a big pool. Don't get out on our account," I say.

Alice and Blair study me like I'm crazy. Then they look at each other.

"I'm Murphy and this is my fiancée, Blair," I say to the guy while descending the corner stairs into the pool.

He gives me a stiff smile and nods while grabbing Alice's arms and pulling her in front of him. "Callen. Nice to meet you."

"Babe?" Blair pulls her hair back into a bun and ties it while giving me a look that says I'm in trouble.

"Yes?" I act innocent.

Blair huffs and makes her way into the pool. "Brrr." She quickly lowers her body into the water up to her neck as we stand on the opposite side of the shallow end as Alice and Callen.

"I don't want this to be awkward later," Callen says, "so you should know that I didn't have a suit, so I'm in my underwear. Alice assured me no one would come home until after we were out of the pool." He slides his arms around her waist, pulling her back to his chest to use her as a shield.

"Uh ... there are extra swimsuits in the pool house," Blair says.

Alice shrugs. "Sorry. I didn't assume they were for my guests."

"And it's a little late now," Callen says.

"Thanks for the warning," I say. "It's better than being naked." I chuckle. "We'll turn away to give you some privacy if you get out before we do."

"Thanks," he says before kissing the back of Alice's head.

I hate how uneasy it makes me feel. She's no longer mine, not that she ever was.

"I didn't know you had a boyfriend, Alice," Blair says. "But I don't know a lot about the help around here."

I pinch Blair's side, and she turns to give me a look like she doesn't understand why I did it.

"Callen coaches lacrosse at the university. I don't share my personal life with strangers, so I wouldn't have expected you to know."

Well, shit. Alice isn't playing nice tonight either.

"What she means is our relationship is casual, so I'm not technically her boyfriend." Callen makes an attempt to ease the tension.

I know why Blair feels animosity toward Alice, but I'm not sure why Alice is giving it back to her.

"Did you play lacrosse in college?" I ask, trying to change the subject.

"I did. Have you played?"

I shake my head. "I played soccer in high school."

"You know what I could use?" Blair says. "A glass of wine. Would you mind, babe?"

"I'll get it," Alice says.

"What? No." I move toward the stairs, but not before she's halfway out of the pool. "You're not working."

"Red or sparkling?" Alice asks, wrapping a towel around her head and another around her body.

"Sparkling," Blair says.

"Anything for anyone else?" Alice smiles at me and Callen.

He folds his hands over his junk and shakes his head as I quickly dry off.

"Babe? Where are you going?" Blair rests her hands on the edge of the pool, peeking out at me.

"To get your wine," I grumble, following Alice, who ignores me even when I'm only two feet behind her. "Forget about the wine," I say when we reach the kitchen. "We'll come inside and leave you two alone. You're right. We weren't supposed to be home."

Alice retrieves a bottle of sparkling wine from the rack and opens the drawer to get the electric opener. "We've been in the pool long enough, so if anyone is getting out, it's us."

I take the bottle and opener from her and set it on the counter behind me, which makes her frown. "You're off the clock."

"So."

"So go be with your boyfriend."

"I'm fine." She reaches for the bottle. "Go be with your fiancée."

I grab her wrist to stop her. She stares at my grip on her, and I can feel her pulse against my thumb.

"Who was she?" Alice whispers. "The person you think I remind you of?"

I move my thumb in a tiny circle against her skin, against her scar. "She was the best two weeks of my life." My heart sinks into my stomach.

"I wouldn't tell your fiancée that." She lifts her gaze to mine.

I release her wrist.

Alice draws in a shaky breath and takes a step back, balling her hands. "I'm sorry you miss her. The past has a way of ruining the future, but only if you let it."

My past is staring me in the eye, daring me to acknowledge it—to acknowledge her.

I glance over her shoulder. So this is how it's going to be? On a sigh, I brush past Alice and return to the pool. "Sorry, Blair. There's no wine left."

"What?" She wrinkles her nose just as I dive into the deep end. "Murphy!"

When I emerge, she scowls. "I didn't want to get my hair wet."

Callen watches us from the corner where he's still covering his junk with his hands.

"Here's your wine," Alice says, setting a glass of wine and the rest of the bottle on the table by Blair's towel.

"Thank you. I guess there was wine after all." She narrows her eyes at me before climbing out of the pool. "Alice, aren't you having wine with me? Please join me. I don't want to drink alone."

"Sorry, I don't drink. Perhaps I can get a glass for Murphy."

Blair pouts. "Murphy doesn't drink wine. He had a friend who drank wine for breakfast and then sort of lost his mind, so it ruined it for him."

Jesus ...

I never said my friend was a "he," and I don't think I used the words "lost his mind." But it doesn't matter. Alice clearly didn't lie about her amateur acting. She keeps a stiff upper lip, not so much as a flinch of recognition or glance in my direction.

"Maybe I can get him a beer," she says to Blair as if I'm not in the vicinity.

"Babe, will you drink a beer?"

"I'm good, but thanks."

"Callen?" Blair looks at him.

"No, thank you."

"Fine." She plops down onto the lounger and lifts her wine glass in a toast. "To me. The only one who knows how to have fun on a Friday night."

"So how did you two meet?" I ask as Alice reenters the pool and everyone ignores Blair.

Callen immediately grabs Alice to use as a shield again, and he kisses her neck. "She was at my son's soccer game by accident."

"How does that happen?" Blair asks.

Alice scrapes her teeth along her lower lip and dips her chin while shaking her head. "Just something stupid. It doesn't matter."

"She was at the wrong field. Her nephew was playing on the field across the street," Callen says.

Alice said she was an only child. Either she lied, or she

has a nephew by marriage. *Was* she married? I need the truth. I gave up on knowing and walked away. But now she's here, and not knowing is driving *me* fucking crazy.

"The following weekend, I saw her again at the soccer complex," Callen says. "She was in line at the concession stand. I think I said something cheesy like, 'Isn't this a lucky coincidence?' And that led to her agreeing to have dinner with me."

Alice doesn't look at me or anyone else. Her discomfort is palpable.

"What does your *nephew* think of you dating a college lacrosse coach?" I ask.

Alice offers a quick glance and a one-shoulder shrug.

"I haven't met him. We're not at the meeting family part of our relationship," Callen says.

"Do you have a brother or sister, Alice?" I slant my head to the side.

"What's with the personal questions?" Blair asks me with a little laugh.

"Didn't you say you have an older brother?" Callen asks Alice. "And very protective?"

My mind is so twisted into knots that I don't know what's up or down.

Alice turns in his arms and kisses him, and not a quick peck. She kisses him like she used to kiss me. The intentional PDA makes me nauseous. Then she whispers in his ear.

"I guess we're leaving," Callen says, like it's an afterthought not meant for anyone's ears in particular.

She wraps her legs around his waist, and he carries her out of the pool and straight toward the guesthouse without grabbing towels, saying goodnight, or offering a look in my direction.

"Well, damn." Blair whistles. "Alice is getting some tonight." She waggles her eyebrows at me before sipping her wine. "I guess we can lose our suits now that they're gone." She stands, sets her glass on the table and unties her bikini top, unbothered by potential neighbors seeing her.

Closure has always seemed like a cliché. But right now, I'd do anything to get closure before the unanswered questions upend my future.

Chapter
TWENTY-FOUR

Alice

Ask him to wait. Forgive him when he doesn't.

Eight Years Earlier ...

WITH MY HEART tightly lodged in my throat, bandaged hand hugged to my chest, and other hand poised to knock on Murphy's door, I took a steadying breath.

After two soft taps and about ten seconds, he slowly opened it. The only thing he offered was a heartbreaking frown as he stood shirtless, shoulders curled inward.

"I don't have a husband," I whispered. Then I drew in a shaky breath to keep the tears at bay. "No kids. No dog." My heart ached behind the bandaged hand on my chest. "I'm not terminally ill. But I ..." I closed my eyes for a breath. "I *am* really fucking lost. And I'm not ready to be found. And I'm sorry that I can't give you more."

I stepped inside, toe-to-toe with him. When I lifted my chin to look into his eyes, he threaded all of his fingers through my hair.

"And I can't stay. But I want to return."

A reluctant smile tugged at the corner of his mouth.

"Will you wait for me?"

He dipped his head, brushing his lips against mine. "I'll wait," he whispered.

Chapter
TWENTY-FIVE

Murphy

Comparison kills confidence.
Not everything is about you.

"I'M FLYING to New York tomorrow to meet with the contractor who's doing my studio renovations. Dad's loaning me his private jet. Come with me. We can watch the Macy's Fourth of July fireworks. We can apartment shop too. Maybe see a show. Dinner. What do you think?" Blair massages my shoulders while I sit at the desk and work on a project.

"I think I've fallen behind and you should take your mom so I can get some work done."

She stops massaging me and plops down on the bed. "All you do is work. It's a holiday weekend."

I laugh. "I *try* to work. But it's hard when everyone around me is not working. We'll have lots of holidays to spend together."

"I'm planning a wedding. *Our* wedding. So don't act like I'm not working."

I sigh, leaning back in the desk chair and lacing my hands behind my head. "Yes. And you have time to do that because it's your only job at the moment."

"What do you think this trip to New York is for? Hello? It's for my studio, which is where I'll make and sell my art, which is *my job.*"

"Bingo. You're proving my point. Tomorrow, you have to fly to New York for your job, and I need to keep my ass planted to this chair to do mine."

Blair pouts. It's an adorable pout, but I can't give in.

"Take your mom. She'll be thrilled to spend a few days in New York with you. Watch fireworks. Take her apartment shopping. I'll live absolutely anywhere you choose, as long as we can afford it."

She sighs, staring out the window. "Fine. But you have to keep an eye on my dad."

"I'm sure he'll be fine, but yeah, I'll check on him."

"1 mean ..." Blair returns her gaze to me. "Make sure he doesn't do anything stupid with ..." She widens her eyes like I'm supposed to finish that sentence.

He's a fit guy in his fifties with an insane amount of money. The list of stupid things he could do is endless.

"Alice. Don't let him get too cozy with the *homemaker.*"

"I'll keep him on a tight leash. Happy?"

"No." She pushes off the bed and straddles my lap. Her expensive perfume that Vera bought her bleeds notes of rose and saffron. "I'd be happy if you were coming with me. My first love was from New York."

I nod. "Chance," I say because she's told me about her

first love and her first broken engagement and her second love and second broken engagement.

"I want to make new memories in New York with you. Right now, all I have are memories of him there with me."

"Good thing you're making it down the aisle this time. Then we'll move to New York, and make all new memories." I smile with confidence.

Sometimes I feel like she's searching for my insecurities, baiting me with her past lovers.

"Why don't you ever talk about the women you loved before me?"

I lift a single eyebrow. "Because I value my life."

"Stop." She laughs while punching my shoulder. "I'm serious. Give me something. A little jealousy is good in a relationship. When you say I'm the first girl to steal your heart, I don't believe you. There has to be someone who took a little piece of it before me. A high school crush? A sexy college professor with black-framed glasses and big breasts?"

I chuckle, unsure if it's specifically Blair who's obsessed with this subject or if all women insist on obsessing over past lovers. Then again, it's possible that my feelings for Alice border obsession.

"Come on, Murphy. Make me jealous. Make me want to get back here as soon as possible, because I can't stop thinking about you and your first love."

"Or you can want to get back to me because you think we're each other's last love and that's all that matters." I feel proud of my comment. It's romantic. Right?

Blair deflates, proving my assumption is incorrect, so I give her something.

"The rental I owned?"

She nods.

"I had a guest. A woman. We formed an unusual bond. I was intrigued by so many things about her; but she was ..." I shrug. "Elusive. And it felt like a mix of love and bad timing. Ultimately, it didn't feel real."

"A guest? How long did she stay?"

"Two weeks."

Blair's face wrinkles. "You fell in love with someone in two weeks?"

"Well, at the time, I would have said yes."

"And now?"

"And now I'm in love with you. The end."

"Murphy, there has to be more. Did she love you back? How did it end? Why did it end?"

"I don't know if she loved me. And it ended"—I twist my lips and search for the answer that I still don't know to this day—"tragically. But I don't know why."

"Tragically? Did she die?"

"No. She left and never came back. I waited, but she never returned."

Blair squints. "Did you call or text her?"

"No. She said she couldn't give me her number until she returned. Of course, I didn't understand why, but she asked me to trust her. And I did. So the only contact I had was through the rental app. But she never replied."

"So she could have died, right? Or she was married. Murphy, she was married." Blair gasps. "That's it. That's why she didn't give you her number. Maybe she planned on leaving her husband for you, but then she changed her mind. Oh, babe, that's so sad. Especially since you loved her and waited for her."

I force a smile. "I'm with *you*, so I think you should call it fate instead of feeling bad for me."

"I do think it's fate." She pecks at my lips. "But it's also bizarre to think you fell in love in two weeks. It took more than six months for you to confess your love to me." She teases the nape of my neck. "But maybe you loved me long before you said it. Did you fall in love with me in two weeks?"

I smile, interlacing my fingers behind her back.

"I mean," she pauses with a nervous chuckle, "don't respond so quickly."

I lean forward to kiss her, but she pulls back. "Murphy, I'm serious. When did you know you loved me?"

"I don't know. It just sort of happened. There wasn't an exact moment that I knew."

"Yet, you just said you fell for this woman in two weeks."

"Blair," I sigh, "why are we doing this?"

"Doing what? Talking? Opening up to each other?"

"Opening a can of worms."

She frowns. "Why is it a can of worms? She's gone, dead, or whatever. What's wrong with knowing about your past?"

"Because you don't just want to know about it. You want to compare everything to us. If I compared everything in your past to us, I probably wouldn't marry you."

She winces. "What's that supposed to mean? Now you sound like my father. Do you think I'm going to break off the engagement?"

I rest my face in my hands and grumble. She pulls them away, forcing me to look at her.

"I'm sorry," she whispers. "I shouldn't have asked. But now I can't un-know that you loved another woman more than you love me. And if she wouldn't have left you, we probably wouldn't be together."

"That's such a stretch, Blair. Why? What is the purpose? *More* than I love you? Why the sudden insecurity?"

She climbs off my lap. "Wow. That's your response?"

I need to strangle something. Instead, I stretch an understanding smile across my face even though I don't at all understand how we got on this topic. "What should my response be?"

"It should be something comforting, like how you were young and stupid, and what you thought was love was nothing more than bored infatuation with a stranger. And when you met me, that's when you knew you had never really experienced love." She crosses her arms over her chest.

"Blair, I have never asked you about your failed engagements. I fell in love with the person you are with me, not with them. But right now, I miss the self-assured artist I met at an art expo in San Francisco. The contagious smile. The flirty batting of your eyelashes, and your unassuming talent blended with just the right amount of confidence. I miss the way you giggled at everything and laughed at people who took life too seriously. That's the woman I asked to marry me. So I don't know if it's just the stress of planning this wedding or your studio or what, but maybe you could use a few days away to clear your mind."

"Yes, Murphy. Meeting with the contractor and apartment hunting without my fiancé seems like a great way to clear my mind." She rolls her eyes and sulks out of the bedroom.

Chapter
TWENTY-SIX

Alice

Temptation is unavoidable,
but not uncontrollable.

NURSE ALICE TO THE RESCUE.

Vera and Blair take a private jet to New York for the holiday while I stay here and take care of Mr. Morrison. He has a cold, and Vera says he's the worst when he's sick.

I'm fairly certain it was their wedding vows that contained the "in sickness and in health" clause, not my employment contract.

"Did you get that chicken from the coop out back? Chase it down? Break its neck? Pluck all the feathers from it?"

I smirk, keeping my attention on pulling the meat from the chicken bones as Murphy refills his coffee mug.

"Or is that just what you tell Hunter, like telling him you made his favorite hand soap?"

"What makes you think I didn't make the hand soap?"

Murphy pulls out a barstool to the island and gets comfortable watching me work. "For starters, common sense tells me you didn't make it. But I've seen you take it out of the sack from the store where you also buy the lavender linen spray that he thinks you make as well."

I lift my head and we have a stare-off.

"Your secret's safe with me." He winks.

Without acknowledging him, I return my attention to the chicken and keep tossing the meat into the stockpot.

"Is your nephew good at soccer?" he asks.

I can't hide my grin. "Yes." I toss the bones into the trash and wash my hands. "Were you good at soccer?"

"I was decent."

"Do you have other siblings or just a brother?"

"Just a brother. How did you meet Blair?"

"I met her at an art expo in San Francisco. What's your brother's name?"

"Why? Are you making a family tree for me?"

"I can if you want me to."

I shake my head.

"What's his name?" Murphy is unrelenting today.

"Arnold," I say.

"Like Arnold Palmer?"

"Like Arnold Yates."

"Alice and Arnold Yates. Interesting. You know, I used to have a cat named Arnold Palmer. He went by Palmer."

"Surprising. You don't seem like a cat guy."

"Why is that? What constitutes a cat guy?"

"Empathetic. Sensitive. Nonconformist."

He laughs. "You don't think I'm sensitive and empathetic?"

"Are you?" I lift my gaze briefly while cutting carrots.

"Blair would say no, but she hasn't been in her right mind lately. Wedding derangement syndrome or something like that."

"Probably the most important time to be sensitive and empathetic is when your bride-to-be is stressed over the wedding."

"Thanks for your advice. I'll take it with a grain of salt." Again, I lift my gaze to his.

"Sorry, was that too insensitive?" he asks.

"Don't you have work to do?"

Murphy sips his coffee. "Yes, I have work to do, so will you stop distracting me?" His grin is not only clownish; it's irresistible. I don't need irresistible.

"Get out of here. I'll bring you a bowl of soup when it's done."

He stands. "Soup? Heck no. It's too hot for soup. I'm not sick. I'll run out and grab my favorite Banh Mi."

I stay in character, the homemaker who didn't fall in love with this man eight years earlier. "Enjoy."

"If you don't want hot soup, I'll let you ride along with me to get a sandwich."

I clear my throat. "Do you think your fiancée would approve of that?"

"It's a sandwich, Alice. Get your mind out of the gutter. I'm a taken man." He smiles like the devil, not like a taken man.

After I finish the soup, serve Mr. Morrison a bowl in bed, and read him a few chapters of a new book (a steamy romance), I poke my head into Murphy's room. "Is the Banh Mi offer still good?"

He turns with a smile and stretches his arms over his head. I let my gaze slide to the T-shirt riding up just far enough to show an inch of his abs. Heat fills my cheeks when I make eye contact with him, and I know he saw me.

"Does Mr. Morrison know you're leaving?" He stands.

"Yes. I told him we were going to lunch together."

Murphy freezes.

I spin on my heel, grinning when he can't see me. "What? It's just a sandwich. Get your head out of the gutter. I'm a taken woman."

"Did Coach Callen put a ring on your finger?"

I continue toward the back door. "I'm going to change my clothes. I told Mr. Morrison that I had a few errands to run. Want me to drive? I'm parked on the street where there are no cameras." I glance back. "Not that it matters, because Blair would never be jealous of you taking her dad's home-maker to lunch. Right?"

"This is sounding less like lunch and more like a full-on affair. Should I be worried that you're trying to steal your boss's daughter's fiancé?"

"Stop. You're setting me up for a good joke that you won't find funny."

He follows me out the door after I change my shoes. "I fear you underestimate my sense of humor."

I laugh without stopping or waiting for him. I don't know why he's following me to the guesthouse instead of waiting for me to change my clothes.

"Say it," he says.

"It's cruel." I open the sliding door.

"But funny?"

I glance back at him. "It won't be funny to you. Just cruel."

"Well, try it." He tucks his hands into his back cargo shorts pockets.

"Why would I need to steal my boss's daughter's fiancé when he'll most likely be put on the sale rack in a few months?"

Murphy slowly lifts his eyebrows. "Are you implying she'll call off the wedding and I'll be a bargain? Marked down like something that no one wants?"

I bite my lips together.

"Damn, Alice. That's harsh."

"I'm—"

He cuts me off with a hearty laugh as he fists a hand at his mouth. "But funny."

I squint, restraining my grin while I assess him for a few seconds. Is it really okay to laugh? "I'm sure you're the one," I say.

His laughter simmers. "Nothing's a guarantee. But you're not really living if you don't take chances. Right?"

After a few seconds, I nod and whisper, "Yeah."

"Change your clothes. I'll wait out here."

I slide the door shut and kick off my shoes before heading into the bedroom to change into denim shorts and a fitted T-shirt. Then I untie my hair and comb it with my fingers. And for whatever reason, I check my makeup and dab a bit of perfume onto my wrists and neck before meeting him outside.

He gives me a quick once-over, but I don't stare at him, silently calling him out like he did to me. Instead, I relish the way my skin tingles from nothing more than one look from him. The most tragic thing about us (and there are a lot) is this awful timing.

As we pull away from the curb onto the street, he rolls down his window. "Do you like biking?"

"Um, sure. Why?"

"I might take a ride later. You could join me."

"I don't have a bike."

"You can ride Vera's. She won't mind."

I laugh. "It's probably a five-thousand-dollar bike. What if I crash it?"

"It's probably closer to a ten-thousand-dollar bike. If you crash it, she'll fire you and hire a new homemaker. Oh, wait. No, she won't, because you are literally the only person who would take this job."

I smirk, shooting him a quick sidelong glance.

"Someday, all this money, the kind that buys ten-thousand-dollar bikes, will belong to you and Blair. Has that sunk in?" I ask.

"It won't feel like mine. I'm signing a prenup."

"Oh, does that bother you?"

"The prenup? No." He shrugs. "I'm a minimalist. And when I met Blair, I had no idea her family had this kind of money. She was living in a dinky apartment in San Francisco. She didn't have a car, took public transportation, and shopped at second-hand stores for most of her clothes. When her art began to sell, she bought a nice car and splurged on some shoes and handbags, but it was all purchased with her own money. I respected that."

"She's staying grounded. That's hard to do when you have access to a private jet."

He hums. "Yeah."

I start to say more, but stop before the words make it to

the air. Murphy seems content with the breeze hitting his face, staring out the open window, and that makes me content as well. When we arrive at the Vietnamese restaurant, Murphy eyes me before unfastening his seat belt.

"What?"

He slowly shakes his head. "Nothing."

We head inside, order our sandwiches at the counter, and find a table near the window to enjoy our lunch.

"Best sandwiches in Minneapolis," he says after swallowing a big bite.

"For sure." I nod while blotting my mouth with a napkin. "Have you brought Blair here?"

"Of course." He eyes me, and it's like he has a secret.

The heaviness of his gaze on me, even when I'm not looking, makes it hard to concentrate.

"You said you met Blair in San Francisco. What made you leave Minneapolis? And how bizarre is it that she's from here too?"

"It was a coincidence. Kismet in her mind." He grins. "And my company's headquarters is in San Francisco. I can work remotely, but I decided a change would be good. It was nice to have more in-person meetings."

"New York will put you even farther away. Are you looking forward to living there?"

"Good question." He glances out the window with a faraway look in his eyes. "Leaving Minnesota is never easy. But sometimes the first part of moving on is ... moving."

When his attention shifts to me, I return a sad smile. "That's good advice."

"No." He grunts. "It's not advice."

He's on the verge of marriage and all the bliss that's

supposed to come with it. Yet, all I see is a tortured soul. Did I do this to him?

I want to reach across the table, squeeze his hand, and apologize for everything I did, but mostly for the only thing I didn't do.

"Do you think Callen is your future husband?" His question jumbles my thoughts.

"Uh ..." I press the pad of my finger to a crumb on the table, giving it all of my attention while I formulate the response to a question I've never considered. "No," I say with every intention of further explanation, but there is none. At least, none that I can give Murphy.

"Keeping it casual, huh?"

"Keeping my whole life casual."

A tiny muscle twitches in the center of his forehead, like he's trying to disguise his reaction. Everything is a disguise between us.

Murphy clears his throat. "How long do you think you'll be Hunter's homemaker?"

"Oh," I say dramatically. "Now that's the one relationship in my life that could go the distance."

The grin on his face looks like it's there against his will.

"I don't know what I'll be doing tomorrow." I shrug. "Today I am here."

"But?"

I shake my head. "No but. No comma. No asterisk. Today I am here. Period."

Chapter
TWENTY-SEVEN

Murphy

If love doesn't break your heart,
perhaps it's not true love.

Eight Years Earlier ...

SHE SAID she wanted to come back to me. Yet, when we made love, we did so with an intensity and desperation of the world ending.

Deadlines be damned. We spent our last days together in bed or in the kitchen, making a meal to refuel before going back to the bedroom.

"Murphy," she whispered, hand curling with a fistful of my hair as I kissed her inner thigh.

"Come back to me," I murmured, reaching for her breast as my mouth tasted her.

Her chest rose and fell in hard, erratic breaths while she

lifted her hips from the mattress. When she closed her eyes, a tear escaped. It wasn't the first, and I knew it wouldn't be the last. What I didn't know was the reason for them.

She gasped when I crawled up her body and pushed inside of her like I could claim something that wasn't mine. And there was no uncertainty about it. Alice was *not* mine.

The only thing that felt real about us was the inevitable wreckage.

"I love you," I said with a labored breath before kissing her.

She curled her fingers, nails digging into my flesh, while turning her head to break the kiss. "Don't," she said, eyelids blinking heavier with each thrust. "Don't love me now. Love me when I'm yours."

God, if only she knew how badly I wanted that, how often I imagined it, and not just when I was inside of her. Every time I walked into the room, she'd grin and take an audible breath as if I were the very air that fed her lungs. It was such a subtle, intimate gesture.

And then there were times when our bodies searched for each other.

When we walked around the lake, she didn't just hold my hand, she hugged my arm. During a meal, she'd say something funny or cute while stretching her leg until her foot rested on mine. Then I rested my other foot on hers, stacking them like we couldn't stop touching each other.

"Whatever it is, I can take it," I said, with her naked body draped over mine as we came down from our high.

"Another orgasm?" she asked in a groggy voice, turning her head a fraction to kiss my chest. "I'm pretty tired. Wake me in a couple of hours."

The same humor that attracted me to her, the playful

one-liners, no longer brought me joy. Every quip felt like a kick in the gut meant to keep me at a safe distance.

The next morning, the day before she had to leave, I brought her breakfast in bed.

"This is risky," she said, stretching her body in one direction and then the other before sitting up against the headboard and pulling my T-shirt over her naked body.

"Why is that?" I asked, setting the tray in front of her.

"Because I don't know if you can cook."

"Am I still in danger of falling off a pedestal? A hundred orgasms later ... really?"

"A hundred?" She giggled while taking a bite of the toast with apricot jam.

"My face has spent so much time between your gorgeous legs, your pussy could charge me rent."

She blushed while slowly chewing. "This jam is amazing."

"It's from the farmer's market. We should go today since you leave tomorrow," I said without allowing anguish to seep into my tone.

"We should go on a date tonight."

"A date?" I reclined on the bed, resting my head on her legs.

Alice grinned. "Something amazing."

"Like bowling?"

She giggled, pressing her fingers to her lips while she swallowed. "So close, Murph. You were just so close. Then with one word, you tumbled from the pedestal."

"Bowling? You don't like bowling?" I propped myself up onto my elbow.

"Why do you look so excited over the idea of me not liking it?"

"Because if you don't like it, that means you're not good at it. We're going bowling. Fuck the pedestal."

"Perhaps I'm *so* good that it feels too easy and therefore boring. *Or* it feels like the most unoriginal date ever."

I shook my head. "No way. Dinner and a movie is the most unoriginal and boring date ever. Bowling is a solid choice. And if we're lucky, we'll arrive and get a warm pair of shoes that someone just returned."

She laughed. "I can't believe you're single. Nothing sweeps a girl off her feet quite like warm bowling shoes. And I want to dress up for our date."

"Bowling shoes go great with a suit." I was so fucking scared our time was coming to an end, and so I took mental pictures of every smile and hoped my mind would remember the sound of her laughter.

"What's that look?" she asked before sipping coffee.

"Have you been swept off your feet before?"

She swallowed and returned a less-than-convincing smile. "Before what? Warm bowling shoes? Sex in front of your neighbor?"

"Before me," I said.

Her hand shook as she set the mug back on the tray and cleared her throat. "Are you going to cry if I beat you at bowling ... in a dress?"

I took her shaky hand in mine and squeezed it. Tears filled her eyes, but she kept them at bay with a nervous laugh. Her pain was palpable, and I wanted to take it away.

"Why are you so good at everything?"

She shrugged, sniffling and fighting to keep a smile. "Quick learner. Good genes. Luck. I don't know."

"Well, I might just cry," I said. "But it won't be from a bruised ego."

She averted her gaze and quickly wiped her tears. "Please don't do this," she whispered.

"Do what?" I set the tray aside and pulled her into my arms, spooning her to me while kissing her neck. "Want you? Miss you? Love you?"

Alice sniffled again before turning in my arms and pressing her palms to my cheeks. "Yeah," she whispered. "Today I'm here. So just look at me like you do, and say ..." her voice cracked.

"Hi," I said.

She closed her eyes as I kissed her. Maybe she wasn't real, but the pain sure was.

Chapter
TWENTY-EIGHT

Alice

The truth can wait, but not forever.

"Are you sure it's a good idea for me to ride Vera's bike?" I ask on our way down the stairs to the garage after checking on Mr. Morrison.

"I think it's an acceptable idea. Do you want me to text her?"

"No. I don't want her to know I'm biking instead of sitting next to Mr. Morrison's bed holding a box of tissues in case he sneezes."

Murphy chuckles. "That visual cracks me up."

As we make our way to the door behind the hidden bookshelves, I glance toward the two-lane bowling alley.

"Do you bowl?" he asks.

"No," I say.

Murphy stops and I almost bump into him. He narrows his eyes. "Really? Who doesn't bowl?"

I point to myself. "Obviously me, since I just said it."

He cants his head to the side. "Want me to teach you?"

"We're going for a bike ride."

"We can do both."

I roll my eyes. "Don't you have a job?"

"Don't you?" He tries to hide his grin by twisting his lips. "One round." He brushes past me to the lanes, picking up a blue bowling ball and handing it to me. "Your thumb goes in the big hole and your middle and ring fingers go into the small holes."

I stare at him for a few seconds before taking the ball. "I said I don't bowl. I didn't say I've never picked up a bowling ball."

"Just trying to be helpful."

"So helpful," I mumble, holding the ball up and taking several steps before releasing it. The ball rolls a few feet before veering off into the gutter. I turn toward him and shrug. "Told you."

He crosses his arms, confusion wrinkling his forehead. "Try again."

I sigh. "Fine." When the ball returns, I line up, take a few steps, and release it. This time, it makes it closer to the pins, but still lands in the gutter. "Ready to take that bike ride?"

Murphy nabs the pencil from the scoring pad and tosses it to me.

I catch it. "What are you doing?"

"You caught that with your right hand."

Curling my lips between my teeth, I shrug.

"That means you're right-handed. Yet, you bowled with your left hand."

I set the pencil on the table. "Let's go. I'd rather wreck a ten-thousand-dollar bike than watch a grown man cry."

"Oh, Alice." He groans, stumbling backward with his hand over his heart. "That's harsh."

"You're proving my point." I laugh, heading to the garage and he follows me.

We ride the bikes around two of the lakes and down tree-lined streets of historic homes in charming and quiet neighborhoods. Then we stop in the Uptown District for ice cream.

"This is weird," I say as we eat double scoops from bowls at a picnic table.

He spoons another bite of caramel pecan into his mouth. "What's weird?"

"If you were my fiancé, and I found out that you went to lunch with the family homemaker, then on a bike ride that included a stop for ice cream, I would not feel good about it."

"Why must you spoil a perfectly good day with ..."

I lift my eyebrows at him. "With what? The truth?"

"The truth?" Murphy laughs. "Are we exploring the truth today?"

I take the last bite of my ice cream and toss the bowl and spoon in the trash. "*Truthfully,* I need to get back and check on Mr. Morrison." I head toward the bikes, then put on my helmet.

"I don't know how much longer I can do this," he says, following me.

"It's not that far to the house. Need me to come back and get you and your bike with my car?"

"You know what I'm talking about."

"I'm not sure I do." My heart races with anxiety as I pedal before he's on his bike. I should have quit my job the day he and Blair arrived from San Francisco. My legs burn, but I keep pushing to keep ahead of him.

As soon as we get back to the house, I enter the code to the underground garage.

"Alice, stop."

"I have to check on Mr. Morrison. Thanks for the ice cream." I descend into the garage, leave the bike next to the rack along with the helmet, and speed walk to the door.

"Was any of it real?"

My steps falter as I reach for the door handle.

"And if you tell me you don't know what I'm talking about, I won't believe you. Because you're right ... I would never take *the homemaker* to lunch and on a bike ride for ice cream while engaged to another woman. But that's not who you are to me. I know you can beat me at bowling and cornhole. I know that you're a terrible dancer, and Vera has never known how I drink my coffee. I know you genuinely love this job because you love to cook, and you have a nurturing soul. And I never told you where we were getting sandwiches today, yet you drove there from memory. But all the things I know about you no longer matter because it's the one thing I don't know that keeps me awake at night. Alice," his voice cracks. "*I waited.*"

I've imagined this moment, but never have I imagined the right words. And just like my mind played it out, I have no words. Everything hurts. Despite closing my eyes, the tears don't stop, so I wipe them away, one at a time. But I can't look at him. Not now.

His phone chimes, and he silences it.

Seconds later, it chimes again.

"Babe, can I call you back?"

I pull in a shaky breath.

"I'm just in the middle of something."

I open the door.

"It's not your dad. No, I'm just—"

I close the door behind me, run up the stairs, out the back door, and straight to the guesthouse.

"There you are," Callen says, sliding off the barstool at my counter.

I gasp.

"Alice, what's wrong?"

I shake my head a half dozen times. "Nothing. It's uh, nothing."

He pulls me into a hug. "Doesn't look like nothing."

It's tempting to fall apart in his arms, but then it can't be nothing.

"I was jogging, and a dog chased me. It scared me. Then the owner called him back. It's fine. I'm fine." The lie makes my stomach twist. Navigating untold truths is easier than weaving lies that will, eventually, tangle around my neck into a noose.

"Damn. I'm glad you're okay." He kisses the side of my head. "I was hoping we could go to dinner. I leave town tomorrow. You hungry?"

I'm not even a little hungry, but I nod anyway. "Let me grab a quick shower." I duck my head and wipe my nose while sliding past him.

"Need help?"

I sniffle and force a tiny laugh. "I'm afraid we won't make it to dinner if you help me. I'll be quick."

When I'm safely behind the bathroom door, I turn on the fan and water, strip off my clothes, and step into the shower. The sobs break free when I cover my mouth with a washcloth and slide down the shower wall.

Chapter
TWENTY-NINE

Murphy

Trust is unrealistic.
It's how foolish people pretend they have control.

Eight Years Earlier ...

IT WAS OFFICIAL. The night before Alice had to leave, I took her on our first date. In honor of the occasion, I made reservations at an upscale Japanese restaurant. And I wore a suit and tie since she seemed to enjoy how I looked the day of my grandfather's funeral.

Cologne.

Perfect hair.

And a small bouquet of pink dahlias.

I knocked on the front door instead of the back door, and she slowly opened it.

"What are you doing coming to this door?" she asked

before her breath caught, then her grin swelled when I handed her the flowers. "Murphy," she whispered, failing to hide the emotion in her eyes as she stepped aside to let me in. "They're beautiful." She took the bouquet and kissed me.

I slid my hands along her silk kimono robe, grabbing her backside. "What's under this?"

She shook her head, retreating from my grasp. "You'll find out later. Let me slip on my dress and shoes."

"I'm rethinking this date."

Alice laughed from the bedroom. "*All* I've been thinking about is this date, except the bowling. You should absolutely rethink that part."

Her enthusiasm and humor calmed my nerves. All I'd been thinking about was her leaving me the following day with nothing more than a promise to come back.

When she stepped out of the bedroom in a black mini dress with buttons down the front and thin straps, the nerves returned in full force. I didn't want her to leave. The risk of not seeing her again hurt too much.

"I'm speechless."

Her cheeks turned pink. "That's what I was going for."

I held out my arm. "Shall we?"

She took it. "We shall."

We bowled, wearing warm rentals, and as expected, she won. I didn't care. It was her laughter and nonchalant shrugs after bowling a strike that I knew I'd never forget. After two rounds, we headed to dinner.

The restaurant was on the thirty-fifth floor of a bank building with a stunning view of the city.

"You know food is my love language. And right now, I could orgasm," she said after the server filled our table with dishes of Japanese fare that looked like art.

I sipped my Negroni. "Do you want to orgasm *now?*" My gaze said I'd happily slide into her side of the booth and hike her dress up her legs to snake my hand between them.

She squirmed in her seat and wet her red lips while nodding. "But I want to wait. It's more fun this way."

"You mean wait until I'm ripping that dress off you because I'm too impatient to unbutton it?"

She pinched the nigiri between her chopsticks and lifted it to my lips. "I look forward to it."

Why did I wait so long to ask her out on a real date? I couldn't get enough of her flirty grins and unbridled laughter where she tipped her head back and rested her hand on her chest.

"No pouting, mister," she said halfway through dinner as I tapped my chopsticks on the side of my plate.

I glanced up at her. "I'm not pouting. I'm ..."

"Pouting." She smiled enough for both of us.

I pulled my phone out of my pocket. "I don't even have your number." I brought up a new contact and slid my phone across the table.

Alice stared at it. "I thought you were waiting for me?"

"I am. Does that mean I can't have your phone number?"

She continued to stare at my phone. "We'll exchange numbers when I get back. Trust me."

After a few seconds of inspecting the flicker of worry across her face, I pulled my phone away from her and slid it back into my pocket. "Feels like you're not coming back."

"Are we getting dessert? Please say yes."

Dessert? My appetite was gone. How could she think about dessert?

As only an actress could do, Alice pinned a smile to her face and filled the rest of the meal with meaningless conver-

sation. I wasn't as dedicated as she was to pretending everything would be just fine, but I gave it a half-assed effort
anyway.

"We should go dancing," she said, hugging my arm as we
strolled to the car in the parking garage.

"My toes hurt just thinking about it."

She giggled. "Give yourself a little more credit. You've
taught me to dance."

I unlocked the car. "I've taught you to sway so you don't
have to step on my toes as much."

"That's what I said. You taught me to dance."

I tried to grin instead of pout, but damn the clock
continued to tick. Dancing wasn't going to change that.
And by that point, I just wanted to crawl under the sheets
with her and convince her to tell me everything or invite
me to come with her—something more than blind faith that
she'd return. I wasn't religious enough to feel comforted by
that.

"I didn't know rain was predicted," she said as we pulled
onto the street and droplets splattered against the
windshield.

"Me neither." I turned on the wipers.

The gravity of our last hours together seemed to leave us
without anything to say. I opened my mouth to speak more
than once, but each time, I closed it just as quickly because
the right words weren't there.

As we approached a bridge over the river, I saw something in the road and slowed down. When I realized my car
was hydroplaning, I let up on the brakes. Still, the car drifted
a bit to the side, and Alice lost it.

"Noooo!" She lunged for the steering wheel.

"What are you doing?" I tried to push her away before

she steered us down the embankment or into the water. I had things under control. There was no need to panic.

Before I got the car stopped along the side of the road, she unbuckled and opened her door.

"What are you—"

I reached for her, but she rolled out before I got to a complete stop.

"Alice!" I called, shoving the car into *Park* and running after her as she slid on her butt down the embankment.

"Chris!" She yelled over and over before diving into the water.

Chapter
THIRTY

Murphy

It's much easier to fall in love than out of love.

I CAN'T UNDO what's been done. Alice knows.

Now what?

As soon as I smell coffee, I know she's in the kitchen making breakfast. The warm wood floor absorbs my steps without creaking.

Just as I reach the dining room, Hunter clears his throat and glances up from his phone, readers low on his nose. "Morning," he says.

"Good morning. How are you feeling?" I sit at the opposite end of the table.

"Much better. Alice made elderberry cough syrup and gave me a dose before bed."

I didn't hear her come into the house last night, but before I can say as much, Alice brings his coffee, carefully pouring it into his gold-rimmed cup while offering me a quick smile.

"Coffee, Murphy?" she asks.

How can she look at me as if yesterday never happened?

I stare at her, waiting for her to break, but she doesn't. So I nod slowly. "Thank you."

She places another cup and saucer in front of me and fills it.

"I talked to Vera this morning, and the women seem to be having a great time. I think we should head to the country club, get in eighteen holes, and spend the rest of the afternoon drinking. They're setting off fireworks later."

Hunter's suggestion hangs in the air as I silently beg Alice to look at me again, but she just turns and floats back to the kitchen as if her conscience has no gravity.

"Put in thirty years of marriage, and you can have an Alice, too." Hunter smirks, catching me watching Alice.

"I appreciate the offer," I say, ignoring his comment about Alice, "but I need to catch up on work before Blair returns."

"I thought you were catching up yesterday."

I sip my coffee, buying a little time. "Sadly, one day wasn't enough."

"Fine. I'll give you the day but meet me for dinner at the country club."

I nod because it sounds like a demand, not a question.

Hunter's phone rings, and he squints at the screen before mumbling, "What now?"

As he answers the call, I use it as an excuse to step into the kitchen.

Alice glances over her shoulder while arranging flowers in a vase. "Can I get you something for breakfast?"

I lean my backside against the island, hands resting on the edge of the counter.

When I don't answer, she takes a second glance back at me. This time, she pauses her hands.

"I was in a mental hospital for fourteen months," she says, facing the vase again, cutting another stem and tucking it into the arrangement. "PTSD. Depression. Severe anxiety. Suicide ideation. But that was then. This is now. Sometimes life sucks; sometimes it doesn't. It's good to see you. It's even better to see that you're in a good place."

She piles the discarded stems into the small bucket and turns, hands folded in front of her. "I'm in a good place too."

Jesus Christ.

My physical response remains masked behind clenched teeth. She was in a mental hospital for fourteen months? What the hell? And now she's good, and supposedly I'm good? That's it?

I swallow past the lump in my throat. "I'm sorry," I whisper because I don't know what to say, and I don't want to make it about me, but I have all these feelings and questions, and I don't know what to do with them.

After a pause, as if she's waiting for me to say more, she nods slowly. "Thanks. I'm sorry too." She drops her gaze to the floor for a second, but then the oven timer buzzes.

I return to the dining room while running both hands through my hair. When Hunter glances up at me, I hide my pain behind a fake smile. I'm a fucking wreck.

For eight years, I've thought about Alice. Only in my dreams did I imagine seeing her again. Now, she's here, canning tomatoes and pickling onions between loads of laundry. And I'm holed up in the bedroom, trying to get caught up on work, but my mind is shit.

Eight years, and here we are.

This is insane. Hunter is at the club. Vera and Blair are in New York. It's *just* the two of us under the same roof, and I feel like a hostage, gagged and unable to speak, afraid of knowing all the details, and equally afraid of not knowing. I lean back in my chair and stare at the cursor blinking on my screen. Then I fixate on the hummingbird, taking nectar from the feeder outside the window.

After the bird flies away, I wad up a piece of paper and shoot it at Blair's yellow leather tote across the room. It lands inside, so I try it again. But I can't focus on anything for more than a minute or two.

Something taps the floor and my gaze flits to the open doorway and the plate with cookies and milk that appear out of nowhere. I lumber from my chair and peek around the corner as Alice sashays in the opposite direction, her pink dress hitting just below her knees, and her wedged shoes making her calves look sexier than ever.

"I refuse to snack alone," I say.

She stops. "You're not alone. You have your work."

I feel weak and emasculated. Anything but brave. I want to know who Chris is or was. Why it took her fourteen months to recover from hydroplaning? What was in the water, if not this Chris person? Did she try to find me?

"I need help," I say.

Alice turns. "I don't know how to write instruction manuals."

"I need help moving on from our last night together."

She fiddles with her apron before smoothing her hands

down the front of it. "You're getting married. I think that's considered moving on."

I pick up the plate of cookies and milk. "You're right. I guess I need help letting go."

Her lips turn downward. "Murphy—"

"I just"—I shake my head—"I just need some of the gaps filled in because I've spent eight years trying to figure it out. So call it closure or whatever, but I can't let it go until I know exactly what I'm letting go of."

She chews on the inside of her cheek.

"I don't want to cause you stress or bring up painful memories. I really don't. So if this is too much to ask, then—"

"It's not," she murmurs. "It's just more than you need. So I guess I'm trying to decide how to help you let go without giving you too much."

I walk toward her, dipping a cookie into the milk and taking a bite. It softens her frown. "There's nothing you could give me that's too much." Dipping the cookie again, I hold it up to her mouth.

It drips milk onto her apron, and she inspects the spot before giving me a raised eyebrow.

I snort while suppressing a laugh. "Oops."

She takes a bite, and it drips onto her chin, so I wipe it with my thumb. She stiffens for a second before slowly chewing and swallowing.

"I've missed you," I whisper.

She takes a step backward. "Blair is—"

I shake my head. "Don't. I can love her *and* miss you. Two things can be true at once. Grief doesn't die. It just learns to coexist with a new reality. In fact," I take another bite of the cookie, "when it's just the two of us, let's not talk about Blair or what's his name."

Her nose wrinkles. "His name is Cal—"

"Shh." I shake my head. "Nope. It's just you and me. Cookies. Milk. Manuals to write. Tomatoes to can. And Hunter's streaked underwear to fold."

Her giggle reaches into my chest and squeezes my heart. "His underwear doesn't have streaks. And even if they did, you knowing that would be weird."

"The guy farts more than a thirty-year-old truck with exhaust issues."

"He does not." She rolls her eyes before returning to the kitchen.

I follow her. "He does, just not in front of you. I never said he's not a gentleman. He holds it in until you're out the door, then he explodes."

Alice shakes with laughter as she finishes putting dated labels on the sealed jars of tomatoes and onions. "You're ruining my fantasy."

"Fantasy? What fantasy?" I cross my arms over my chest and lean my shoulder against the fridge. There are *so* many things I want to ask her, but I don't know where to begin. So I opt for anything that will bring a smile to her face.

"Mr. Morrison has a real charm about him. And while he sneaks no less than a hundred peeks a day at my legs, I love the way he curls Vera's hair behind her ear before he kisses her cheek and whispers, 'I love you,' in that ear. And Vera always blushes like they've been dating for weeks instead of married for years. It's sweet." She caps the marker and faces me.

I glance at my watch without actually paying attention to the time. "I'm taking a quick break before getting back to work. Let's get in the pool."

"Can't. I'm on the clock."

"Who's going to know?"

"Anyone who looks at the security cameras."

"We'll pause them."

Alice scoffs. "No. *We* won't be pausing anything. Enjoy your swim."

"It feels like a crime that you've never shown me your synchronized swimming moves."

She sets the jars in the divided storage bin. "Look up the word synchronized and you'll discover it means two or more things occurring at the same time. Then you'll think about it for a moment and realize there's a reason synchronized swimming doesn't have an individual field."

"Are you mocking my intelligence?"

"No. Am I embarrassed for you? Perhaps."

I chuckle. "I'll be your synchronized swimming partner."

She slides the bin full of jars off the counter, so I take it from her and carry it to the root cellar in the basement, hoping Chris wasn't her synchronized swimming partner. Was Chris a man or woman?

"Thirty minutes," I say, setting it on the empty shelf.

She closes the door behind us and heads back up the stairs. "Then I'll have to dry my hair."

"It's a little after one. I'm meeting Hunter at the country club for dinner, so he won't be home until eight or later tonight. I think you have plenty of time to dry your hair."

She heads toward the laundry room, and I grab her wrist to stop her. I feel all kinds of things I shouldn't feel. Her eyes flit to my hand on her wrist and then shift to my face. "It's a bad idea."

I smirk. "I can think of worse ones."

Chapter
THIRTY-ONE

Alice

Pain doesn't disappear.
It multiplies, divides, disperses,
and even hides for a while.

It's a thirty-minute dip in the pool. Yet, I've tried on all three bikinis a half dozen times. Murphy is marrying Blair. I'm ~~in love~~ having sex with Callen. I like my job. It's been eight years. And the list of reasons I don't need to fuss over what bikini to wear goes to infinity.

When I reach the pool, he's casually doing back strokes. He lifts his head to look at me. And when he smiles, I jump in so he doesn't see my whole body blush. Before I lose my nerve, I go straight into a series of pikes, arches, thrusts, and twists.

Murphy gives me a slow clap and whistles when I finish. After I swim to the shallow end, I return a dramatic bow.

"Damn. And here I thought you were feeding me a line of shit about synchronized swimming."

I slick back my hair and wring it out over one shoulder. "Okay. Your turn."

"My turn?" He jabs his thumb into his chest.

I nod.

"You're supposed to teach me."

"I just did."

He laughs. "That's not teaching, but fine. I'll show you my moves. Prepare to be impressed." He dives under the water and does a handstand in the shallow end, followed by several somersaults in the deep end. Pushing off the bottom of the pool, he shoots into the air with his arms out like the aquatic edition of YMCA.

When he finishes, I reciprocate the enthusiastic applause and whistle. He shakes his head like a dog, his grin on the verge of cracking his face in two.

"Not gonna lie, I've been practicing," he says.

I roll my lips together and nod, eyes wide.

"Are you mocking me?"

I shake my head.

He narrows his eyes, moving toward me like a shark. "You are."

I shake my head faster. "No!" A squeal escapes my chest when he scoops me up and tosses me into the deep end. When I come up for air, I swipe my arm along the surface, splashing water in his direction.

He laughs, turning his head to the side.

The straps around my neck are not totally untied, but they're loose, so I adjust them and retie it. "You about made me lose my top."

Murphy lets his focus slip to my chest before our eyes

meet again, and he smirks. It feels both wrong and familiar. We didn't fade. The attraction didn't die. We simply ended. It's like the emotion and passion have been on pause. Does he feel it too? Is it why moving on feels like going nowhere?

"I can think of worse things," he says in a husky voice that makes my insides turn to molten lava.

How many times can a heart break? I feel like mine has the ability to crumble into infinitely small pieces. He was so concerned about my marital status because he's a good man with morals. Now, I'm feeling the same, but his relationship status isn't in question. It's solidified with thousands of dollars in a venue reservation, caterers, a live band, and a big diamond ring on the finger of a woman who I want to hate, but can't manage to fully do.

My smile fades as I climb out of the pool and wrap a towel around my body. Murphy follows me, drying off as I avoid eye contact. When he steps directly in front of me, demanding my attention, I stare at our bare feet until I find the courage to lift my chin.

I know that look in his eyes. It's like no time has passed. He's going to kiss me. And I want to let him. When he wets his lips while staring at mine, I offer something else.

"I was engaged."

His gaze lifts.

"He died." I don't know if there will ever come a day when those two words don't rip open deep wounds. "A month later, I rented a lovely little house for two weeks in Minneapolis."

Murphy's brow tightens as he swallows hard.

"For two weeks, I pretended it was all just a bad dream. In fact, I pretended he never existed. Because people who never existed can't break your heart." Tears burn my eyes, and I draw in a shaky breath. "Then I met a guy who was *the best* escape." I smile, wiping my eyes before my emotions break free. "He was funny and sexy."

Murphy returns a painful smile.

"And kind of shy, but confident when it mattered. An extroverted introvert. He had phenomenal taste in music and the most fascinating talent. A man who knew how to handle his wood."

He grunts a tiny laugh.

"My break from reality turned into something so real that it felt like an alternate universe. How could I feel *so* lost and yet found at the same time?"

Murphy doesn't try to fill a single breath of air between us with words that won't change anything. He just lets me *feel,* reminding me why my heart opened wide enough to let him in while grieving Chris. Murphy's patience is more intimate than a kiss.

"I wanted you to have the best version of me. And I thought"—I shake my head—"I thought I could face reality again, and push through the grief, knowing that you were on the other side. But that's not how grief works. It's grueling and unforgiving." Again, I blot my eyes before tears escape. "It's like falling into the water, and the only thing that can propel you to the top is your feet pushing off the bottom. But the bottom was so deep, I could hardly breathe, and—" My voice cracks.

Murphy reaches for my face, and I shake my head, taking a step back and swallowing a sob. The pain in his eyes compounds the ache in my chest.

"It felt like cinder blocks tied to my feet. I couldn't move. All I could do was hold my breath until my lungs burned. And I felt *so* guilty over you and our time together. I thought I deserved everything that was happening to me."

He takes a hesitant step toward me. I know I should turn and run. Get dressed. Dry my hair. Do my job.

But I yearn for the comfort of his arms, so when he wraps them around me, hand on the back of my head, holding me against his chest, I let him.

"Nobody deserves what happened to you. I'm *so* very sorry," he whispers.

I could stay in his arms forever, and that scares me, so I pull away and wipe my face. "I uh ... should get back to work."

Murphy frowns. "Yeah, me too."

"Don't forget to turn the cameras back on."

He nods, glancing up at one of them just outside the mammoth sliding door. "Alice, had I known—"

"You didn't," I say because I did everything to hide my grief, my reality. "Had you known, you wouldn't have been anything more than a guy renting me a place to stay for two weeks. And I don't regret anything except," I shake my head.

"Except what?"

"Nothing," I whisper. "No regrets. Right? Isn't that how we should live?"

He shrugs a shoulder. "I suppose if the world were perfect. But it's not, and neither are we. So my list of regrets is long and ever-growing."

With a sad smile, I tighten my towel around my body and turn to head back to the guesthouse.

"Alice?" he calls.

I stop.

"My regrets? You're not one of them."

Chapter
THIRTY-TWO

Murphy

If you can't remember how it ended,
did it really end?

I SPEND the rest of the Fourth with Hunter. Then I keep my head down, work, and eat at my desk, biding my time until Blair and Vera come home.

Alice was engaged, in love with another man. And she was right. Our time together wasn't real. She fell in love with the escape. I was the escape. On our last night together, the wall between real life and a contrived reality broke. Why? I don't know, and I can't change it anyway. It's time to put that time of my life to rest and forge ahead with my future and the woman I've known for much longer than a fortnight.

By one o'clock, I look at Blair's location. She's still in New York at the airfield. I gather my dirty dishes from breakfast and lunch and return them to the kitchen, listening for

Alice, hoping to avoid seeing her. When I succeed, I can't just be happy that I'm avoiding her. Instead, I wonder where she's at. Then I hear laughter, so I follow it all the way to Hunter's study.

It's story time.

My curiosity is stronger than my willpower to avoid her, so I stand around the corner from the partially opened door and eavesdrop. Last I knew, she was reading him a romance novel, per Vera's suggestion.

"I think women write men how they want them to be, not how they are," Hunter says. "We're not ... what's the word? Swoony?"

Alice giggles. "But you could be."

"Do tell, young lady. How do you suppose I become *swoony* at my age?"

"Actually, you already have some serious swoon game."

He barks a laugh. "Like what?"

"Every day you tell Vera you love her."

"There's nothing special about that. Men should love their wives."

"Yes, but you whisper it in her ear when you think no one is watching. And I know that doesn't seem like much, but it's the little things that mean the most."

"Go on," he says. "I'm listening. What else do I need to do?"

"I can't tell you. These have to be your little things. And you surely have more of them, because Vera is still with you."

"Have you been swooned?"

Alice chuckles. "Yes."

I'm not sure I can listen to her talk about the man she lost. Yet, I can't seem to pull myself away from the door.

"What's the most unforgettable thing a man has ever done to sweep you off your feet?"

"It's ... nothing. Let's just finish this chapter. You haven't fallen asleep. Just close your eyes and stop talking."

"I'll stop talking when you tell me."

She sighs. "I fell for a guy who would stop just before our lips met for a kiss, and he would grin and whisper, 'Hi.'"

"Hi?"

"I know. It's hard to explain. But it was intimate, like he wanted to take that extra second to make sure I knew it meant something more than an uncontrolled act of passion."

"Hi?" Hunter questions again.

Alice giggles. "I'm just saying, it's the little things. Legit, the tiniest gestures are *swoony.*"

I lean my head back against the wall and close my eyes. Me. I'm the guy who said "hi" before I kissed her. And I've never done that with anyone else. Why did I follow the laughter? I didn't need to hear her say that. It's easier to get over her if I don't think of what we had as real. But *that* just made it so fucking real.

"Hey, sexy. Miss me?"

I swivel in my desk chair and grin at Blair standing in the doorway. "As a matter of fact, I did."

She kicks off her heels and saunters toward me in her tight jeans and white blouse, straddling my lap. I slide my fingers into her long, blond hair and kiss her because I love her. I inhale the saffron and rose because I love that too. We're getting married. And that's all that matters. If only I could stop mentally reciting the reasons. If only I could say that I thought about her nonstop while she was gone.

"Shut the door," I whisper in her ear before kissing her neck. Maybe all I need is to bury myself inside of her and forget about everything and everyone but her.

"Baby, I have so much to tell you."

I begin to unbutton her blouse. "We'll talk later."

She pulls my hands away and giggles. "Stop. I'm serious."

I blow out a long breath and lean back, scratching the back of my head. "Okay then. Let's hear it."

"Well," she climbs off my lap and plops onto the bed, crisscrossing her legs, "the studio plans are beyond my wildest dreams." Her voice escalates into pure giddiness.

I can't help but smile.

"And I hope you were serious about letting my mom and me pick out an apartment because I found one within walking distance of my studio, and I put down a deposit to hold it. Look at these pictures." She taps her phone and hands it to me.

I scroll through them. "Looks good." I hand the phone back to her.

She deflates. "Good? Baby, did you see the hearth over the fireplace? It's a work of art."

I nod. "That's what I meant. It looks like a work of art."

Blair rolls her eyes. "You suck. I'm glad I took my mom. She knows how to be appropriately happy for me."

"What was her *appropriate* response?"

"Jumping up and down and squealing. Then we headed straight to Restoration Hardware and ordered furniture."

I nodded. "Great. Thanks for doing that."

She grins. "You're welcome."

I gesture toward the door. "Now, can you close the door and take off your clothes?"

Her nose wrinkles. "What's your deal? When I suggest we have sex during the day, you get uptight about my parents being awake and hearing us, but now you're ready to just go at it at"—she inspects her watch—"four in the afternoon?"

"I've missed you."

"Aw ..." She makes duck lips. "I missed you too, baby. But I want to get a workout in before dinner."

"Great idea. I'll let you ride me." I lean forward and reach for her hand.

She pulls away and scrambles off the other side of the bed. "Tonight." She blows me a kiss.

I wait for her to change her mind, but the only change she makes is into her leggings and sports bra.

"My parents are going out to dinner tonight, so we'll have the house to ourselves for a few hours. How does that sound?"

I scrub my hands over my face and look at her with a manufactured smile and a tiny nod.

"I'm jogging to the park and doing some stretching there before heading home. Give me an hour?"

Again, I nod.

"Enjoy your dinner," she says to her parents in the hallway.

"Alice is making a quiche for tomorrow morning," Vera says. "If you want her to make you two dinner, let her know before she leaves for the night."

"Murphy and I will fend for ourselves, but I'll tell her on my way out the back door," Blair replies.

I stare out the window and wait for Vera and Hunter to pull onto the street. A few seconds later, Blair jogs down the sidewalk. I should stay in my room and wait for her to return. Maybe we'll shower together.

Unfortunately, I've never been good at doing what I should do, so I head to the kitchen. "I hear you have the night off."

Alice jerks her head up like I've startled her, then she seethes, quickly looking back down at the cutting board filled with diced onion and blood.

"Oh, shit," I say, grabbing a towel.

"It's f-fi." She passes out, and I catch her before she hits the floor.

"Alice?" I ease her onto her back and wrap her cut finger with a towel before pulling out a drawer to prop up her feet.

Her eyes slowly open.

"Welcome back. I think you'll need a couple of stitches."

She hugs her wrapped hand to her chest. "I ruined the quiche," she says in a weak voice.

"I don't think you need to concern yourself with that. Let's go get this taken care of."

"I've got it." She winces, trying to sit up. "Oh god, is it bad?"

I laugh a little. "I take it you don't handle blood well."

"Not mine. Ugh, I feel nauseous."

"Just don't look at it. Look at me. Chin up." I lift her off the floor, and she drops her gaze to her hand. "Alice, look at me."

She swallows hard, skin pasty white. "Just call me a cab."

"I'm not calling you a cab," I say, carrying her down the stairs to the garage.

"It feels weird," she says in a desperate tone. "Did you look at it? Is it still attached? Is part of my finger still on the cutting board. Oh god ..." She closes her eyes, each breath more labored than the previous one.

It's not funny, so I try not to laugh, but I've never seen this side of her. I set her on her feet, keeping one arm around her waist as I open the passenger door.

"I'm going to pass out again. I need the seat to be leaned back."

"I've got you."

She closes her eyes and groans like a wounded animal as I push the seat recline button. Then I fasten her in, and we head to urgent care.

I call Blair on the way. "Hey, baby," Blair says, panting. "I'm not even to the park yet. What do you need?"

"Alice cut her finger. I'm taking her to urgent care."

"I'm ... I'm sorry," Alice mumbles.

"What did she say?" Blair asks.

"She's not doing well with the blood, but she's trying to apologize to you even though there is no need to apologize."

"Ouch. Well, I hope she'll be okay."

"Nothing a couple of stitches won't take care of. I'll see you when we get back."

"K," she says before I disconnect the call.

"Ugh, I ruined your night. I'm so sorry."

"You have not ruined anything. And it's my fault for startling you."

"Not true. I ruined tomorrow's breakfast."

"Hunter loves his steak rare. I'm sure he'll enjoy his quiche a little bloody as well."

"Stop," she tries to laugh, but it sounds more like a moan.

When we reach urgent care, I help her inside. It doesn't take long to update her medical records, but the waiting room is crowded. Alice slides down in the chair and tries to lean her head back. Her face is still ghostly.

"Lie on my lap or lean against me before you pass out again," I say.

"I'm fine," she says in a weak voice.

"You don't sound fine." I wrap my arm around her, forcing her to lean against me.

She's called back before other people, perhaps because there's blood involved, or maybe they don't want her passing out in front of everyone else.

"I hope I don't lose my finger," Alice says, curled up in a ball on the exam table while we wait for the doctor.

I bite back my grin. "I hope not either."

"Did I ruin your plans for the night? Were you and Blair going out to dinner too?"

"Nope. We're staying in. And I don't think this will take all night unless you get transferred to the hospital for surgery."

Her head whips in my direction. "Do you think that will happen?"

"No," I say with a chuckle.

She frowns.

"Do you want me to call Callen?"

"So you do think I'm going to lose my finger?" Her eyes narrow.

"I think the effects of your minor blood loss could last for a while."

"I'll be fine. If I pass out," she sighs like she might do just that, "I'll eventually come to. Besides, he's out of town. I don't think he needs to get on a plane for my finger."

After a quick knock on the door, a young woman in a white coat steps inside. "Hi, Alice. I'm Dr. Friedman."

The nurse follows her.

"I'm sorry. Blood makes me queasy. Well, my own blood," Alice says.

The doctor smiles while donning a pair of gloves. "That's okay. Feel free to look away or close your eyes."

As the nurse unwraps Alice's hand, the doctor inspects the finger, and Alice tips her chin up, looking at the ceiling.

"Alice, I think we're going to clean that up and just use a little glue. No stitches. How does that sound?"

Alice swallows and returns a tiny nod while keeping her focus on the ceiling. The doctor gives me a brief glance and a tiny grin.

It's a quick procedure and we're back in the car and on our way home in no time.

"The color in your face looks better," I say, shooting her a sidelong glance.

"Thanks for the compliment." She stares out the window.

I chuckle. "Anytime."

"I overheard Vera telling Mr. Morrison that she and Blair found an apartment. That must be exciting," she murmurs.

"I heard that too."

Alice turns toward me, but I keep my eyes trained on the road. I overheard something, too, and now I can't stop thinking about kissing Alice Yates and whispering "hi" before our lips touch.

"Can I ask if you're better now? Fourteen months of intensive therapy seems like a lot. And if you don't want to talk about it, that's fine."

"I love the way you refer to a psychiatric hospital as 'intensive therapy.'"

"Sorry."

"Don't be. I think I'm going to use *intensive therapy* from now on. It's a little less scary than a psychiatric hospital. And yes, I'm better now. You don't have to tiptoe around me like everyone else."

"Does Callen tiptoe around you?"

"No, because he doesn't know about that part of my life."

"Why not?"

"Because I don't want him to tiptoe around me. Geesh, Murph. I thought you were following the conversation better than this."

I grin. She hasn't called me "Murph" since she stayed at my rental.

When we reach the house, I pull the white SUV into the drive closest to the guesthouse and hop out, jogging around the front then opening her door.

"I've got it," she says, reaching for the seat belt at the same time I do.

I retreat a step to let her slide out of the vehicle. Then, with my hand cupping her elbow, I gently guide her to the door.

"The quiche," she says as I open the door.

"I'll clean it up and suggest everyone go to brunch in the morning."

"I don't want you cleaning up my mess," she says, easing onto the sofa with her hand hugged to her chest like she's lost an entire digit.

"Welcome to my world," I say. "And yet, you continue to do things for me. This is the least I can do." I crouch before her, resting my hands on the cushion beside her legs.

She seems to hold her breath under the scrutiny of my endless gaze.

"That night ..." I briefly close my eyes, shaking my head.

"I don't remember that night," she whispers. "How did it end?"

I open my eyes into tiny slits. "You ... you don't know?"

She slowly shakes her head.

I blink, expressionless, motionless, until my throat bobs in a hard swallow. "We were on our way home from dinner. You were leaving the next day. It was raining, and I hit the brakes." I shake my head. "I didn't hit them hard. We weren't in any danger, but we skidded a little and you panicked, opened the door, and jumped out just before the bridge. I stopped the car and chased after you as you slid down the embankment, yelling for Chris."

Our gazes meet, and I take a moment, unsure if I can tell her without losing myself again. Maybe it will feel like a story with different characters—fictional ones.

Chapter
THIRTY-THREE

Murphy

Not every ending is a happily ever after.
It's not your fault.

Eight Years Earlier ...

Mud clumped to my dress shoes, so I discarded them before diving into the water after Alice. Who was Chris? Where was she going? It was dark, and the night sky mixed with rain seemed to swallow her whole. I blinked the water from my eyes as my arms and legs propelled me forward into the abyss, hoping to catch her.

"Chris!" she cried, slapping her hands against the surface.

I hooked my arm around her waist and used my other arm and legs to pull us toward the shore.

"Let go of me!" She wriggled in my hold, and several times she broke free and I had to chase her.

By the time I got her to the shore, she was crying uncontrollably. "Alice?" I tried to snap her out of whatever state she was in, but my attempts were futile.

She kicked and screamed as I carried her up the hill, slipping onto my knees every few steps as the rain continued to make a mudslide of the embankment.

"Get away! Don't touch me!" She flailed her arms, hitting me in the face more than once.

When I released her, she fell to her butt and hugged her knees to her chest, rocking back and forth on the shoulder a few feet behind my car. I glanced around, hoping someone would stop and ... I wasn't sure. Help me? Help her?

Who was Chris? Did I need to call 9-1-1? And say what?

After stabbing my hands into my hair and shaking my head while watching this unrecognizable woman rock in the fetal position, I searched the front seat and pulled out her phone. When I squatted in front of her, she ignored me while chanting, "Don't drown. Don't drown."

I softly peeled her index finger from her shin and used it to unlock her phone. Then I searched her contacts and found a woman named Krista Yates. I took a chance and called her.

"Hello?"

I plugged my opposite ear. "Hello?"

Again, she said, "Hello."

"Is this Krista?"

"Yes."

"Uh ..." I stared at Alice. "Are you related to Alice?"

"I'm her mother. Who is this?" Her tone hardened.

"Uh ... I'm a friend. She's ... unwell."

"What? Where is she? Oh god. Is she in the hospital?"

"N-no, ma'am. But she's sort of lost it. And she's saying Chris's name and chanting, 'Don't drown.' And I don't know what to do. When I try to touch her, she starts yelling and kicking and screaming."

"Let—" The woman's voice shattered with a sob. "Let me talk to her."

I held the phone to Alice's ear. After a few seconds, she stopped chanting but continued to rock back and forth. Then she nodded and her voice shook in an "o-okay" as she shivered.

I pressed the phone back to my ear. "Hello? Are you still there?"

"Text me your address. We'll be there as soon as possible, but it's going to be four or more hours. Can you take care of her?"

I didn't know, but I nodded and said, "yes" anyway. Then I tossed the phone in the car, squinting against the rain. "Alice, your mom's on her way. Okay?" I scooped an arm under her bent knees and wrapped my other arm around her back.

She shook, her sobs softening, and her fight dying. On the way home, she sat in the seat with her knees hugged to her chest, whispering, "Don't die."

I carried her into the house and wrapped her in a blanket on the sofa. Her eyes were blank. It was as if I wasn't there; it was as if she wasn't there.

For those four hours, I sat on the coffee table in front of her, waiting for the nightmare to end, but it didn't.

She didn't so much as flinch with the knock at the door. I opened it, and her mom rushed past me, red hair pulled into a messy bun, face streaked with tears.

A tall man in a hooded rain jacket offered a sad smile. "I'm Ryan, Alice's dad. Thanks for calling us."

"I'm Murphy," I said with a nod as he stepped inside.

"We haven't known where she's been. We just knew she'd eventually come home. How did you two meet?" he asked, squinting with concern as Alice's mom kneeled on the floor in front of the sofa to console Alice.

It took me a moment to register what he'd asked. I felt dazed and confused. "Uh ... I own this place. She rented it from me. We were—"

"Let's go, baby," Krista said, helping Alice to her feet.

When she looked at me, I thought for a second that it was all a bad dream, and she would be fine. Then her face contorted into an unrecognizable scowl.

"Don't look at me," she gritted through clenched teeth. "I'm not yours. Do you understand me?"

Her mom winced right along with me. "Sweetie, shh. You're not well. He hasn't done anything."

"DON'T EVER TOUCH ME!" Alice screamed before her knees buckled, and she sobbed as her dad rushed to catch her. "I'm n-not h-his ... he c-can't have me ..."

"Sweetie, he's not trying to take you. He called us. He's just trying to help," Krista said, stroking Alice's hair before her dad scooped her up in his arms.

I could barely fucking breathe, but I managed to clear my throat. "Uh, let me see if I can get her things gathered quickly."

Her parents gave me appreciative nods, so I stepped into the hallway just outside of the bedroom. Leaning the back of my head against the wall, I closed my eyes burning with tears, and pinched the bridge of my nose.

What the hell is happening?

I sucked my lips together and choked on a sob. Then I quickly wiped my eyes and headed into the bedroom, grabbing everything of hers I could find, shoving it into her bag. I did the same thing in the bathroom.

"Thank you," her mom said, taking the bags from me. "What do we owe you?"

Owe me?

I couldn't speak past my heart in my throat, so I shook my head. She offered a sad smile. "Well, again. We can't thank you enough. Bye." She opened the door, and they left.

I was so fucking scared that she wouldn't come back, but never did I imagine it ending like that.

Did I ... break her?

Chapter
THIRTY-FOUR

Murphy

The heart has an infinite capacity.
Sometimes we wish it didn't.

"I'm so sorry," she whispers, quickly swiping at a tear on her cheek.

"Don't." I shake my head, sitting back on my heels as my hands slide off the sofa. "Don't apologize."

"He drowned." She tips her head to the ceiling and closes her eyes while taking a long breath. "And I was—"

My phone chimes. "Fuck," I mumble, pulling it from my pocket.

"Blair is looking for you?"

I stare at the screen and nod.

"Thank you for taking me to urgent care."

I type a quick reply and slide my phone back into my pocket. "I don't have to go yet. Keep talking."

"I think ..." She turns and stares out the window. "Perhaps we've said everything there is to say. I lost a lot. And maybe you did too. But we've moved on." Her gaze returns to me. "Sometimes I get lost in what might have been, but it only keeps me from moving forward. You said it yourself. Sometimes the only way to move on is to actually move. If my being here is too much, even just for the summer, I'll leave. It was never my intention to turn your life upside down. Not then. Not now."

I stand and drag a hand through my hair. "Worst timing," I mumble.

"Us?" A smile plays along her lips as I nod. "What if it's perfect timing?"

I grunt my objection to her "what if."

She drops her gaze, picking at the edge of the bandage around her finger. "When Chris died, I didn't cry. Not a single tear. Everything inside of me rejected the idea that he was gone. And when that no longer worked, I pretended he never existed. No love. No death."

I slide my hands into my pockets, resisting the urge to touch her and comfort her.

"My parents were worried I wasn't facing the truth." She laughs. "As usual, they were right. But I didn't see it. All I saw were people telling me what to think and how to feel, so I left. Drove all night and ended up in Minneapolis. I spent the night at a hotel and decided to find a rental. I found you."

Maybe she's right. We've said all that needs to be said. Everything else feels like torture.

"What if I needed you to help me breathe again?" she asks.

"That's not how it felt the night your parents took you away from me."

Alice frowns. "I know," she whispers. "And I know this feels like terrible timing to see me again, but what if it's what you need to really move on? Get married. Be happy. You said you needed closure. Now, you have it."

I have it? Is she joking? This isn't closure. I don't look at her and think how lucky I am to have dodged that bullet. It's no longer about the past. I don't want to make the wrong fucking choice for my future. What if I can't exist in this world knowing she's here, baking bread, dancing to oldies on vinyls, and flirting with rich, married men?

It's been eight years, and I haven't really let her go. And now I have a chance, but all I want to do is hold her tighter than ever before. Yet, these feelings somehow coexist with my love for Blair, and it makes no sense, but it's my truth. My truth feels like punishment.

"I'm so sorry for all that you've been through," I say.

Alice swallows and offers a sad smile. "Thank you. I'm fine now. Really. And I'm thankful that fate, God, whatever has brought us here." Her smile stretches a bit more into something hopeful. "I think I've needed closure too."

"Finding me engaged to Blair is closure?"

She averts her gaze for a beat, a tiny line forming between her eyebrows. "Finding you happy and in love is ..." Her fingers blot the corners of her eyes. "All that I ever wanted for you."

I wish I could share a similar sentiment, but I can't. Not truthfully. My wants are more selfish. They involve going back in time and changing something. What? I don't know. Had it not been raining. Had I not braked at that exact moment. Had we not hydroplaned. Then what? She wouldn't have been triggered. We would have returned to my place and spent the night making love until she had to leave the next day. But then she would have returned to me. Right?

"Why did the car hydroplaning trigger you?"

She eyes me for a second, lips corkscrewed. And just as her lips part to speak, there's a knock on the glass door. Our heads turn in that direction at the same time. Blair smiles and waves before sliding it open.

"Oh, my goodness. How are you feeling?" She steps inside and slips off her red flats.

"I'm okay," Alice says, holding up her hand with the bandaged finger. "It's actually quite embarrassing. No stitches, just glue. Thank goodness. But I don't do well seeing my own blood." Her nose scrunches. "And I'm sorry about the kitchen. I'm actually fine now. If I wear latex gloves, I can clean up the mess."

"No, no." Blair shakes her head while sliding her arm around my waist. "I just cleaned it up. My parents will never know."

I don't know why it surprises me that Blair did that, but it does. It shouldn't. I'm marrying her for many reasons, and one of them is her generosity.

"I can't thank you enough," Alice says, with the same flicker of shock on her face.

"Is there anything else I can do for you? Have you had dinner? I can make you something or order food to be delivered?" Blair asks.

"Uh," Alice shakes her head and smiles, "no. I'm fine. Really. But thank you. I've taken up enough of your night by stealing Murphy to drive me to urgent care. Go. Don't waste another minute thinking about me."

Easier said than done.

"Well, you know where to find us if you change your

mind." Blair laces her fingers with mine. And I hate it. I also *hate* that I hate it.

Alice's gaze lands on our hands for a few seconds, and when she notices me looking at her, she quickly glances away. "Thanks again," she murmurs.

As Blair pulls me toward the sliding door, I wait for Alice to look at me, again, but she doesn't.

Closure my ass.

"You, Murphy Paddon, are a good man. The best," Blair says, hugging my arm as we walk to the main house.

"Thanks. It was pretty hard work driving her to the urgent care and then back home. But the warrior in me just came out."

She giggles. "So sexy. Let's talk more about this warrior. I might need you to save me before the end of the night."

As soon as we step inside the back door, she wraps her arms around me and kisses me with an open mouth. I love her. I really do. And what guy doesn't like it when his girl gets turned on by his imaginary super powers?

She grabs my hands and places them on her ass without breaking our kiss. Then she teases my dick with the heel of her hand. It stirs like waking a teenager at six a.m. on a Saturday morning. And like a parent frustrated with said teenager for not getting up, Blair breaks our kiss and frowns.

"What's going on, baby?"

"Nothing," I say.

She grunts a laugh. "Well, yes. I gather *nothing* is going on. My concern is why?"

Why am I only getting a partial erection for her? That's such a good question and an embarrassing situation.

"I don't like the idea of your parents potentially walking in on us while you're stroking my dick."

Yep. This is a perfect example of what a good guy (the best) I am. When I can't stop thinking about another woman, I blame my fiancée for putting her hand on my dick in the wrong room of the house.

"My parents will come in through the basement. We'll hear them." She shakes her head. "What is your deal? You've been so off lately. Literally a few hours ago, while my parents were still here, you were ready to jump me in the bedroom. But now you're in super cautious stealth mode?"

How do I explain that earlier I wanted to fuck her to forget about Alice, but now I can't fuck her because I know forgetting about Alice tonight is no longer possible?

Then I think about her cleaning up the kitchen after Alice's accident, and I feel extra guilty. So yeah, I'm going to figure out how to get the job done using her kitchen generosity as mental foreplay.

I scoop her up in my arms, and she squeals. Then I carry her to the bedroom to make love to my fiancée like it's a chore to check off my to-do list.

Chapter
THIRTY-FIVE

Alice

There is logic and love. But they can't coexist.

"Thank you," Vera says when I deliver a small arrangement of roses to her office off the primary bedroom suite on the second floor.

"You're welcome." I smile, replacing the vase from several days ago with this new one.

She pulls off her black-framed readers and sets them next to her computer. I don't know what she does in her office on her computer. Wedding plans, I suppose.

"I'm not talking about the flowers. Although they are simple and elegantly arranged, just as I like them." She offers an approving smile.

"Oh?" I smooth my hands over the white apron.

"Whatever book you've been reading to my husband.

Well, it's working." She smirks, a blush blooming along her cheeks.

My eyebrows lift, and I laugh. "Well, that's good to hear."

"Keep up the good work."

"I will." I take several steps toward the door and pause. "Could I make dinner early tonight. I have somewhere I'd like to be at seven. If not, it's—"

"Of course, dear." She slides her glasses back onto her nose without asking me anything about my request.

"Thanks," I murmur.

When I reach the bottom of the stairs, I hear a "Psst," and I stop, arching my back to look behind me into Hunter's study.

"Can you help me?" he asks in a hushed tone.

I step into his study, eyeing Murphy on the sofa, his ankle resting on the opposing knee. My gaze ping-pongs between the two men.

"Close the door," Hunter says, so I do. "Murphy's trying to show me how to dance so I can surprise Vera. But it's too weird dancing with a dude."

I suck my lips between my teeth and nod slowly.

He puts a record on his turntable.

"Uh, where's Blair? I'm not the best dancer," I say.

"She's getting a pedicure and massage," Hunter says just as Eric Clapton's "Wonderful Tonight" plays. "I just need to see it in motion." He turns and eyes Murphy who lumbers from the sofa and gives me a shy smile while holding out his hand to me.

I look at Mr. Morrison, and he gestures with his head for me to take Murphy's hand, so I do. His other hand slides to my lower back.

"Don't step on my feet," he whispers.

I bite back my grin as he leads.

"Op ... sorry." I cringe, stepping on his foot two seconds later.

"Are you counting?" Hunter asks Murphy.

"I'm not. But if you need to count, go for it."

"Not helpful," he grumbles. "So eight counts to the right in a sway then eight to the left, or should I dip her?"

Murphy dips me then lifts our hands and turns me in a slow circle. "If you feel like dipping and twirling, it's never a bad idea."

I can't keep a straight face.

"Goddammit! Who's calling me?" Hunter checks his phone. "I have to take this. Just keep going. Give me five minutes. I'll be back, and we can start from the top again." He lifts the turntable needle to play the song from the beginning. "Hello?" he answers his phone and exits the room.

Murphy narrows his eyes again when I step on his toes—his naked toes because Hunter must have dragged him in here spur of the moment in shorts, a T-shirt, and bare feet. He grabs my shoulders to stop me from moving. Then he crouches before me and unbuckles the ankle strap of one shoe while his other hand rests on my calf before removing my shoe.

I hold my breath.

He repeats with the other shoe, but this time he leaves his hand on my calf.

My heart drums, pulse thundering in my ears, sliding one foot out and then the other. His head remains bowed as his hand inches higher, behind my knee.

And a little higher.

My lips part, eyelids closing in a heavy blink. There is no part of my body that doesn't crave his touch.

This is so wrong.

My fingers curl into tight fists, keeping them from reaching for his hair to pull him to me.

He audibly swallows and stands. I force my breath to leave my lungs in tiny, controlled, and muted increments.

"Better." He grins, standing and guiding my arms around his neck.

Better? Is he joking? I'm sweating from head to toe.

I can't tear my gaze from his, as I silently demand he explain what just happened. But he says nothing. Eyes intense, a little dark.

After swaying for a bit, Murphy takes my hand and twirls me again, breaking the intensity of the moment. I lift onto my toes and pirouette dramatically.

He grins. "Nice."

I giggle, stepping back into his embrace, pretending nothing happened—falling into character. "I don't know why you think I'm good at everything."

Murphy hums. "Good question." His eyes shift, inspecting my face before stopping on my lips, stirring the flames again. I step on his toes again because I'm the worst dancer when he's looking at me like we're back in time, dancing on the creaky wood floor in his rental.

He's engaged.

I have Callen.

If those two reasons aren't enough to step away from his embrace, there are at least a hundred other good ones.

As if he can read my thoughts, Murphy releases me. The song is almost over anyway. He pulls in a long breath through his nose, lacing his hands behind his neck while eyeing me.

"Alice," he says my name like it's bitter coming off his tongue.

The guilt in his eyes spurs me to put on my shoes. Then I smooth my hand down my ponytail and pin a cordial smile on my face. "Tell Mr. Morrison I've requested the evening off, so I have to keep working if I want to leave early. He can plant his feet and sway with Vera. It's the thought that counts."

Murphy eyes me, the lines of regret along his forehead deepening. Without a word, he slowly nods, releasing his arms to his sides.

Whoever tried to simplify love into boy meets girl, they fall in love, the end, should be shot. Real life is more complicated. Love is fucking messy. We try to rationalize it and make rules. We take vows and oaths like our hearts don't have a say.

I can be logical or I can be in love. But I'm certain I can't do both.

Not now.

So I'll choose logic because I destroyed Murphy once by choosing love. I can't do it again.

I spend my evening at the playhouse, grinning uncontrollably and even shedding a few cathartic tears. Where would I be today had I followed my passion for acting instead of following in my mother's footsteps? I never would have met Chris. He'd probably be alive. And I wouldn't know Murphy Paddon. That world is hard to imagine.

When I return home, there's a suitcase inside my front door, but it's not mine.

"Hello?" I call.

Nothing.

I check the name on the tag.

Krista Yates

"Mom?" I shuffle toward the back door, but she's not out back. Perhaps she went for a walk around the lake.

The real question is, what is she doing here? I text her.

> Where are you?

She replies.

> Visiting with your neighbors.

Neighbors?

"Oh no ..." I cringe. She's at the main house.

I head straight to the back door and let myself in, slipping off my canvas sneakers and adjusting the belt of my fitted denim jeans. Then I find everyone on the second-floor covered balcony, sipping drinks.

"Hello," Vera says when I open the door. "Come have a seat. What can I get you to drink?"

"Sweetie," Mom says, eyes wide as she stands, like she's waiting for me to throw my arms around her and celebrate her surprise visit.

"I'm fine. Thanks, Vera." I return a tiny smile and soft nod while turning down her drink offer.

"Who's this girl?" Hunter winks at me as I skirt around

226

the perimeter of chairs to reach my mom. "I don't think I've seen you with your hair down since the day we met."

Keeping a smile plastered to my face, I release a tiny laugh. From the loveseat on the opposite side of the balcony, Blair eyes me, her legs draped over Murphy's lap, her hand possessively on his chest.

"What an unexpected surprise," I say to my mom through clenched teeth as we hug.

"Is there any other kind of surprise?"

Everyone laughs.

"I suppose not." I sit in the swivel chair next to hers.

"I knocked on their door, looking for you of course, and the next thing I know, Vera invites me in for wine. Now I see why you love this house manager position."

Vera and Hunter beam with pride.

Blair clears her throat. "Actually, your daughter is a homemaker."

Murphy shoots her a look and squeezes her leg.

"What?" Blair shrugs. "It's a niche job. I respect that."

"What's the difference?" Mom asks.

"Just semantics," I say. "We should get out of their hair, Mom."

"No rush," Vera says. "How was your night off?"

"Yes," Mom chimes in. "Where did you go?"

"I uh, watched a play at the playhouse." I stare at the mesmerizing flames of the gas fire pit table, but I feel Murphy's gaze on me.

"Alice used to love acting," Mom said. "She played Hermia in *A Midsummer Night's Dream* in high school. But after graduation, she chose a more stable path like me and studied engineering."

"You're an engineer?" Hunter asks.

"Yes," Mom answers. "A biomedical engineer."

"Alice, you took this job but you're an engineer?" Vera gawks at me, mouth agape.

"No." I shake my head.

"She was in a car accident, and afterward she decided to go down a different life path." Mom reaches toward me, resting her hand on my arm.

I lift my gaze to accept all the pity glances, and no one disappoints.

Thanks, Mom.

"Oh my gosh. I'm sorry to hear that." Vera squeezes Hunter's hand as if to remind him that later they will have to play a guessing game as to why I dropped out of school after a car accident.

"Were you hurt?" Blair asks.

Again, Murphy nudges her, and again she frowns like it's a fair question.

I lift my arm and point to the scar on it. "Just a cut on my arm from escaping the vehicle that sank to the bottom of the river with my fiancé. The rest of the injuries were emotional." I shrug. "Nothing a year in a psych ward couldn't take care of."

Silence.

Mom's lips part, and she tries to form a smile with them, but her sudden uneasiness steals her ability to move. She started it.

I stand, holding out my hand to her while letting my gaze sweep across the balcony of spectators. "I'm kidding," I say with a grin and a wink.

It was fourteen months, not a year.

Blair and her parents laugh and resume drinking their wine, but Murphy gives me a dead stare that makes my grin falter for a beat before recovering. No one should be shocked. Surely, rich people know that nothing worth having in life comes without surviving a certain level of insanity. After all, Vera has me reading explicit romance to her husband and wearing dresses and shoes that make him horny. Hunter ordered her a new electric Porsche because the one he bought her two months ago isn't the right shade of red in her opinion.

I'm not the crazy one on this balcony.

"Oh, Krista, I was going to show you my massage chair since you said the car did a number on your back," Vera says, standing and setting her wine glass on the table.

"Massage chair? Where do you have a massage chair?" Blair asks. "How did I not know about this? I want to see." She untangles her legs from Murphy's and follows them.

"I'll meet you at the guesthouse," I say to my mom, but she's too enthralled by Vera's expensive chair to concern herself with my whereabouts.

"Mr. Morrison, I'm off the clock, so you're not allowed to look at my ass." I tease, squeezing past his outstretched legs.

He returns a hearty chuckle. "I wasn't."

I shoot him a flirty grin over my shoulder. "You were."

"Did you really lose your mind?" he asks.

I hold my grin. "I'm your *homemaker*. I think that speaks volumes about my sanity. See you in the morning, Mr. Morrison."

Halfway to the guesthouse, I take a hard left, down the terrace, through the fence, and across the one-way parkway to the lake. I need a walk, a moment to clear my head and organize my thoughts before dealing with my mother.

Sunrise and sunset are my favorite times to stroll along the path around the lake because it's less crowded.

"Wait up."

I close my eyes for a second when I hear Murphy's voice behind me.

"I think we're done waiting for each other," I say.

"Alice, that day you thought I was drowning in the pool—"

"You feel like an ass because my fiancé drowned before I could save him. It's fine. I wasn't triggered. Just doing a public service."

"Are you angry with me?" He catches up, and I feel his gaze on my cheek, as I keep my pace.

"No. I'm angry at ... nothing. No one. I'm not angry. You're putting words into my mouth. And where's your wife?"

"I don't have one."

I stop, slowly deflating as he steps in front of me. My focus stays on his chest because I can't look at him.

"For the record, I waited for you," he says.

"I did too," I whisper, lifting my gaze.

Two vertical lines form between his eyes. "What do you mean?"

I shake my head and step past him to continue walking.

"Wait. No. You can't say that then walk away."

"Uh, I did. And I am."

"You didn't wait for me. You left me. And I'm not blaming you. What happened to you is horrible. I just need things between us to be clear, and what's clear is I waited for you."

"Murphy, I don't think things will ever be clear between us. They will forever be about as clear as that water." I nod to the mossy green water edged with algae. "But if you must know, I returned to Minneapolis for you, but you were gone.

The rental was sold. Your neighbors knew nothing of your whereabouts, and the one gallery I found that once had your art didn't know where you'd moved. So I waited. Rented an apartment. Got a job. And settled into the area. Then I waited. I waited and waited. Until ..."

"You're not being serious."

I give him a quick sidelong glance and smirk. "Well, I wish I weren't. I'm not usually so sappy and pathetic."

He grips my arm, making me stop and look at him. A couple walking their dog pass us on the left.

"You waited until what? Until when?"

I'm still waiting.

"Until my boss's daughter came home for the summer with her fiancé."

Murphy squints, shaking his head. "That's a lie. You were with Callen."

"I'm not marrying him."

"You're mad because I'm marrying Blair?"

I roll my eyes. "Of course not."

"Then what?"

"Then nothing. You followed me."

"Because I was concerned after what your mom said."

I tip up my chin. "I'm not your concern."

"It's just a public service."

I don't want to grin, but damn him for saying that. "Shut up." I start walking again.

"I'm scared," he says, staying a few steps behind me.

"Of the boogie man?"

"No."

"Of Blair leaving you at the altar?"

"No. I'm scared I'm going to royally fuck up my life before I ever get to the altar."

"Sounds like a you problem."

"It's an *us* problem."

I laugh. "There is no *us*."

"And yet, here we are."

"Because you're following me."

"Then stop walking away."

"So you can catch me?"

"Maybe."

My heart lurches into my throat. Why is he saying that? He doesn't mean it. I break into a jog.

"Want me to chase you?"

I don't answer. I *can't* answer.

And he doesn't chase me.

Chapter
THIRTY-SIX

Alice

Moms are like best friends—
only brutally honest.

"WHERE DID YOU GO?" Mom asks when I return.

"For a walk around the lake. I didn't know how long you'd be enjoying Vera's massage chair."

She twirls her red hair around her finger and grins. "It's a nice chair."

I toe off my shoes and grab a glass of water. "So what brings you to Minneapolis?"

"You, of course."

"You're here to see me for no particular reason?" I gulp half the glass of water.

"I am. It's called being a mom. I didn't stop loving you and wanting to be with you just because you decided to become an adult."

"What are you talking about?" I set the glass on the counter and sit on the opposite end of the sofa. "I have *yet* to decide to be an adult. I hear it's overrated."

She laughs. "Horribly overrated. I actually have PTO to use, so I took five days to visit my favorite person in the world."

"But Henry Cavill was busy, so you're visiting me instead?"

"Exactly." She tugs the decor pillow out from behind her back and throws it at me.

I catch it and giggle. "I'm honored. And I'm glad you're here. Had I known, I would have taken some time off. They'll still probably let me work some half days so we can hang out."

"Can they be without their *homemaker* for very long?" She shoots me the hairy eyeball.

"This might be the best job ever. It's like a job in the theater only there is no standing ovation. I have a costume with an apron, and I wear my hair in a sleek 1950s ponytail."

"Well, now I want to see your performance."

I smirk. "I bet you'll get invited to breakfast or dinner where you can see me in action."

She sighs. "My daughter, the homemaker. I couldn't be more proud." I sense a lot of sarcasm in her tone.

"Well, I have no rent. And I make a lot more than you do, so mock me if you must, but it's a damn good job."

Her eyes widen.

"But if I could request that you not overshare every little detail about my life, I'd appreciate it."

"Sweetie, the car accident is hardly a *little* detail. And you're the one who told them you were in a mental hospital. Why did you do that?"

"Because I like toying with them. Getting a reaction. And I knew they'd be more likely to believe that it was a joke than the truth."

"You're a pill, young lady. And I was nervous about seeing the man who called us to come get you the night you had a breakdown. Murphy, right? Have you said anything to him yet?"

I nodded. "Yeah, it's out in the open, at least between us. But now it's just weird."

"How so?"

"Because he's marrying Blair."

"So?"

"She doesn't know about us."

"I'm sure he doesn't want her to. So what's the big deal?"

I take a quick breath, readying the words to spew from my mouth on instinct. Then I let them die in silence because she doesn't know. The day we talked about it on the phone, I avoided answering her question because she asked it in such an incredulous way.

"Alice?"

I lift my gaze.

Her brow furrows. "You don't—" She shakes her head slowly.

"I was going to go back to him. *For* him. But then I fell apart before his eyes, and fate had other plans for me. And for him."

"You," she points toward the main house, "love that young woman's fiancé?"

When she says it like that, it sounds so bad. And maybe it is bad, but I'm not trying to love him.

"Don't look at me like that. I'm not stealing anyone's

fiancé. But yes, there are unresolved feelings. So I'm just resolving them," I lie.

"And how exactly are you doing that?"

That is an excellent question.

"First, I'm being a good friend to both of them. When he wants to vent about things like cake flavors, I listen without interfering. And when she's PMSing, I remind him she's under a lot of stress, and he needs to go easy on her. I'm basically the glue holding that whole family together." No one has to put me on a pedestal. I'm perfectly capable of climbing to the top all by myself.

"Is that so?" Mom narrows her eyes.

"Yes. And I make most of the meals, which means I've had ample opportunities to poison her, but I have not."

She snorts. "Well, that's a relief. So you actually like her?"

"I mean, I don't *not* like her. Of course, when she's hanging from his neck and suggesting they shower together, I want to kill her, but in an irrational, very temporary sort of way." I end with a toothy grin.

Mom frowns. "Have you found a therapist here yet?"

"Therapist? No. When I have a weak moment, I AI that shit. I just type in 'Should I kill my ex-lover's fiancée?' and every time, the answer is no. It's way cheaper than an actual therapist. And usually it takes a while to get into their office. Blair would be dead by then."

"Alice Yates. What is wrong with you?"

I laugh. "Nothing. I'm just kidding."

"You have your father's humor. And that's not a compliment."

"Well, he was a homemaker too. And we homemakers

don't get enough social interaction to have anything but a morbid sense of humor."

"Is that your way of blaming me for the divorce?"

My head jerks backward. "What? No. Of course not. He cheated on you. That's not your fault."

She takes a calming breath, shoulders relaxing. "Don't break up their marriage."

"They're not married. And I wouldn't do that."

"They're almost married. In your mind, you need to think of them as married. Understood?"

"Blair is 0-for-two in engagements converting to marriages."

"She's been dumped twice?" Mom's face wrinkles with concern.

"She's the one who has broken off her previous two engagements."

"Well, don't you be the one responsible for number three."

"Did I mention I have a secret lover?" I change the subject before my mother makes me feel any worse about myself.

On cue, she perks up. "A secret lover?"

"Clearly not a secret now, but yes. He coaches lacrosse at the university. His name is Callen, and he's divorced with two kids."

"Have you met his kids?"

I shake my head.

"Do you want to?"

"No."

Her face falls, and I feel her disappointment.

"We're not there yet. Maybe we'll never get there. All the more reason to hold off bringing me into his kids' lives."

"Do you think you're afraid of commitment?"

"No. I think Chris died. Murphy is engaged. And Callen has a family. Let's call it commitment cautious."

"That's fair. Is Callen as handsome as Murphy?"

"He's exactly what you'd expect a lacrosse coach to be. Ruggedly handsome. Although shorter than Murphy. And he doesn't ..." I suck my lower lip in while rethinking my inclination to overshare.

"He doesn't what?"

I shake my head.

"You can tell me." She pulls her knees into her chest, gazing at me like a friend, not my mother.

"Callen doesn't look at me like Murphy does or did."

"What do you mean? You don't think he's as attracted to you?"

I shake my head. "No. It's not that. Callen looks at me like he wants me, like he's attracted to me. Murphy looks at me like I'm magical."

"Magical?"

I can't help but smile. "Yes. He looks at me with wonder. And sometimes he doesn't look at me at all because he's blushing. Handsome but shy. Then other times, he has such confidence it makes me weak in the knees. I think that's it. He's unpredictable in the best way possible."

"You mean *was* and *did*."

"What?" I squint.

"You mean he was that way. And he did those things. Gave you those looks. In the past."

My friend is gone, and my mother is back.

"Yeah. Of course, that's what I meant."

"Maybe Callen just doesn't know you well enough.

Perhaps if you give him time, he'll get that wonder in his eyes when he looks at you."

"Maybe," I whisper.

Murphy looked at me that way from the first moment he saw me. Maybe he looks at Blair that way, too. He should. He's marrying her.

Chapter
THIRTY-SEVEN

Murphy

Honesty is an okay policy, but it's nuanced.

"You've never looked more handsome," Blair says as the tailor pins minor adjustments to my suit for the wedding.

"What about me?" Hunter asks, standing a few feet away in his half-sewn suit.

"Dear, you already know you look handsome. This isn't your first suit," Vera says dismissively while focusing on her phone.

"This isn't my first suit either," I say.

"It's your first big boy suit," Blair says before sipping her wine. "And don't give me that look. I'm just stating the obvious. You know I fell in love with your jeans and wrinkled T-shirt."

"The suit I have still fits me. And I'm a *big boy*, so ..."

The tailor clears his throat and mumbles, "I don't think it counts if it's off the rack."

"The hell it doesn't," I mumble. "Ouch," I grit through my teeth.

"Sorry, sir," he says.

He's not sorry. He poked me on purpose.

"Your owliness is a real ick, babe." Blair wrinkles her nose.

"My owliness? And what is an ick?"

"I know you're unsettled right now. But we'll be in New York before you know it. So, can you just stop moaning and groaning about everything? It's an ick. A turn off."

"Oh, lord, son." Hunter shakes his head. "Don't be an ick. I've dumped too much money into a third wedding to let my daughter change her mind *again*."

"Hunter!" Vera snaps.

"I'm kidding." He tips up his chin, scratching his neck while sliding his gaze to me. "I'm not kidding," he whispers.

"What if I have a few icks with you too," I say to Blair.

Silence.

It's so quiet I can hear the tailor gulp, the pin sliding through the fibers of the imported Italian fabric.

Vera presses a hand to her throat like she's choking on her response.

Blair narrows her eyes, head cocked to the side. "Oh, *really*? And what might those be?"

"Run," Hunter whispers.

"I didn't say I did. I just asked *what if* I did? Would you want me to mention them?"

"Seriously, son. Run!" Hunter says with more urgency.

Vera frowns at her husband.

"Yeah. Let's hear them." Blair sets her wine on the

marble coaster atop the dark wood table next to the velvet sofa.

"Don't be stupid," the tailor whispers.

"No." I pull back my shoulders because I'm not running out of here with my tail between my legs. "I don't have anything to share right now. But it's nice to know that if or when I do, you're open to listening."

Am I owly? Yes. Why? I think it has a lot to do with a certain homemaker. Honest to God, I love Blair. But I can't stop thinking about Alice. I can't stop wanting to touch her, feel her skin against mine. Maybe it's infatuation—my own moment of temporary insanity. And as I think this, I feel terrible because everything in my head sounds selfish and insensitive.

Maybe not the tailor, but I need someone to give me sage advice. My father would have done it. He'd say something like, "Murphy, you already know everything you'll ever need to know in life."

I know my head hurts. My heart aches. And my instincts are shit.

There are the things that people *should* do in their lives. Then there is Murphy Paddon, who does the opposite. Most of the time, I regret it. But sometimes, I get it right. The odds are not in my favor.

The trip home is uncomfortable, to put it mildly. Hunter makes me ride in front with him. When I glance back at Vera and Blair, daggers fly toward my head. After Hunter parks in the garage, he reaches for my arm just as I open my door to get Blair's for her. He gives me a quick headshake. When the women disappear into the house without a backwards glance at me, he releases a deep sigh.

"Do you smoke cigars, Murphy?"

"No."

"Well," he opens his door, "you do today. Come on."

I head toward the door.

"Nope," he says, nodding toward his Corvette. He sits in the driver's seat and retrieves cigars from the glove compartment.

With a laugh, I sit in the front seat.

"Don't inhale. Just enjoy the flavor then let it go."

I light it and feel confident that I'm not inhaling. It's when I go to release it, I realize there's a little inhaling taking place.

Hunter laughs when I cough. "I'm sorry your dad's not here."

"Did Vera put you up to this? Did she ask you to sit me down and offer to be my new father figure?"

He looks at the ceiling and exhales a plume of smoke. "Yup."

I laugh, and the grin on my face isn't forced. No "owly" Murphy at this moment.

"I love your daughter," I say, meaning every word.

"I know you do. But she may still change her mind."

I nod then try not to inhale again. This time I manage to blow out without coughing. Does it taste good? No. But sometimes we do things because it makes other people feel good. I don't know if Blair and I will make it to the altar and both say, "I do." But I like Hunter. He's unapologetically himself, even when it's frowned upon or offensive. Blair hates that about him. I can respect it without agreeing with everything he says.

"Would your father have liked my daughter?" he asks.

"My dad liked everyone. He was an artist too. So he would have been drawn to Blair's passion."

"She's a good person," he says. "I know we don't see eye to eye on a lot of things, but I'm proud of her. We've tried to give her everything, but she's always found more joy in forging her own way, achieving success on her own. She'll be a good mother and wife."

Again, I nod. He's not telling me anything about Blair that I don't already know. She's beautiful, talented, and kind. Any man would be lucky to have her.

"So"—he takes a puff and blows it out—"what are your ... what was the word? Icks?"

I chuckle. "You first."

"Murphy, my wife hired a homemaker for me. She's perfect."

"Your wife or the homemaker?"

Hunter doesn't look at me, but he smirks.

"My ick with Blair is she's been engaged three times but never married. And I feel pretty arrogant thinking I'm different."

"You're confident. She needs that. Hell, she needs you to drag her to the altar by her hair if need be."

This is the perfect example of things he says that angers Blair, but I find humorous. I'm more laid-back than my fiancée. It's easier for me to enjoy life without running it through a filter, dissecting everything to determine if it offends someone before I let myself laugh. I try to tell her intention and context matters, especially with her father's generation.

"By the way, thanks for the dance lessons. I got laid." He holds out his fist.

Golfing and sharing inappropriate jokes are one thing, fist-bumping after he nails my future mother-in-law is another. Still, I bump his fist.

"I got laid the same night too." I offer my fist.

He scowls at me. "Too far, Murphy. Too far." Then he opens the door and climbs out.

I chuckle then wait a few minutes and head upstairs to see if I'm still engaged. Before I reach the main floor, Blair appears at the top of the stairs in her workout wear.

"I'm going to exercise so my body doesn't go on your ick list." She descends the stairs and tries to slide past me without our bodies touching. I wrap my arm around her waist to stop her.

She huffs, lip protruding in a pout.

"I'm sorry. There is no ick list. You're perfect just the way you are."

"Liar," she says, rolling her eyes.

I nuzzle my face into her neck. "I'm not lying."

"You need to shave. And you smell like cigar smoke. Yuck." She tries to push me away.

"Wanna know a secret?" I ask.

She refuses to smile, but she stops trying to wriggle out of my hold. "What?"

"My dad used to make things out of wood. He had a lathe and carving tools in his garage. My mom resented all the hours he spent with a 'tree stump' instead of her. I was fascinated by it, so he taught me."

Blair's forehead wrinkles. "You're a woodturner?"

I nod.

She blinks several times, face soured. "Why have you never told me this?"

"Because I don't do it anymore. And since my dad died, I let that part of my life die too."

"Murphy, I'm an artist. I create things out of clay. You

met me at an art expo, and you never thought to mention that you're an artist too?"

"You're far more talented. I never wanted to sound like I was competing with you."

Her head juts back. "Why are you telling me this now?"

"Because I told your dad that my dad would have liked you because he was an artist too."

"So the only reason you're telling me is because you don't want my dad to tell me first? Jesus, Murphy. What is wrong with you?" She jerks out of my hold and continues down the stairs.

I drag a hand over my face. There is nothing I can do right today. Perhaps I should take a nap and try again tomorrow.

Chapter
THIRTY-EIGHT

Alice

Only fools judge others for their mistakes.

"Where's your mom?"

I look over my shoulder at Murphy in his swim trunks and baseball cap. Wiping the dirt from the garden off my hands, I sit back on my heels.

"Visiting your nephew?" he asks.

I stiffen.

"You have a brother, right? You met Callen the day you were watching your nephew's soccer game. Right?"

"Yeah." I clear my throat. "No. My mom is shopping. Waiting for me to get done working so we can spend time together."

"But she's going to visit her grandson, right?"

"You're awfully concerned about someone you've never

met. Is this because you have nothing better to do since pissing off your fiancée this morning?"

Murphy frowns. "She told you about the ick?"

"No." I stand, brushing off my butt. "Before I came outside, I overheard her venting to Vera."

"Eavesdropping?"

"No. I'm just not deaf."

His gaze sweeps along my entire body. "Is wearing that dress to work in the garden weird?"

I laugh. "It would be if you did it. You're too tall, and the skirt would ride up your ass."

"Funny."

"Think you can do me a quick favor before you relax by the pool?" I ask.

"Why are you saying it like all I do is relax by the pool?"

I shuffle toward the guesthouse, assuming he'll follow me. "Why are you so on edge?"

"I'm not on edge. I'm owly."

I giggle. "Sorry. *Owly*."

"What do you need me to do? You're eating into my short break. I have to get back to work soon."

"I'm beginning to see why you're on Blair's shit list. Did I not make your coffee strong enough this morning?" I open the sliding door and kick off my canvas gardening sneakers.

"I'm on everyone's shit list today. Blair's. Vera's. Hunter's. And I'm sensing you're putting me on yours too. When will your mom be back? Maybe I can piss her off, too, and bat a thousand today."

I shoot him a narrow-eyed look before leading him to the bathroom. "Vera said she's fine with me changing the showerhead in here, but I can't get the old one off. Can you?"

Murphy parks his hands on his hips and inspects it for a few seconds while I inspect him in his low-hanging trunks and no shirt.

Tight abs.

Sinewy arms with blue veins.

He grips the showerhead and tries to turn it. Then he shakes out his hands and tries again. This time, it loosens, and he removes it for me.

Damn. That body.

His face comes into my visual frame, and I realize he's bent to the side, ducking to put himself in my line of sight which is glued to his half-naked torso.

I swallow hard. "Th-thanks." I take the showerhead.

"I know I'm the bad guy today, but it's not as if my actions have been unprovoked. And when you look at me like that, my last fiber of control feels really fucking close to snapping."

"I'm not looking at you—"

"You are." He kicks the bathroom door shut and backs me against it.

My breath dies in my chest, suffocating my response. What the hell is happening?

"Two weeks," he says in a tone that sounds like a mix of anger and pain as he rests his hands on the door above my head. The heat of his body penetrates my dress and permeates into my veins. "Two. Fucking. Weeks."

I ball my hands at my sides to keep from touching him because he's not mine.

"Callen. Your boyfriend. I *hate* him."

I lift my gaze. "Well, fuck what you think, because I want to kill your perfect fiancée."

Murphy smirks before ducking his head and brushing my cheek with his scruffy jaw until I feel his breath at my ear. "Now that we've cleared the air, unbutton your dress."

My insides liquify under the heat of my skin. I know better. So does he. Did I survive death and a mental breakdown only to destroy another woman's life?

No.

Still, I unclench my fists and slowly work the buttons of my dress, stopping just above my navel, chest heaving with impossibly hard breaths as Murphy's lips brush along my neck, not kissing, just touching. Then they feather along the swell of my breasts to the edge of my satin and lace bra.

Wetting my lips, I part them on a heavy blink.

His mouth hovers over my nipple on the outside of my bra. My fingers ache to dive into his hair.

"God..." I seethe, smacking my hands flat against the door when he bites my nipple and gives it a firm tug before sucking it just as hard. My knees collapse inward, and I swear I'm a breath away from orgasming just from that.

He doesn't move his hands from the door, not one touch beyond his lips and teeth. After releasing me, he repeats the same thing with my other nipple.

I hiss. It hurts and feels good at the same time. My eyes pinch shut, each breath harsher than the one before as I arch my back. He lifts his head, our lips so close to touching that I feel like his last breath is my next.

"Button your dress and get back to work," he whispers, letting his hand slide down the door to open it.

I gasp a silent breath and step away from the door so my back is to him. Closing my eyes, I button my dress and wait for him to leave. When I hear the sliding door, I fall toward the sink, hands on either side, holding me up. The pink-cheeked reflection in the mirror is unrecognizable. She's not me.

I wouldn't let another woman's fiancé do that to me.

Would I?

Chapter
THIRTY-NINE

Alice

If Hell exists, there's a waiting list.

KARMA IS VERA. Tonight they are one and the same. She invites my mom and me to join everyone for dinner—the dinner I make, of course. And "everyone" includes Murphy's mom.

I'm a dirty ~~homemaking~~ home-*wrecking* whore hidden behind a blue floral house dress and an apron that's been in the Morrison family for years.

"This is weird. I knew it would happen, but it's still weird," I say, whisking the Dijon dressing. I'm not sure I made it with the right ingredients. I'm meeting Murphy's mom tonight and my thoughts have gone to shit.

"What's weird?" Mom asks with a laugh while cutting the sourdough bread.

"We're having dinner with the people who hired me to serve them dinner. It's weird."

"It's a meal. They seem to adore you. Just think of it as your house, and you've invited them to dinner. Then making and serving the meal won't seem so weird."

I nod. She's right. That's a better way to look at it. Of course, it won't help my nerves when I see Blair, Murphy, and his mom seated at the table. It's like Blair or his mom will see it on my face and instantly know that he had my nipples in his mouth earlier today.

"Jesus, it's hot in here." I wave a hand over my face.

"It's not that hot. Are you getting sick?" Mom asks.

If only.

"No. It's probably just standing over the stove too long. Here. Let's serve our guests." I hand her two small salad plates.

"We should have gone out to eat. I suddenly feel guilty for inviting you to dinner and asking you to cook it," Vera says as we serve the salads.

"You have a lovely kitchen. It's a real treat getting to cook in it," Mom says, placing salads in front of Vera and Hunter.

Dang it! I was going to serve them, but she beat me to it, so I'm stuck serving Blair and the nipple biter. Murphy doesn't even try to avert his gaze. Just the opposite. I feel it like it's glued to me. The midday sun in a desert.

"Sit down, Mom. I've got the rest." I nod toward the two free chairs opposite Blair and Murphy.

"You sure?"

I nod. "Uh-huh."

"Krista, Alice, this is my mom, Janelle. Alice works for the Morrisons and her mom is visiting for a few days," Murphy says.

"Lovely to meet you both." Janelle smiles, playing with her hoop earring under her long, dark hair streaked with gray.

"You too," Mom says, sitting across from Janelle, who's sandwiched between Murphy and Blair.

As soon as I scurry back to the kitchen, I tug open the freezer and take a deep breath, welcoming the cold air on my exposed skin.

"Get a grip," I whisper.

When the rest of the meal is on the table, I sit next to my mom, which puts me directly in front of Murphy.

"Your daughter is a phenomenal cook," Hunter says.

"Thank you." Mom blots her mouth. "I wish I could take credit for it, but Alice has always loved cooking. She's curious. And whatever she sets out to do, she does it exceedingly well."

I glance at Murphy, and he smirks while chewing. He's thinking about cornhole and bowling. This conversation should have my back straight and chin up. Who doesn't love a little praise? But I can't look at Blair, and when I think she's looking at me, I swear she knows.

Did he leave with a guilty conscience and immediately confess? No way. Surely not.

"Blair is talented too. Not as much in the kitchen, but she's found herself a good man who loves her for all the right reasons," Vera says, giving her husband a little smirk that has everything to do with me.

"I can't wait to have another daughter," Janelle says, wrapping her arm around Blair to give her a side hug.

Blair tips her head to press it to Janelle's. They're so cute I want to vomit.

"How are the wedding plans coming along?" Mom asks.

Vera and Blair perk up, and then it begins, nonstop wedding talk. My mom and Janelle join the conversation with stories of their weddings and Blair's upcoming bridal shower. Hunter finishes his meal and zones out, focusing on his phone.

Finally, I excuse myself. "I'll get dessert. Mr. Morrison's favorite—lemon sorbet."

"Alice, I like tiramisu and you know it," he says without lifting his gaze from his phone.

"That's right. Lemon sorbet is your wife's favorite. Oops."

When he finally looks at me, I wink and retreat to the kitchen.

"Ugh ..." I sigh, dropping my face in my hands when I'm tucked out of sight. Is it September yet?

After seven glass cups are filled with lemon sorbet, I carry them on a tray to the dining room. My mom's laughter has hit the second glass of wine volume. It might be time to cut her off, but Janelle is laughing just as much. Of course my mom would get along with his mom.

"Traitor," Hunter mumbles when I set the sorbet in front of him, but he can't keep a straight face because he's too much of a flirt.

Vera gives me a look that says I should ignore him.

"Were you renting out your guesthouse before Alice started working for you?" my mom asks.

"No. We have no desire to deal with that kind of rental property," Vera replies.

"Murphy could probably give you some tips," Janelle says.

"Oh, yes. He owned a house not too far from here," Mom adds.

"How does Krista know about your rental property?" Blair asks with a smile through gritted teeth.

My mom wrinkles her nose.

Murphy clears his throat, pressing his napkin to his lips for a beat. "I'm not sure how it came up, but it did."

Shit.

"Mom, isn't it time for you to take your walk around the lake?" I stand, eyeing my mom with a tight grin. "You know how important a ten-minute walk after each meal is to keep your glucose in check."

"Oh, are you diabetic?" Vera asks.

"No." Mom plasters on a fake grin and stands because she knows I'm not happy with her. "And that's probably because I take a ten-minute walk after every meal."

"Good for you. I wouldn't be able to drink that much wine and walk around the lake without falling in. Alice, perhaps you should walk with your mom," Vera suggests.

"She's good." I hold on to her arm. "I'll see her out then clear the table and clean up the kitchen."

"It was nice meeting you, Janelle," Mom says.

"You too." Janelle smiles like she just made a new best friend.

Blair stands too, jaw fixed while she tosses her napkin aside. "You know what? I think I need a drive. Dad, let's take one of your convertibles for a drive."

"Oh, that sounds like fun," Vera says. "But no smoking, dear."

"Then it won't be that much fun," Hunter deadpans.

"I guess we're going for a ride." Murphy finishes his last bite of sorbet.

"No, babe. I think you should walk your mom out then hang out in the bedroom and do your work or whatever else you do, like own rental property and turn wood, and tell everyone like it's no big deal, except me." Blair narrows her eyes.

They have a stare off, but he waves the white flag first. "I'll stay here."

I pull my mom toward the back door. "Good job, Mom."

"What? I didn't say you stayed at his place."

"Shh." I open the back door. "Go to bed."

"I thought I was going for a walk."

"You are. Walk straight to the guesthouse and go to bed. I have work to do, and Vera is right. You've had too much to drink to walk around the lake. Nighty night. Love you and your big mouth."

She sticks her tongue out at me. Yep, she's tipsy.

I smirk and close the door. When I return to the kitchen, Murphy's scraping the leftover food from the dinner plates into the garbage.

"You're grounded. Go. I've got this."

"Everyone left. I'm back in the doghouse. Might as well make myself useful."

Everyone left.

We're alone.

"I'm sorry my mom said that. In her defense, she had too much to drink, and it's a fair assumption that your fiancée would know you owned rental property less than a mile from here."

He keeps his head down while cleaning the last plate. "It's not her fault. I take full responsibility. And Blair knows I owned a rental, but she just recently found out. That's on me. I shouldn't have waited so long to tell her. But I'm an adult and fully capable of weighing risks."

Me. I'm a risk. What we did earlier was a risk.

I don the pink gloves from under the sink and run dish water. "Well, you should not have taken the risk that you took earlier with me."

"You're right." He sets the plate on the neat pile next to the sink.

I didn't expect him to agree so wholeheartedly. It steals my breath for a few seconds, a little gut punch.

At a loss for words, I focus on scrubbing the dishes and setting them in the strainer as fast as Murphy can dry them. I'm obviously hurt by his admission, yet he makes no effort to say it differently or apologize, which only makes me angrier. And I don't even know why I'm so mad. He's not my fiancé. I willingly unbuttoned my dress. I wanted it to happen.

A good man would feel regret. Right? No. A good man wouldn't do it in the first place. But that feels equally awful because Murphy is a good man. That's why we fell in love in less than two weeks. That's why eight years later, these feelings are still alive, sprouting, taking root, and searching for sunlight to grow again.

As the silence stretches, my stupid emotions build. But I refuse to cry. He's *not mine*. Blair should cry. Not me.

Would it kill him to say something? *Hey, it was fun, but wrong. No hard feelings?*

Or ...

I'm an asshole for cheating on my fiancée. I'm going to break up with her immediately.

He won't say that because he loves her. This isn't contrived. It's real and messy. I'm sure anyone on the sidelines would think of a dozen better moves to make, but it's like me yelling at Chris to wake up and swim to the surface, to fight, and live. It's always easier to live a perfect life when it's not yours.

"I don't trust you," Murphy says.

I freeze while tugging off my gloves.

He dries his hands, leaning against the island. "And I"—he chuckles while shaking his head—"I feel emotionally mature for having the courage to say that to you because I'm ashamed. It's been eight years. You've spent *so* long overcoming everything you went through. And I've moved on. Yet, when I'm with you, I'm scared out of my fucking mind that you're—" His voice catches and his throat bobs as his eyes redden.

Chris died, but Murphy is the emotional carnage.

"I hurt you. And you think I could do it again." I set the gloves aside.

He stares at his feet, then he nods.

"But it's more than that. You love her."

Another nod.

"Then it's settled. You'll marry Blair as planned. And in twenty years, she'll hire you a homemaker, and you'll not even remember my name."

"Fuck you," he says, missing the humor in my joke.

"I think that's a bad idea since you're engaged."

"Well, that's *all* I want to do."

My jaw unhinges, but nothing comes out.

Murphy pushes off the counter and cups my face, bringing his lips so close to mine I almost whimper when he stops. His thumb traces my lower lip. "Hi," he whispers.

Damn him.

I barely get "hi" out before he kisses me. My mind swims, and tears burn my eyes because he's erasing eight years with one kiss. We're back in his rental listening to Lesley Gore sing "Misty." Reality goes out the door. Life is sweeter when days are filled with oldies on vinyl and afternoon delight.

Somewhere there's a tiny part of my brain holding on to rational thoughts, and they're fighting to remind me of trivial things like Murphy is not mine. But the other ninety-nine percent of my mind homes in on one thing: his tongue making deliciously languid strokes against mine.

We don't miss a beat when he lifts me onto the cold, white marble countertop. I want this to be an alternate universe where we're doing nothing wrong because it feels too good. I've been an unsettled wanderer for eight years, because this man is the only thing in my life that has felt right since Chris died.

He begins to unbutton my dress, his mouth moving to my neck. I close my eyes and let my head lull to the side to give him better access. His hands give up on my buttons after three, and he snakes his hands up the skirt of my dress, curling his fingers around the waist of my panties and dragging them down my legs.

"Lie back, beautiful," he whispers in my ear.

I have no self-control, so I do what he asks. He sets my underwear on the counter, then guides my wedged pumps to the edge. Then he kisses his way up my leg while planting his hands on my inner thighs to spread my legs wider.

My back arches and I grip his hair in anticipation.

Oh god ...

He's going too slowly. Why must he torture me? He's ... all ... most ... there ...

"Hello?"

HOLYFUCKINGHELL

I jackknife to sitting and fly off the counter. It's my mom coming in the back door.

Murphy is way cooler than I am. He takes my underwear and starts to slide them into his pocket.

I scowl at him, ripping them from his grip and tucking them into my dress pocket. Then I shove him and hiss, "Go!"

Working the last button to my dress, I meet my mom just before she steps into the kitchen.

"Oh." She jerks backward. "You scared me."

I scared her? Okay. Sure.

"What's up?" I ask, smoothing the apron down the front of my dress.

"You weren't answering your phone. And I couldn't find any Advil in your bathroom." She squints, lifting the inside of her wrist to my forehead. "Are you running a fever? Your cheeks are burning red. I definitely think you're getting sick."

"Uh ..." I retreat a step and push her hand away. "I'm fine. I got the dish water too hot."

She gives me a wary look.

"Hey, Krista," Murphy says, popping back into the kitchen like he's been somewhere else, doing only good things.

"Hi, Murphy. Listen, I'm so sorry about bringing up your rental property. I should have—"

"Don't sweat it." He fills a glass with water. "I should've told Blair earlier. It's not that she didn't know; it's just that she recently found out. After my dad died, I went out of my way to not look back. Clearly, not telling Blair sooner was taking it too far." He smiles before sipping his water.

"Well, thank you for understanding. Listen, I won't keep you, but my dear daughter wasn't answering her phone. And I have a slight headache, so I need Advil, Tylenol or something like that."

"Oh, sure. Let me see what I can find," he says.

"No. Really, I'll get it." I head toward the hall bathroom, but Murphy does, too, like it takes both of us to find a bottle of pain pills.

"Your in-laws and fiancée will be back soon. Just go to your room. I've got this." I flick my wrist to shoo him away just as I step into the bathroom. I find a bottle of Advil and turn, but he's right here, blocking the doorway.

I frown. "What are we doing?" I whisper.

"You missed a button." He reaches forward and fixes the missed button while forcing me backward and kicking the door partially shut.

"What are you—"

He kisses me, gripping the back of my legs and lifting me onto the vanity. It's a punishing kiss just like his hands sliding to my ass, squeezing tightly, pressing my bare core firmly against the bulge in his jeans.

God, I want him so badly I could cry.

He kisses my jaw, and I drop the bottle of pills then grip the edge of the vanity, shamelessly rocking my pelvis to grind against him.

"I hate her so much," I say with a tight voice between labored breaths.

His mouth curls into a grin as he nips at my neck, keeping a bruising grip on my ass. "You don't." He thrusts his hips into me. "But I fucking love how hard you're trying to."

He's right. I don't hate Blair, but I want to because then I don't have to hate myself so much. I'm afraid it's too late to save my soul or his.

A nauseous feeling kills the butterflies in my tummy and extinguishes the burning need in my veins when I think about Blair wanting make-up sex later, or Murphy needing to get off after our two close encounters today.

I shove him away, hop off the vanity, and retrieve the pills from the floor. Then I peer up at him as if everything is his fault even though it's probably mine. "If I make breakfast in the morning and hear Mr. Morrison say one word about how loud you and Blair were, I'm going to piss in your coffee."

He lifts one eyebrow.

"Understood?" I double down.

Murphy slowly brings his pointer and middle finger to his temple in a tiny salute.

I roll my lips together to keep from grinning at his gesture.

But seriously, please don't have sex with her!

That plea stays in my head because it's an unfair and unrealistic request, which is quite fitting for the fantasy world I like to live in with Murphy. My brain has reverted to childish behavior with its fingers shoved in its ears while chanting, "lalalalala."

Chapter
FORTY

Murphy

Choices suck. Avoid them at all costs.

WHEN WE WERE YOUNG, my parents would take me
and my sister to Dairy Queen every Saturday during
the summer. My sister was boring as hell, always
getting a vanilla crunch cone. But I stewed over my
decision. Banana split or peanut buster parfait? Mom
would roll her eyes and tell me to hurry up because
people were waiting in line behind us. Dad would
invariably jump in and order one so I could order the
other and we'd share. He'd say, "Life is short, buddy.
Why choose?"

He lied.

Life isn't *that* short. And since then, I've discovered the
hard way why choices must be made.

I just never imagined I'd stew over love. Actually, I'm not

sure stewing is the right word. I've backed myself into a corner, and I will not get out of it unscathed.

"Still in the doghouse?" Hunter asks as we practice on his putting green next to the pickleball court.

"Yep." I tap the ball into the hole.

"You should buy her something. Nothing cliché like flowers or jewelry. It has to be something that feels well-thought-out, like a Chihuahua or a new car."

I chuckle, scratching the back of my head as he makes a long putt from the edge of the green. "I'll uh ... keep that in mind. Thanks."

"Everything you said to her was probably true. But you need a little more tact."

"Like you?"

He smirks, tossing another ball onto the green. "When you've been married as long as I have, you can get away with more."

"Like hiring a homemaker?"

"Alice is a dream. I hope this guy she's dating doesn't try to marry her anytime soon."

Me too.

"I don't think you have to worry about that. She's pretty focused on serving you at your throne," I say.

"Who's serving who at what throne?"

My head whips around when I hear her voice.

Alice's light pink and white dress sashays with each step as she carries a basket of fresh cut flowers toward the house. Perfect auburn ponytail bobbing like a show pony.

"Murphy was just asking me what my secret is to a happy marriage. I told him he needs to worship Blair like I worship Vera, and he'll have a long, happy marriage." Hunter delivers his bullshit with a devilish grin.

"I couldn't agree more." Alice bats her eyelashes. Her tone has an edge that makes my grin falter.

After she's out of earshot (I hope), Hunter whistles. "There is nothing as sexy as a woman in heels."

"I think they cause bunions. We should normalize wide-toed flats being the new sexy."

"Christ, Murphy. I knew you were pussy-whipped, but castrated too?"

I laugh, handing him the ten thousand-dollar Honma putter that goes with his "older" matching irons he spent over 50K on. "I need to get some work done before Vera and Blair return from the salon, since it looks like I'll be going to the animal shelter or a car dealership before the end of the day."

"Go for the car. I don't want a dog pissing on my floors."

"You should have thought of that before doling out advice. The dog fits my budget better than the car," I holler, walking away.

Alice isn't in the kitchen, but there's a jug of iced tea on the counter. I pour myself a glass and head to the bedroom to work. Do I take a big detour in hope of running into her? Absolutely.

"It was nice seeing your mom," I say, for a lack of anything more original.

Alice transfers laundry from the washer to the dryer. "Yes. I'm sure you've missed seeing her the past eight years. Though she mentioned you didn't send a Christmas card last year."

"I'm making small talk."

She starts the dryer and turns, leaning against it. "Why?"

"Because I need to work, but I'm procrastinating."

Her perfectly lined red lips twist, and she clasps her

hands in front of her, taking slow steps to me. It's not an exaggeration when I say her nearness takes my breath away. I slide my hands into my pockets to keep them from touching her.

"Where's Mr. Morrison?"

"Putting away the putters. Why?"

If she's wondering if we have time to hide in a dark corner and kiss, we do. Sin begets sin. At this point, I'm in so far over my head, what's one more kiss?

"It's story time," she says.

"That is so messed up."

She smirks and unbuttons the top two buttons of her dress. "I think you're jealous. Maybe when he's down for his nap, I can read you a story. Do you have a favorite genre?"

Such a fucking tease.

"Let me guess. Anything with a ripped bodice on the cover?" Alice has always played out of my league.

I glance down the hallway for any sign of Hunter. Then I drag my thumb across my lower lip to mask my grin. "When's your boyfriend coming home?"

"Yesterday."

That's unfortunate.

"Why? Do you want to double date? Maybe go to a movie?" The challenge in her eyes only makes it harder to keep my hands in my pockets.

"That would be fun." I rock back and forth on my heels.

"Or ..." She releases a third button of her dress.

For fuck's sake, Hunter doesn't need to see that much cleavage.

"Maybe," she continues, "the homemaker could cook a nice dinner, then we can play cornhole or bowl. Teams. Callen and me against you and Blair."

"What does the winner get?"

"Winner gets to sleep with the homemaker."

I freeze, then clear my throat to keep from tripping over my words. "I'm not sure Blair would think of that as a prize."

"Oh, Murphy. I think you're too busy ogling me to see your fiancée sneaking a peek. She's an artist. Artists are curious. Perhaps a little kinky."

I stretch my neck from side to side. Alice loves a good reaction. She's waiting for me to take the bait.

"Are you enjoying this?" I ask.

"Absolutely." She winks and saunters toward Hunter's study.

This doesn't feel real. Alice and Blair. My past and my future have collided in the present, and I don't see a way out of this without ripping my heart in two and hurting everyone around me. It feels like I'm falling and there's a tummy-turning excitement when I think a parachute will deploy.

The adrenaline.

The euphoria.

But what if there is no parachute?

I return to my bedroom and manage to clear my head long enough to complete a project that's due tomorrow. The small successes matter more than ever. They give me the illusion of control.

"Hey," Blair says, closing the bedroom door behind her with her hands gripping paper bags from fancy clothing stores.

Vera knows Blair doesn't splurge on herself that often, so when they're together, she showers her daughter with gifts.

"Looks like a successful day." I say, nodding to the bags.

When I look at her, my heart aches. What am I doing?

And why can't I stop? Is Alice a drug? Drugs destroy families.

Blair tosses the bags onto the bed. "I suppose." She plops down and frowns, gathering her hair over one shoulder to braid it. It's what she does when she's nervous. "I hate that we're fighting."

"Are we? I just assumed you were upset with me, not an actual fight. I'm not upset with you."

She deflates like I'm weighing her down with all the blame. It's not my intention.

"I'm sorry. I wasn't trying to be insensitive or keep anything from you. It might take some time for me to perfect running every thought through a filter. But I'll try because I'm sure it sounds worse than I mean it to sound. I don't have icks or whatever you call them. Stress is my excuse, but it's not a good one, and it's not your problem."

Blair runs her fingers through her braid to undo it. "How can you say that? Your problems are mine, and mine are yours."

Had Alice felt that way eight years earlier, would we still be together? If she would have trusted me with her past and the trauma, would I have been able to prevent her from going to a psychiatric hospital?

"Why so many lines on your handsome face?" Blair finds her favorite spot straddling my lap. She runs her fingers along my forehead, tracing the craters of worry. "You're not going to call off the wedding, are you? This isn't a cruel joke where you're trying to teach me a lesson, right?" She laughs, but it's not without a hint of true concern.

"I would never call off our wedding to teach you a lesson."

"You'd crush me, baby," she whispers. "I wouldn't

survive not spending forever with you." Her hands press to my cheeks.

They're gentle.

Warm.

Familiar.

I rest my hands on her hips. The proximity to her I've craved since we met no longer feels right. Then again, nothing feels right. Whatever internal gauge or natural instinct I'm supposed to have feels broken.

Chapter
FORTY-ONE

Murphy

Never underestimate the power of the last bite.

"You're on your own, babe." Blair wraps her arms around my neck and kisses me before slinging her handbag over her shoulder.

"On my own?" I wipe the sweat from my brow with a towel, drinking electrolyte water in the kitchen.

It's been a week since Blair and I "made up" of sorts. Alice has performed her homemaker duties without giving me too many second glances, and I've tried to pretend that I'm not thinking about her nonstop.

"Mom's taking me to a wine tasting at Aunt Tammy's house, and Dad just left to have dinner at the club with friends. Alice asked for the night off, so you're on your own for dinner. Maybe order something to be delivered." She glosses her lips just as Vera steps around the corner.

"She's watching a play again. I think she said her nephew is in it," Vera says, sliding her phone into her purse.

"Where's the play?" I casually ask.

"Uh, I assume at the children's theater," Vera says.

"Why? Are you going to wait for her to get back to make you dinner?" Blair snorts.

"Think she would?" I smirk, and Blair rolls her eyes as expected.

"Before long, we'll be married and living in New York without a *homemaker*. You'd better get used to takeout food."

"Noted." I shoot her a toothy grin.

As soon as they pull out of the driveway, I head to the children's theater. Why did Alice lie to me about being an only child?

I laugh when I see the sign out front with the performance title. *Alice in Wonderland.*

The theater is less than half full. So it doesn't take me long to find Alice's long, wavy auburn hair in the third row from the stage. I sit in the back and read through the program with the list of cast members. If Alice's real last name is Yates, and she has a brother, then his son's name should be Yates too. But there is no one listed with that last name.

During the standing ovation, Alice scoots out of her aisle, clutches her purse, and walks up the stairs to the exit. On a double take, she spies me and stops. As soon as I stand, she continues out of the theater and the building as if she didn't see me.

"Don't act like you don't know I'm here," I say, following her to her car parked along the street.

"I'm pretending you didn't follow me because that would be creepy." She unlocks her door.

"Curious. Not creepy. You told me you were an only child. Yet, you have a nephew. I'm confused."

She sighs, rounding the car to get out of the street. "I'm an only child."

I wait, but that's all she gives me, crossing her arms over her chest.

"You just like watching plays? That makes sense because you said you acted. And your mom confirmed that."

After a beat, she nods.

"I just want to know you. *Really* know you."

"You're engaged to another woman."

"And I've cheated on her. So the least you can do is help me understand why."

Her jaw drops. "Help you understand?" She coughs a laugh. "I didn't back you up against a door and tell you to unbutton your dress. I didn't kiss you, lift you onto a counter, and pull off your underwear. I didn't cheat—"

Callen.

He's not so casual. I can see it on her guilty face. Maybe she's not engaged, but she's taken. Callen wouldn't be okay with what happened between us. And I wouldn't blame him.

"Yes." Her shoulders relax. "I like watching plays."

"So what were you doing at the soccer fields the day you met Callen?"

Alice frowns. "I'm sorry. I know you want to know me because you feel like you can't trust me. And I can't undo the past, no matter how much I try to make you understand it." She holds out her hand. "I'm Alice Yates. Can we start over?"

"Start over?" I laugh. "Like erase the past? Which part of it? Just the tragic parts? The two weeks we spent together?

273

The day you unbuttoned your dress for me in the bathroom? The encounter in the kitchen? The other bathroom?"

Her hand drops to her side.

"If I pretend none of that existed, then my feelings for you—which I can't avoid—are incredibly inappropriate," I say.

"They are anyway."

I shake my head. "Alice," I lace my hands behind my neck and drop my head, staring at my feet, "I think about you nonstop. When I'm supposed to be working. When I'm running in the morning. Every time I see the swimming pool. When Hunter plays music in his study. Morning, noon, and night." I look up. "I fucking think about you when I'm in bed with my fiancée. Not because I want to. I don't. I love her, and that should be enough to stop thinking about you for one goddamn moment, but it's not. Do you have any idea what that's like?"

Tears well in her eyes, so she averts her gaze and wipes them. "Yes," she whispers.

"Can you tell me one truth?"

She sniffles and looks at me.

"Was I just an escape, an actor in your play, an illusion in your two-week break from reality? Or were we real?"

She flinches.

"I feel like"—tipping my head toward the sky, I rest my hands on my hips and sigh—"I'm lost. Buried in a dozen perfectly wrapped, nested boxes. And to find what I'm looking for, I have to rip everything apart."

Alice furrows her brow, then returns several tiny nods. "I ripped everything apart." She laughs, but it sounds like a partial sob. "Then I burned it to the ground with myself in the middle."

I don't hear the cars on the streets, the people passing by. And everything around me blurs until it's just us in a bubble.

"For what it's worth, I wouldn't trust me either."

I sag in regret. Why did I say that to her?

Alice smiles, and it feels like an invisible lifting of my chin, as if I shouldn't feel remorse.

"There's a reason why you're engaged and I'm living on the outskirts of someone else's happily ever after."

Jesus ...

"Alice—"

She shakes her head. "Don't. When I was unwell, I honestly didn't think I'd make it to thirty. After Chris died, breathing felt like a luxury I didn't deserve. Literally everything in my life gets compared to death. When I didn't have a job, I thought, 'Well, at least I'm not dead.' Marriage? A family? Love? That feels incredibly indulgent for someone who probably shouldn't even be alive."

"What?" I say like someone knocked the air from my lungs. Without hesitation, I grab her face, forcing her to look at me. Then I lower my forehead to hers. "Don't ever say that. Do you hear me?"

She grabs my wrists and swallows hard.

"*Do* you hear me?" I repeat.

"Yeah," she whispers.

I lift my head and press my lips to the spot it had been.

"I should go," she says.

"No. Let's get something to eat. Grab a drink. Take a walk. Whatever. Just ... don't go yet."

Indecision lines her brow. "You don't have to burn everything down like I did."

My thumb brushes her cheek. "What if I do?"

We walk to a nearby café, and she orders a salad while I get a piece of turtle cake with ice cream.

"Do you want me stealing your salad?" I tease her when she reaches across the table and sinks her fork into my cake, scooping up a generous bite.

She opens her mouth like a shark and shoves in the cake. When she grins with ice cream dripping down her chin, my heart feels as gooey as the caramel. "Help yourself," she mumbles with her mouth full.

"It's not too late to go back to your passion."

She squints.

"Acting."

"Mmm." She nods. "What do you think I'm doing now? Every day, I put on a costume, do my hair and makeup, and take the stage. Only the stage is a multi-million-dollar home. And I get subtle compliments and access to a pool instead of a standing ovation."

"That makes me an actor too?" I ask.

She sips her hibiscus tea and shrugs. "Sure. We're all actors in this thing called life. We take on roles: spouse, parent, child, friend, boss, employee ... lover." Her lips twitch with a hint of amusement, but it fades just as quickly. "We don't even know why we're here. To make the world a better place? To love? To procreate? To simply exist? Or is it a game? No one knows. But we don't know what else to do. So here we are doing whatever the 'thing' is. And we have traditions and rules to live by that are supposed to make it easier and perhaps give life more meaning.

"But I feel like I'm not supposed to be here—" She quickly gives me a hard headshake before I can protest. "So in some ways, the rules feel like they don't apply to me. And that's freeing. However, you're following a path, so the rules should matter to you."

"What rules?"

"The kind that says you should love, honor, and cherish the one you've chosen and be faithful to her, forsaking all others." She reaches her fork across the table again.

I block it, sliding my bowl away from her. "Nope. You don't get to guilt me like that, then steal my cake. I don't care that you think the rules don't apply to you. I'm enforcing the no-sharing rule until you apologize for ruining a perfectly good night."

Alice giggles. "I'm sorry."

"Prove it."

"How am I supposed to prove it?"

"Kiss me."

Her cheeks flush. "Stop."

I take another bite and close my eyes. "Mmm, this is *so* good and almost gone."

She reaches for the bowl, and I shield it by curling my arm round it.

Taking another bite of her salad, she squints at me.

I scoop the last big bite into my spoon, and her gaze shifts to it. In the next breath, she tosses her napkin on the table beside her plate and moves to my side of the booth. I peer down at her, and we have a stare off. When she leans in, I duck my head to kiss her because I need to feel her mouth against mine.

At the last second, she presses two fingers to my lips. "Say it," she whispers.

It takes a few seconds to figure it out. Then I smile and murmur, "Hi," against her fingers.

She mirrors my grin and drops her hand. It's a slow kiss. One of her hands rests on my leg and the other slides along my neck until her fingers tease my nape.

Flick. Flick. Flick.

My irresponsibility threatens to ignite the fire that will burn my world to the ground.

After I pay the check, we find a side street to stroll down, hand-in-hand.

Callen who?

Blair who?

What marriage?

Nope. None of that. Just two lovers reuniting after years apart, falling into step once again in a secret affair. Reality is an afterthought when one's heart speaks louder than the mind.

"Don't pretend that doesn't give you a hard-on," she says, nodding to a pile of wood in the yard to our right where a recent storm took down a tree.

"I think you know what gives me a hard-on."

She nudges me with her arm, and I right myself before stepping off the sidewalk. "I'm serious. Your father would be so disappointed in you for giving up on your art."

"You never met my father. How do you know he's not in Heaven still picking splinters out of his fingers, proud of me for coming to my senses and finding a different hobby?"

"Oh? What's your new hobby?"

"I don't know. Some of us don't have natural talent at *everything.*"

"I can only imagine." She smirks, tucking her chin.

"Is that a humble brag?"

"No." She giggles.

"I think it is." I release her hand and wrap my arm

around her neck, pulling her into my side, teasing my knuckles over her head like an older brother would torment his younger sibling. But, it doesn't last long because, in the next breath, I slide all of my fingers into her hair and kiss her in the middle of the sidewalk.

Flick. Flick. Flick.

There's smoke and heat. When we ignite, I won't be able to stop.

Chapter
FORTY-TWO

Alice

The past is always there.
It's reliable and unchanging.

My least favorite role is "mistress."

If I could really hate Blair, it might make it easier. Even when I try to focus on the two men she abandoned before Murphy, I still can't reach the right level of disregard for her feelings.

But ...

And this is a big *but*.

When I was a young girl, we had a dog that ran away. Three months later, while riding my bike several streets over, I saw a boy who looked about my age playing fetch with my dog in a front yard. I raced home and told my parents. We drove to the house, and my dad explained that we lost our dog, and she didn't have her collar on the day she ran away.

The boy got tears in his eyes because he had fallen in love with my dog. His parents hugged him and told him no matter how much he loved the dog, she wasn't his, and she belonged to her rightful owners.

I felt sad for the boy, but the joy I felt over having my dog back was all that mattered to my young heart.

So here's the "but." Despite my inability to hate Blair and not care about her feelings, Murphy feels like mine. However, even this has a caveat. I never gave my dog a choice to stay with that boy or come back home with me. Maybe my dog liked that boy better. Perhaps that boy gave my dog more treats or took her on longer walks.

Murphy has a choice.

I won't ever question his love for me. It's deep in his eyes and bleeds from every smile he gives me, every whispered "hi," every brush of his fingers across my skin. *But* he loves Blair too. He's been with her longer. And he might trust her more than he trusts me.

"Miss me?" Callen surprises me with a bouquet of roses as he waits at my door Friday afternoon.

How is he to know that every day I pick roses, poke my fingers on the thorns, and arrange them in vases that cost more than I make in a month? Still, it's a lovely gesture.

"Thank you," I say, taking the flowers in one hand while wrapping my other arm around him.

"Dinner? Or skip dinner and go straight to dessert?" he asks before kissing my neck.

I close my eyes, and all I see is Murphy running his hands through his messy hair, giving me a shy grin as I step into my car after dinner at the cafe and walking through neighborhoods where no one knows us.

All I feel is my heart stretching my ribs thinking of how

different my life would be had I found him before he met Blair.

"For the record, I tried calling you. This wasn't supposed to be a surprise, but I'm glad it happened this way." He reaches for the door and kisses my lips at the same time.

I pull away, checking my pockets. "Crap. I left my phone on the kitchen counter of the main house. I'll meet you inside. Okay?"

He takes the flowers from me. "Hurry. I'll be in bed."

I smile, but not like my usual smile for him. It's a consolation smile. I jog toward the house, but slow to a walk when I'm behind the hedge bushes. Everything inside of me doesn't want to be with Callen tonight, but how do I tell him that?

After I slip off my shoes and round the corner, I gasp, nearly tripping over Hunter's body on the kitchen floor. "Mr. Morrison?" I drop to my knees and check for a pulse. "Help!" I yell before feeling for a breath.

Nothing.

No pulse.

No breathing.

"HELP!" I scramble to my feet and grab my phone off the counter to call 9-1-1. With it on speaker, I start chest compressions.

"9-1-1. What is your emergency?"

"I need an ambulance. He's"—I compress over and over—"not breathing."

The operator verifies the location and says something else to me, but I don't catch it because *my* heart is beating just fine. In fact, it's so loud in my ears, it drowns out everything else.

Where is everyone? I fed them dinner less than an hour ago.

"Help," I say in a weaker voice as tears sting my eyes and sweat beads along my brow. "Don't die. Please don't die."

Am I pressing hard enough? Fast enough? Is it doing anything?

I lose all sense of time, drowning in dread.

Drowning. It's like he's drowning.

"Don't die, Chris," I whisper.

I hear voices, but it's like everything is echoing underwater. Someone stops me, pulling me away from him as paramedics tend to him. One of them cuts open his shirt while the other prepares the pads of the defibrillator to go onto his chest.

"Don't die," I whisper, staring at him unblinkingly. "Swim."

Behind the paramedics, Blair and Vera sob with their hands over their mouths. That's when I realize it's Murphy holding me back from Hunter.

I turn in his arms. His lips move. I think he's talking, but I don't know.

"I didn't save him. I let everyone die."

He flinches.

I wriggle out of his hold and stumble past him toward the back door. "I have to go."

Vera's going to miss him. And all the things he did to drive her crazy will leave the biggest holes in her heart. She'll regret everything she ever said to him that was anything but kind.

Chapter
FORTY-THREE

Murphy

Tragedies are so tragic because it's never the right time
for everything to fall apart.
Time is our worst enemy.

WE TOOK a walk around the lake after dinner. Hunter didn't go because he had indigestion.

It takes a moment to realize what's happening. Vera and Blair scream. I call 9-1-1, but just as they answer, the paramedics come through the front door. Alice must have called them.

They ask her to step back, but she ignores them, so I have to pull her away while she whispers, "Don't die. Swim."

Blair and her mother are falling apart. My future father-in-law is dead on the floor. But the only thing I can focus on is Alice. I'm losing her again.

This can't happen.

She escapes my hold, but I can't let her go, not with that distant look in her eyes.

"Don't do this," I say, grabbing her shoulders, pressing her to the back door before she can open it. "Do you hear me?"

For the first time, her wild eyes shift and lock with mine.

"Alice, no one is drowning. Okay? He's okay. You're okay." My voice cracks under the lies and desperation. I whisper, "Okay, baby?"

She blinks, sending fat tears down her face.

I have never felt so internally conflicted in my life. I can't be everywhere at once. Is this it? Is this the moment I have to choose? It's a new level of fucking cruelty.

"I need you to focus on me. You. Are. Okay."

Callen's truck is on the street. I never thought I'd want him here as much as I do now.

"Don't move. Stay right here. Okay?"

Tears cling to her long eyelashes.

"Alice, answer me." I press my hands to her face and kiss her.

She doesn't respond.

"Alice," I whisper over her lips. "Hi," I say on a breath like a prayer.

She moves her hands to my wrists and leans in to kiss me. I sigh through my nose in relief. Then I pull back and smile past the pain and panic. "There you are. There's my Alice. Stay right here. Okay?"

After a beat, she nods.

I give her one last kiss on the forehead and hurry back to the kitchen just as they're loading Hunter onto a gurney. Blair flies into my arms, sobbing.

"He has a heartbeat," Vera says, blotting her eyes. "I'm riding in the ambulance."

"I have to go too." Blair releases me.

I nod. "I'll drive the car and meet you there."

Her face contorts into a cry again, Vera wraps an arm around her while they head out the front door. I return to the back door where Alice is staring at her feet, unmoving like a statue. It almost looks like she's asleep.

"Ready?" I take both of her hands and bring them to my mouth. Kissing her knuckles one at a time.

"Ready," she whispers.

"Hunter's heart is beating. He's alive because of you."

She squints like it's too much to process.

"Let's go." I lead her to the guesthouse and open the sliding door.

"Baby, what took you so long? Take off your clothes and get your sexy ass in here," Callen calls from the bedroom.

"It's not just Alice," I say.

He appears around the corner a minute later, shirtless, jeans on but not fully fastened. My jaw clenches briefly, but I don't have time to be mad or jealous. Tonight, I'm incredibly fucking thankful that he's here because I have to leave, and she can't be alone.

"What do you know about her past?" I ask.

He eyes her. "What do you mean?"

"She had something tragic happen. And certain things trigger PTSD. Hunter just had a heart attack, and that triggered it."

"Jesus," he says pulling Alice into his arms.

She leans into him like a limp doll.

"I have to get to the hospital. Stay with her until I get back. Got it?"

Callen eyes me, and something passes between us. I'm sure I'm doing a shitty job of hiding my deep concern. I'm sure he sees every emotion I've ever felt for her, bleeding from my face like a flashing sign.

"Of course, I'll take care of her," he says with a tighter voice.

I turn and run back to the house to get the car. When the adrenaline wears off, I'll break open a bag of marshmallows and roast s'mores over the dumpster fire that is my life, but for now, I have to keep going—keep everyone else from falling apart.

Chapter
FORTY-FOUR

Alice

If you're going to fuck everything up,
do it royally.

CALLEN GIVES ME A BATH, then he wraps me in my robe and makes a cup of tea as I sit on the sofa and stare at the mesmerizing flicker of the electric fireplace under the television.

"Thank you," I murmur when he hands me the mug.

"You're welcome." He sits next to me on the sofa, resting his elbows on his knees, head bowed. "Are you okay?"

I think about it for a few seconds. "Yes."

"Can I ask what happened in your past? Is this about your friend who died? And can I ask how Murphy, your *boss's daughter's fiancé*, knows more about your past than I do?" He peers over his shoulder at me.

"My fiancé died, not my friend." I give it a moment to

sink in. When Callen's gaze flits from the mug back to me, I continue. "I needed to escape life. So I rented a place not far from here. Murphy was the owner, the vacation rental host."

I observe Callen and the subtle shifts in his expression. The details don't matter, but I'm not sure he'll believe that.

"Were the two of you *close* during your stay?"

I sip my tea then return my attention to the fireplace before answering with a tiny nod.

"How close?"

I don't answer.

"Because the look he gave me earlier made me feel like an outsider, like I wasn't the guy who was supposed to be in your bed."

"I'm not sleeping with him," I say as if parsing hairs at this point really matters.

"But you want to?"

"Callen ..."

"It's a simple question, Alice. Do you want to fuck another woman's fiancé?"

I flinch.

"Wow." He stands, rubbing his temples. "If you have to think about that answer, then I have mine."

"Callen—"

He holds out a flat hand and closes his eyes, taking a deep breath. "I'm sorry for your loss years ago, and for what triggered you tonight. If you ask me to stay, then I'll stay. But if you want me to go, then I will. And I don't have to come back, if you're ready for whatever this is to end."

I don't know what this is.

I don't know what I'm doing.

I don't know who I am.

Callen walks past the sofa then stops and leans over the

back of it, pressing his lips to the top of my head before whispering, "You have my number."

The next morning, I wake at my usual five o'clock time, and I go through the motions. Meditate. Jog around the lake. Shower. Breakfast.

I arrive at the main house just before seven. Exchange shoes. Tie my apron. Smooth a hand along my ponytail. I cling to routine like my life depends on it. But my steps halt when two tired eyes meet mine.

Murphy slowly stands from a stool at the kitchen island. His hair is chaotic like it's been a long night. Wrinkled white T-shirt. Dark jeans. No shoes.

I open my mouth to speak, but he holds a finger to his lips before jerking his head to the right. After a second, I wordlessly follow him to the basement stairs. We take a sharp right at the bottom until we reach the bedroom at the end of the hallway. Sometimes Vera comes down here to hide from Hunter. She says it's the most quiet room in the house.

Murphy closes the door after I step past it.

I turn to face him, wringing my hands together. "How is Mr. Morrison?"

"Are you okay?" Murphy asks like my question doesn't matter. The anguish on his face hits me like a twenty-foot wave coming onto shore.

"Yeah," I whisper.

He pushes off the door.

"How's Mr. Morrison?"

Murphy brushes his knuckles down my left cheek. I

close my eyes and lean into his touch. When his hand disappears, I open them again. The intensity of his gaze locked to mine makes all the questions vanish.

It's eerily quiet, except for my heart thrashing around in my chest as he slides his arms around my waist to untie my apron. Not a muscle in my body protests, not a flinch of hesitation or flicker of doubt.

Did Hunter die?

Where are Vera and Blair?

And why can't I make finding the answers to those questions my number one priority?

After he discards the apron onto the floor, Murphy ducks his head and whispers, "Hi," in my ear.

Shivers skate along my skin when he kisses my neck while unbuttoning my dress. After he slides it off my shoulders, I reach for the hem of his T-shirt. He grabs the back of it at the neck and pulls it over his head. Our mouths collide, tongues exploring familiar territory.

With deft fingers, he unhooks my bra and I discard it to the floor. Murphy gently clasps my wrists behind my back, making my back bow. My hard nipples brush the smattering of hair on his chest, causing the ache I feel at my core to intensify into something stronger than I imagined. And dear god ... how I've imagined.

He drops his head, kissing and nipping my neck while tightening his hold on my hands so my chest pushes out just a little more.

"Ohhh ..." I cry for a brief second before biting my lower lip to silence my reaction when he sucks my nipple into his mouth and tugs it with his teeth. He moves to the other side and does the same thing.

I bite my lip until I swear I can taste blood. I don't

remember the last time I've been this aroused, on the verge of orgasming. My knees wobble, and he grins against my skin while releasing my nipple and hands at the same time.

I stab my fingers into his hair, curling them into tight fists to pull him to me for another deep kiss. His hand dives into the front of my underwear, stealing what little breath I have left in my lungs as two fingers thrust into me.

"Don't you ever fucking try to leave me like that again," he says in a deep, unwavering voice, our foreheads pressed together while we share labored breaths, mine hitching every time he drives his fingers deeper.

Like that.

He's not asking me to be his. He's asking me not to lose my mind like I started to do last night after giving Hunter CPR, like I did the night the car slid on the road in the rain.

Murphy removes his fingers and hunches before me, sliding my underwear down my thighs.

I hiss, and then my jaw unlocks in a silent cry as his tongue spears between my legs. "Oh ... god ..." I pinch my eyes shut and curl my fingers into his hair, yanking it hard as pleasure claws along every nerve fiber in my body. When I stumble backward in my wedge pumps, he falls forward onto his knees, grabbing my ass like he's starving for me, humming his pleasure, fingers digging into my flesh.

My knees buckle, and I lower to the edge of the bed, but Murphy keeps his face planted between my legs, releasing one of them from my underwear so he can spread me open, devouring me with his unrelenting tongue.

I arch my back, body twisting and contorting while one hand keeps ahold of his hair and my other leverages the bedding beneath me.

"Murph ..." I pant. "Murphy, I'm ..."

He releases his grip on my leg, and I hear the soft grinding zip of him unfastening his jeans as his tongue flicks my clit one last time, and I orgasm.

My head thrashes from side to side, heart drumming erratically in my chest, a deafening echo shooting to my ears. "Yesss ..." My abs tighten, body pulsing as I feel like I'm transported to somewhere only we know, that place we used to go eight years earlier.

Just as my vision returns, he towers over me, shoving his jeans and briefs down just far enough to release himself. This is the Murphy I remember. The ravenous, impatient man who can't be bothered with removing all his clothes before thrusting into me.

"Oh, Jesus!" I gasp when he does just that.

"Alice," he drags his tongue up my chest, and his hand slides behind my knee, "you're so fucking gorgeous. I want to die inside of you, baby." Murphy sucks the skin along my neck while his pelvis rocks into mine.

His hooded eyes snag on my breasts when he lifts his torso, hands flat on the mattress next to my head. The bed grinds, creaking as it slides a fraction, padded headboard softly drumming against the wall.

"Why are you blowing up your world?" I whisper, eyes heavy, heart bursting from my chest, wanting nothing more than to claim the man inside of me.

Behind my eyelids, I see us eight years ago on the sofa, Murphy driving into me while Leslie Gore's "You Don't Own Me" plays on the turntable. We released within seconds of each other, and he murmured in my ear, *"But I want to."*

I don't know what this means or if it means anything beyond an uncontrolled attraction we've had since the day he greeted me in the backyard with Arnold Palmer. But I know Murphy Paddon will be okay. I didn't break him.

He moved on with an enormous capacity to love. His heart stretches beyond its limits. Mine just sort of ... breaks.

When we kiss, it feels like the rest of the world vanishes. Maybe it feels that way because I've simplified my world, giving little regard to all yesterdays and tomorrows. But Murphy has a life. A *real* life. He has more to lose. More people who he can hurt. Accountability and responsibility.

Have we come full circle? Am I his escape? Does he need this for perspective?

The questions die when we release; my fingers loosening their grip on his back. For thirty seconds, everything is perfect. Utter contentment. Every cell in my body vibrates from pure joy and euphoria.

"Murphy." His name tumbles from my lips.

What have we done?

Before vulnerability and regret have a chance to fill the space between us, he rolls to the side, hugging my body so close to his there is no space for anything else.

If he's warring with his conscience or second-guessing leading me down here, I'd never know it. I feel nothing but his patient lips pressed to my forehead and gentle hands caressing my bare back.

"Hunter had a heart attack. They placed a stent. And he should recover just fine, thanks to you," he says.

I don't know what to say. Did I really do anything? All I remember is the feeling of drowning.

"Are Vera and Blair here?"

"No. Vera stayed at the hospital last night. Blair came home after the procedure, but she headed back to the hospital before you got here. Hunter wanted his Hermes throw blanket and Sea Island cotton sheets."

I kiss his chest next to my hand over his heart. "I hope you comforted her. Held her. Loved her."

Seconds turn into minutes, and he doesn't respond. They weren't questions, anyway. I just don't want him to think I can't understand how much she means to him even if I'm the one in his arms.

I slide out of his hold and collect my clothes from the floor, stepping past the door to the bathroom across the hallway. When I return, Murphy's dressed, sitting on the end of the bed, head bowed, hands folded between his legs. I seem to have this effect on men.

"I want to clean the wood floors where the paramedics came into the house. Make sure all the laundry is clean. New sheets. Replace flowers in the vases. Get groceries." I shrug. "I want everything to be perfect when they come home."

He narrows his eyes for a beat before relinquishing a nod. "He won't come home for a few days. You should go to the hospital. He'd love to see you. And Vera and Blair would too. They are incredibly grateful that you were here for him."

"I wasn't here. Not when it happened. I forgot my phone and came back to get it. Callen surprised me and said he tried calling me. That's when I realized I'd left my phone. Maybe they need to thank Callen, instead, for coming to see me."

Murphy stands and takes two easy strides toward me. He frames my face. "Alice, you are incredibly special. And I feel like everyone knows this except you. Tragedy is an unavoidable part of life. But I think the biggest of all tragedies is feeling unworthy." He brushes the pad of his thumb across my lower lip before kissing me.

Every kiss with Murphy feels like a last kiss.

"Baby," he whispers, "I need you to feel worthy. I want you to dream." His lips catch my tears the moment they escape.

"I can't."

"Why?" He ghosts his lips along my cheek.

I close my eyes and grip his shirt to steady myself. "Because I'd dream of you."

Chapter
FORTY-FIVE

Alice

Compassion is free. Loyalty comes with a price.

"THERE'S MY GUARDIAN ANGEL," Hunter says from his hospital bed, wearing the most humbled expression I've ever seen on his weary, unshaven face.

Before I can answer, Vera wraps me in her outstretched arms and whispers, "Thank you *so* much."

When she releases me, I smile past the lump in my throat and nod.

For an even bigger gut punch, Blair does the same thing. Only she's too choked up to speak. When she releases me, she quickly blots her eyes.

My gaze remains glued to her until her smile fades a bit, and I realize I'm staring at her too long. Would they thank me if they knew what I did six hours ago in the basement with Murphy?

Would I still be a hero? Or a villain?

If I do what Murphy wants me to do—feel worthy and dream—then I have to accept my role in life again as more than just a series of fleeting moments that don't mean anything. I have to be accountable.

I'm not ready for that.

"I feel a raise is in my future." I tease, sliding into character with a smiley face, delivering each word like a well-rehearsed skit. It's the art of living in an alternate universe.

They laugh, but Hunter cringes.

"Sorry. I didn't mean to make you laugh. I bet it hurts." I stand next to his bed and squeeze his hand. Then I pull a book out of my handbag. "I thought you might like a story read to you."

"Oh my gosh," Blair says. "Mom, I think that's our sign to grab dinner. I'll call Murphy and tell him to meet us somewhere that's not hospital cafeteria food."

Vera sidles up to the other side of his bed and kisses his forehead before whispering, "I love you."

He has hearts in his eyes for her, even after all these years. It melts my insides.

"Can you stay with him until we get back?" Vera asks.

"Of course."

When they exit the room, I pull up a chair and sit next to his bed.

"We're bound for life, now. It's like you donated a kidney to me."

I grin, shaking my head.

"If I tell you something, can you keep my secret?" he asks.

"I can." I cross my legs and fold my hands in my lap.

"I saw you."

"Saw me?"

He glances past my shoulder, gaze unfocused. "I saw you giving me CPR. From above. Like I wasn't in my body."

My lips part to speak, but there are no words.

"You called me Chris."

I immediately feel cold and lightheaded.

"Who is Chris?"

I blink a few times before shaking my head.

"I just told you something I've told no one else. And I never will because they already think I'm crazy. Give me something back. Tell me something you've never told anyone else."

Wringing my hands together, I take a deep breath. "Chris was my fiancé. He died in a car accident. It was raining, and we started to hydroplane. The car flipped over the side of the bridge into the river. I got out. He died."

He narrows his eyes. "I'm sorry."

"Thank you," I murmur.

"But I knew some of this."

I stare at my hands. "Yes." I lift my gaze. "But no one knows I was driving."

The lines above the bridge of his nose deepen.

"I lowered my window before the car was fully underwater. And I unbuckled both of our seat belts. Then I went out first." I wince just from the memories. They're still there. Not as vivid, but not completely gone. "I thought he was right behind me." My voice lowers to a whisper. "But he wasn't."

Hunter doesn't rush to respond. Some things don't need acknowledgment beyond a warm smile.

"Do you want me to read to you?"

"I'd love that," he whispers with a smile.

I begin reading the first few pages of chapter fifteen, and just when I think Hunter has drifted off to sleep, he grins. He has a crush on the main character, Jessica Day, a sexy assassin in love with her psychiatrist. I resume reading:

She continued ironing his argyle socks. "You need to get laid. Normal people don't think like you. When was the last time you had sex?" Jessica asked.

Luke ignored her. It was his usual MO when she tried to pry into his life.

"I bet you're a missionary man. By the book: seven-point-five minutes of foreplay, thirty seconds of clitoral stimulation to get her lubed up, and exactly thirty-five thrusts until climax followed by ten minutes of spooning, a kiss on the cheek, and maybe even a gentlemanly 'thank you' before insisting she leave so you can get your necessary eight-point-five hours of sleep."

"She's sexy and sassy as hell," Hunter mumbles.

I grin and continue reading until he falls asleep, but this time I don't wake him. Neither of us has anywhere to go or anything to do except wait for Vera and Blair to return.

Two hours later, they do just that. But this time, Murphy is with them.

I stand, straightening my dress and hiking my handbag over my shoulder.

"How long has he been asleep?" Vera whispers.

"Not long enough," Hunter says, opening his eyes.

"How are you feeling?" Blair slides past me to hold her father's hand.

"Like I might live."

"Thanks for staying with him." Vera squeezes my hand. "I think you should take some time off. Hunter won't be going home for at least a week, and we'll either be here with him or dealing with wedding plans. I can arrange to have someone water the garden."

I can't look at Murphy with the words "wedding plans" echoing in the room. So I smile at Vera. "Thanks."

"You deserve it," she replies.

"Who's going to read to me?" Hunter asks, earning him scowls from both his wife and daughter.

I blow him a kiss. "Stay out of trouble. And be nice to the nurses."

"Blair, I need to take a work call," Murphy says, holding up his phone.

I don't make eye contact with him as I shuffle out the door and make a beeline for the elevator.

Smack!

His hand darts through the closing doors to stop them. "Alice, are you running away from me?" He steps onto the elevator, tucking his phone in his pocket.

"Nope. Just excited to take a little time off." I lean against the back wall, hugging my handbag to keep him at a safe distance.

"What are you going to do with your time off?"

"Shop for a dress to wear to your wedding. Since I'm basically family now, I'm sure I'll be invited."

His lips twist with a slow nod, hands casually tucked into his back jeans pockets. "Your optimism is outstanding."

"Optimism?"

The doors open and I step past him. He follows me, keeping a few steps between us.

"Do you think she's still going to marry me?"

"I think you have as good a chance as anyone." The warm air whooshes past me when the automatic doors open to the parking lot.

"That would be quite something. She let two men go who probably adored her and never cheated on her, but you think she'll keep me after what's happened?"

Just as I reach the sidewalk, I turn. "You're telling her?"

"Well, yes. I would never marry someone without being completely forthright with them. Would you?"

My stomach drops.

"Do you not want me to tell her?"

I shrug but shake my head at the same time. "I ... I don't know. Seems like a really bad time to lay this on her."

"When would you suggest I mention it? At the wedding? Rehearsal dinner?"

I frown.

Murphy deflates. "I love you."

I wait.

And wait.

"But?" I ask.

Murphy shakes his head slowly. "Alice, there's no but. Those three words stand on their own without an explanation. I don't need an excuse to love you."

"You love her too."

"I do."

Every time we're together, it gets harder to keep a brave face. He makes me want something real.

"You've loved her longer."

"I've loved her for three years and four months. I've loved you for eight years and two months."

I frown.

"Don't give me that look. I knew the day your dad carried you out of my house that I might not ever see you again, but nothing would stop me from loving you for the rest of my life."

"You can't marry her *and* love me."

"I can."

Damn him and his all-encompassing heart.

"Doesn't mean I'm going to."

I can't stop thinking about Hunter, Vera, and Blair. They have me on a pedestal the way I used to have Murphy on one. The betrayal would be crushing.

"Then do it. Marry her and love me."

He furrows his brow.

"Bye, Murphy." I turn, gripping my keys and holding my breath to keep it together.

He doesn't trust me, but they do. I never imagined wanting someone's trust so much, but I do. I want the Morrisons to feel good about hiring me since they now have this overwhelming gratitude.

Chapter
FORTY-SIX

Murphy

If life were easy, what would be the point?

MARRY HER AND LOVE ME?

What kind of advice was that?

Had Alice not reappeared in my life, I would marry Blair, have a family, and live a beautiful life. No questions. No doubt.

This is where there's an all caps BUT.

Alice is back in my life, and my heart has not forgotten about her, nor has it stopped loving her.

When I met Blair, I was attracted to her talent, her beauty, and how she felt like a breath of fresh air when I desperately needed one. I felt confident and cool. My game was on point. My charm turned way up.

However, when I met Alice that day in the backyard of my rental, I was nervous, fumbling my words, blushing, and for two weeks she had me acting and feeling like a young boy crushing on the prettiest, most talented girl in school.

Eight years later, she makes me feel like that young boy again. Maybe it's because she's been a mystery. But I don't know if I can solve her, and that's why I can't completely trust her. So I'm spying on her like I did when she was my renter.

Where is she going?

What is she doing?

And why?

While Blair splits her time between visiting her dad, finalizing wedding plans, and overseeing the construction of her gallery via video calls, I obsess over Alice's every move.

Yesterday, she sat on a park bench, reading a book while kids played on the equipment and kicked soccer balls in the grass, and Canadian geese shit all over the concrete walking path that led to a fishing pond. I didn't stay the whole time like a bona fide stalker. After satiating my curiosity, I went back to work.

Today, she's meeting with a realtor to tour a house for sale in Edina, where the housing is not exactly cheap.

Is she moving? Quitting her job?

Why a house? Why here? If she quits her job, can she afford to live here?

This all should get filed under "It's None of My Fucking Business," but having sex with her, a few days ago, felt like I was making her my business.

I don't stick around and risk her seeing me when she leaves the house. Instead, I message Blair. We need to talk.

~

When I arrive at the restaurant, Blair waves me over to a table on the patio.

"This is such an unexpected surprise," she says before kissing me.

I hold out her chair for her to sit down again. "A lot has been going on, and I thought we should call a time-out, slow down, and talk."

She releases a sigh that's so big her shoulders drop an inch. Then she reaches for my hand, giving it a squeeze. Her glossed lips tip into a soft smile. "I took a pregnancy test."

I've only had a handful of defining moments stand out in my life. The last one was eight years ago when my car hydroplaned after dinner with the most mesmerizing woman I've ever known. I thought nothing would change the course of my life more than that.

Until now.

Blair continues. "Waiting for the result was excruciating. I was scared out of my mind. I know we've discussed having kids—soon even—but Dad just had a heart attack, and the wedding isn't for six more weeks. What if I'm nauseous and miserable? And what about my gallery? And moving to New York? I didn't want to do any of this while carrying a baby. The stress wouldn't be good for me or our baby." Again, she sighs. "Then I realized nothing else matters. I was like ... we're having a baby. We can do this. I can do this. And a year from now, ten years from now, it won't matter if the timing is a little off."

I swallow hard, feeling a war in my fucking soul, the boundaries of my heart reaching their limits. With a smile, I slowly nod, lacing my fingers with hers because sometimes we make decisions, and sometimes decisions make us.

She focuses on the server delivering food a few tables

away, and her smile fades. "The longest two minutes of my life took me to hell and back. And just when I allowed myself to feel a spark of excitement, a sunrise of new possibilities, it was negative."

It takes a moment, several long blinks, before her words make sense.

She wipes her tears as soon as they slide down her face. "It's so stupid. How can I feel brokenhearted over something I didn't want?" She sniffles. "But then I did. And now it hurts."

I scoot my chair closer to hers and pull her into my arms. "I'm sorry," I say. And I am. I'm sorry for a million different reasons, even if I don't regret all of them. Does that make me a bad person? Flawed beyond redemption?

Can I be sorry for hurting her without regretting the love I have for Alice? Our time together? Does the heart always walk a righteous path? Or is it the one thing that makes humans inescapably fallible?

"You make everything better," she whispers, hugging me like I'm the only thing holding her together. "I've never been so sure about anything or anyone in my life as I am about you."

Blair—*my* proverbial pregnancy test—was everything I thought I wanted until life presented another option. And now I can't reconcile any of this. Every decision feels wrong and cruel. If I break Blair's heart, I don't know if I can live with myself, and now I don't know if I can ever feel deserving of happiness that involves Alice.

Chapter
FORTY-SEVEN

Alice

Is anyone really "deserving" of anything?

"Can we talk?" I say to Murphy, peeking my head around the corner into his bedroom.

Blair and Vera are at the hospital this morning because Mr. Morrison is being released today. Murphy has avoided me lately, and I have to assume it's because he's staying with Blair.

He turns in his chair, eyeing me intently for a few seconds before nodding. I miss his smile. It's been a while since he's looked at me with that grin that makes me feel adored.

"Are you going to tell Blair about us?"

He narrows his eyes. "Why?"

"Because I need to know if I'll be keeping this job."

Murphy leans back in the chair and rakes his fingers through his hair. "I need to."

That's not helpful.

"Are you wanting to know if I'm going to marry her?"

I shake my head. "I just want to know if you're going to tell her. And if you are, that's fine. I understand. But your decision affects my life. If you need to tell her, I would never ask you not to. It's just, I have a decision to make, and I need to know if I have job security or not."

"Rumor has it, you can work for the neighbor," he says.

My nose wrinkles. "I thought of that. But it would feel like a betrayal. And honestly, if you tell Blair, I don't think I want to be that close to the Morrisons, out of respect."

He drops his gaze to the floor. "Do I deserve you?"

My heart sinks into my stomach as much as it did the day I found Hunter unconscious on the kitchen floor. What kind of question is that? And how do I answer it? "Murphy ..."

"Every time I get this idea in my head about you, something happens, and it just blows up on me. And I'm not blaming you." He grunts a painful laugh, refocusing on me. "I don't think anyone is to blame. But I poured my heart out to you years ago, determined to keep you forever, then you were taken away. Years later, I convinced myself it was time to really let you go because you weren't coming back. Then you did. So, despite my reservations, I jumped again without regard for anything or anyone else, and it's like my parachute deployed, but I've gotten tangled up in it, and now I'm just free-falling, and when I land, it's going to hurt so fucking bad."

I don't understand, so I squint as though I'm trying to read between the lines, but it's all too blurry.

Murphy gives me a sad smile. "I tried to tell Blair. I gathered every ounce of courage I could muster and met her for lunch a few days ago. I knew it was going to hurt, but you are *so* worth it. You deserve to be loved the way my heart has longed to love you since we met. And I struggled with the idea of wanting you and her. But then I realized that's not true. I love two women, but I only *want* to be with one."

He laughs, but it's not a good laugh. "The end. And they lived happily ever after. Right?"

Nothing about his foreboding tone and eerie sarcasm feels like a segue to a happily ever after.

"Blair thought she was pregnant. She found out she's not. She's heartbroken. And I am her lifeline."

I swallow back the bile that works its way up my throat, but it doesn't quell the nausea.

He doesn't look at me, and I don't know what to say. Minutes pass. How many? I'm not sure, but the heaviness in the air just gets thicker and more suffocating as the silence drags on.

"Can I ask why you need to make so much money?" He changes the subject, and I take a second to process his question. "You have a free place to live."

"I want to buy a house."

"So you have space between work and your personal life?"

"Well, it's not a bad idea."

He squints. "That's not really an answer. More like a second thought."

"How did you feel about the possibility of Blair being pregnant?"

His face relaxes, and he slowly shakes his head. "Numb. Speechless. And ..."

"And?"

"Crushed," he whispers. "Then ashamed."

"I'm so sorry."

His gaze snaps to mine for a breath before he pushes out of the chair. My heart knocks harder against its cage with each step he takes.

"Why would you be sorry?"

"Because I think I took the wrong job," I say.

"You saved a man's life."

"I'm destroying yours."

Anguish brands his face. "Don't say that."

"Am I wrong?" I laugh. "We had sex. It was good. We were really good at it eight years ago, too. But I'm sure Blair gets your dick up just fine. She's artistic. She has good breeding. She—"

"Are you serious?" He rests a hand on his hip and stares at the ceiling. "Breeding? I should be with Blair because she has good breeding?"

"No. But it's not a bad thing."

Murphy pins me with a look. "Say that to my fucking face without grinning. Look me in the eye and tell me that *breeding* is a serious consideration for spending the rest of your life with someone."

I roll my lips together.

"Nope. Don't do that. Don't hide your grin. Don't pretend that you don't see the ridiculousness of such a statement."

"We're done talking." I pivot and click my heels along the floor toward the laundry room.

"We're done talking when I say we're done talking." He stalks behind me.

I wrinkle my nose and mimic under my breath, "We're done talking when I say we're done talking."

311

"I can hear you." He grabs my arm and spins me around just as I step into the laundry room.

This isn't funny. It's heartbreaking, yet I can't seem to wipe the grin off my face.

"Stop laughing. It's not funny." He narrows his eyes. "And you know *good* is not the word that describes us when we have sex."

"I'm not having sex with you," I say, despite his face inches from mine. Despite my breathy words. "You can say 'hi' a million times. But it's not happening. I'm done being the other woman. I'm a homemaker, not a home-wrecker."

His lips twitch. "Is that so?"

I tip my chin up and give him a quick nod.

"I'm not in the mood anyway." He turns and disappears around the corner.

My jaw drops. *What?*

I jolt toward the door as a few choice words get ready to take flight.

"Hi," he whispers, perched around the corner, scaring the hell out of me.

I gasp just as his mouth seals to mine. His kiss is all-consuming. *He's* all-consuming. Every ounce of self-control dies, taking my conscience to the grave with it.

It's not until I stop trying to resist him that he lets me go. We stare at each other through wild eyes and labored breaths.

"Why do you want to move to Edina?" he asks, then rubs the red lipstick from his mouth with the back of his hand.

I squint. "I never told you I was looking at a house in Edina."

His jaw clenches.

"I *never* told you that."

"Can you answer the question?"

"Can you tell me why you followed me?"

After a little standoff, he crosses his arms over his chest, but it's not going to protect him.

I deflate. "Just marry her and forget about me."

He grabs my arm again when I brush past him, but this time, he doesn't force me to face him. "I want to trust you."

"Why?" I stare at the floor.

"Because I want to be with you, but if I can't trust you, it's never going to work."

"Blair is—"

"I don't want to marry Blair!"

I stiffen with my breath held, mind reeling because he's so angry.

He releases my arm and steps back into the wall, dropping his head against it. "I don't want to marry Blair," he repeats in a calmer tone. "And you fucking know that."

I lift my head, and without turning to face him, I murmur, "My son lives in Edina."

Chapter
FORTY-EIGHT

Murphy

Stop planning. God is laughing at you.

CLICK. *Click. Click.*

Alice's steps fade as she retreats toward the kitchen. Her confession echoes in my head like a weather radio with poor signal. Some words pass through the noise, while others get lost in the static.

Edina.

Son.

I hear my name again and again until I peel my head from the wall and stare at the hand on my wrist.

Blond hair.

Familiar scent of rose and saffron.

"Babe, did you hear me?" Blair smiles. "We're parked out front. Come help my father inside, even though he doesn't think he needs help." She rolls her eyes.

"You're home," I mumble, following her as she pulls me to the front door.

"Yes. They released him early. What's your deal?" She laughs. "Why were you just standing against the wall?"

"Um," I quickly shake my head. "I was just thinking."

Blair opens the passenger door to Vera's Porsche.

"I don't need your help," Hunter says.

I reach for his arm.

"Son, you're not hearing me."

I release him and take a step back.

"You're being so stubborn," Blair says, hooking her arm around his.

Hunter seems okay with her help, so I trail closely behind them into the house.

"Stop," he says, shaking off Blair's hold as we pass the kitchen.

"Welcome home, Mr. Morrison." Alice delivers a sparkling smile like she didn't just blow my fucking mind.

"Smells amazing. What's for lunch?" He shuffles his feet into the kitchen and sits at the island while she cuts herbs.

"It's not lunch. It's rosemary for my next loaf of sourdough bread. I thought you'd be home closer to dinner. I'll get started on lunch right away." She winks at him, and he gobbles it up with his shit-eating grin.

"My father will have a salad for lunch with chicken or fish. No more red meat," Blair instructs, while handing him a glass of water.

He frowns at the water and then at her, but she returns an overly sweet smile.

I, on the other hand, keep my attention glued to Alice, but she doesn't return the slightest glance. It's as if I'm not in the room.

"Red meat my ass," Hunter says. "That's bullshit. It's not the red meat that's trying to kill me."

"Then what is it?" Blair crosses her arms over her chest while leaning against the counter next to him.

"Stress."

Blair scoffs. "Stress? What stress? You have people waiting on you hand and foot. If you wanted to stop working today, you'd never want for anything the rest of your life."

"And you get your dick sucked once a week," Vera says, floating into the kitchen with a sly grin before hugging the back of Hunter.

"Gross, Mom!" Blair scrunches her face.

Hunter looks at me as if to ... gloat? I'm not sure. When I return my attention to Alice, she doesn't flinch.

Head down.

Hands steadily chopping the rosemary.

"I'd rather die from choking on a piece of steak than eat chicken and fish the rest of my life."

"Calm down, darling. You'll give yourself another heart attack," Vera takes his hand.

He stands. "You are going to suck my dick?"

"Stop!" Blair covers her ears.

Finally, Alice's lips lift into a tiny grin, but she doesn't look up.

When Vera and Hunter disappear around the corner, Blair drops her hands to her sides. "Let's move out tonight and just elope."

Before I can say anything, not that I have anything to say, she flips her hair over her shoulder and pivots. "I have to call Alison about the bridal shower this weekend."

When it's just the two of us, I take the knife from Alice.

She jerks her head up. "What are you doing?"

I take her hand and lead her to the back door.

"Murphy—"

"Shh." I pull her out the door and past the gardens to the guesthouse.

As soon as we're inside her sliding door, I release her hand and pace the room, massaging my temples. "You have a child?"

She's much calmer than I am. Too calm. Easing onto the barstool at the counter, she nods. Then she crosses her legs and folds her hands over her knee, slowly bouncing her foot in those strappy wedge heels that Hunter loves.

"How? When? Why aren't you raising him?" I rapid-fire questions without stopping my pacing.

"Because his father drowned in a car accident, and his mother ended up in a mental hospital."

I halt. "Alice, you had a child when we were together?" That's why she had to go back. She left her child behind. "I'm so," I shake my head. "I'm so sorry."

She returns a smile that's a little sad, but not hopeless. "He seems happy. Good parents. Sisters. He plays soccer, and he likes theater."

The pieces of the puzzle move into place. "You didn't meet Callen at your nephew's soccer game. You met him at your son's soccer game."

Alice smiles and nods.

"Does he know he's adopted?"

She shrugs. "I don't know because I've never talked to him or his parents. They gave the adoption agency permission to share their information with me if I ever wanted to contact them. But my parents and I didn't give permission for my information to be shared with them for obvious reasons. Who wants to find out the mother of their child was in a mental hospital?"

"So you just," I frown because it's heartbreaking, "go to his games and plays? You watch him from a distance, but you've never spoken to him?"

"All I want is for him to be happy, and he looks really happy. I don't want to disrupt his life because it seems like a good one. But," she bites her lip and tears up, while still managing a smile, "I like seeing him. It makes me feel like his guardian angel. And that's what mothers are. Right?"

"He must have been really young. How old was he when Chris died?"

Her eyes narrow into tiny slits. "He wasn't born yet. I was pregnant when Chris died, but I didn't know it yet."

"He died. A month later, I rented a lovely little house for two weeks in Minneapolis."

"Alice," I whisper, slowly shaking my head, trying to make sense of everything, "how do you know he's Chris's son?"

Her bobbing leg stills, spine straightens. "B-because he is."

"But how do you know?"

She shakes her head a half dozen times. "Because he has dark hair like Chris and ... and ..." She ghosts the pads of her fingers along her cheeks. "He has freckles like Chris had when he was a young boy."

I blink. It's all I can do because the rest of my body feels immovable.

"Alice?"

Her wide-eyed gaze shoots to mine.

"I have brown hair."

"But—"

"And I had freckles when I was younger."

Her eyes redden and she quickly blots the corners while clearing her throat. "It doesn't matter," she whispers. "I wasn't well, Murphy."

"It *doesn't matter?*" My jaw drops.

Alice shakes her head, averting her gaze.

"Alice, that boy could be mine, and your reaction is *it doesn't matter?* Well, it sure as hell matters to me!"

She winces. "Don't do this," she whispers. "You don't know what I went through."

"Do what? Care that I might have a child out there who doesn't know I exist? How can you not know? Didn't they do an ultrasound?"

She looks at me, and I feel the pain in her eyes, but it does nothing to temper my anger. "They did, but not until it was later, which made it harder to pinpoint the date of conception. But I just knew."

"You knew it had to be his? Were you having sex every fucking day like we were?" I hate how harsh and insensitive my words sound, but I haven't had time to process this like she has.

"We weren't real," she mumbles.

"Alice," I drag a hand through my hair and grunt a laugh, "either you're better or you need to go back into treatment. We were real, and you damn well know it. Stop bullshitting me. That boy you follow, the one for whom you want to move to Edina? He could be my child. That's pretty fucking real. So don't act like it can matter to you, but it's not supposed to matter to me." I start to say more. Lord knows there is *so* much to say, but I bite my tongue and leave before I say something I can't take back.

She's right. I don't know what she went through. I wasn't there. And I hate no one in particular for the awful fucking truth.

Chapter
FORTY-NINE

Alice

It sucks being someone's first choice,
but not their only one.

I KNEW.

At least, I knew until I saw Cameron Beckett with his freckled face. I spent years wondering if he was Chris's son or Murphy's. I *knew* he could be either man's son. But I wanted him to be Chris's because the alternative felt like a betrayal to so many people.

I'd seen pictures of Chris from when he was a child with freckles. And that was it. I knew those freckles had to be his. When the agency gave me the Becketts' location and contact information, it seemed like fate that his family lived in Minneapolis. That's where I had moved to look for Murphy.

I'm not sure I believe in fate anymore.

When I return to the main house, Vera's in the kitchen making a salad.

"I'm sorry. I had to run back to the guesthouse. Let me do that."

She smiles, shaking her head. "I can make his salad. I *want* to make it."

When our gazes meet, I know my job is coming to an end, but I smile anyway.

Vera blinks away her tears before refocusing on the knife in her hand and the chopped cucumbers on the cutting board. "He almost died," she says, her voice weak and vulnerable. "And I realized this game we're playing is so stupid. It was funny at first. Neither one of us had to make a compromise. But that's not a real marriage. Right?" She lifts her head again.

All I have to offer is a slow nod.

"I'd really like you to stay until after the wedding. I need the help. Then we'll find you a new job. We know lots of people who would love to hire someone like you." She laughs a little. "And I'm sure they won't make you wear those ridiculous dresses and an apron."

I slide the rosemary from the edge of the cutting board and brush it off my hand into the bowl of sourdough. "Actually, I think the dresses are fun. Maybe I want you to find someone who would like me to wear these dresses when I work for them."

Vera grins, blotting the corner of her eye with the back of her hand. "Thank you, Alice. You have been the best thing to happen to our family."

My smile falls off my face like a boulder tumbling down a mountain.

"You need to teach me all your tips. I want to learn how

to bake bread and make chocolate chip cookies that are the perfect shade of golden brown. Gooey on the inside, crunchy on the outside. Hopefully, in the not too distant future, I'll be a grandma."

My hands shake as I cover the bowl of sourdough with the towel. "I'm sure you'll be a wonderful grandmother," I say without missing a beat, like a seasoned actress.

"Who's going to be a wonderful grandmother?" Blair asks, shuffling into the kitchen, head bowed to her phone.

"Me, silly. When you and Murphy give me grandbabies."

Blair lifts her head, and they have a silent exchange. She must have told Vera that she thought she was pregnant.

"Murphy got us a hotel room tonight. He says we need a night to ourselves." Blair bites her lower lip to control her grin.

"Sounds like a lovely idea," Vera says.

Yep. Sounds *lovely*.

"I'm going to pull some weeds in the garden," I say, jabbing my thumb over my shoulder.

Vera wrinkles her nose. "It's boiling outside. Shouldn't you do that in the morning or later this evening instead?"

Yes. She's correct. That's the best time to do it. But right now is the best time to sweat and take out my frustrations on invasive little soil creatures.

After I change into shorts and a tank top, because I can't stay in character when I'm this frustrated, I rip, pull, and pluck weeds from the garden. My fingers curl like talons, raking the soil between plants. The warm earth packs under my fingernails as I inhale the sweet scent of dirt. Sweat drips from my forehead.

"Ask me to choose you."

I pause, hands clenched around weeds and dirt, but I don't turn. "Why?"

"Because I just want to hear you say it."

"Well, we don't always get what we want. Do we?"

"No. We don't."

"Choose her," I grumble, tossing the weeds into the bucket.

"Because she has good breeding?"

"No. Because you already chose her. Let your word mean something. And if she tries to end it with you, fight for her. She doesn't need you to be perfect; she just needs you to be on her side. So, choose her."

"What if I choose you?"

"Then you're an idiot."

"Why?"

I turn, wiping the sweat from my brow with my arm. "Because she's not going to lose her shit every time there's an emergency. You won't have to hold her together. And you can live in New York or San Francisco or wherever the hell you want to live because with her the possibilities are endless." I jab a dirty finger into my chest. "But I'm going to be wherever that young boy is for the next ten years, watching him grow into a man because that's *all* I want to do. That's it. I don't need to travel. I don't need a fancy career. A husband. I don't need anything except rainy soccer days and weekend matinees at the theater. My future is spectating. Not interfering. Not taking something that is no longer mine."

Murphy's expression sags and he looks away. "What's his name? Can you at least tell me that?"

"Cameron."

"Cameron," he echoes. "What's his last name?"

I shake my head. "Go to New York, Murphy. He's not an orphan. He's a young boy with a family who loves him. Two younger sisters. A Bernedoodle. Friends. He deserves the best, and that's exactly what he has."

Murphy twists his lips and eyes me for a few seconds before nodding. Then he pulls something from his pocket and hands it to me.

I squint past the sun in my eyes and reach for the shiny thing—the ring. I left my engagement ring at his rental in the cabinet with the wine glasses. He's kept it all this time.

"I waited," he says. "Even when I moved on, a part of me waited. To be with you? To see you? To give you the ring? Or maybe just to know you're okay? I don't know. But I waited."

I don't try to hide the tears as I stare at the ring and listen to his words. "I'm okay," I murmur.

"I know you are." He turns and heads back to the house while I swallow the pain that comes with closure.

I stare at the ring in my hand. *I found it* in his closet two days before the accident. Chris said I ruined the moment by being so snoopy. So I jokingly said I wasn't going to marry him anyway. It was a lie that became our horrific truth.

Chapter
FIFTY

Murphy

Lies are a slow death. The truth is a quick one.

"I've lost count of just how many times you've swept me off my feet," Blair says before sipping her wine in the dimly lit Italian restaurant with soft music and the aroma of garlic and spices filling the air.

I smile, calmly cupping my bottle of beer in one hand while my other flexes in and out of a tight fist on my leg.

"Promise me we'll always date. Even when we have kids and we're exhausted. Promise that you'll get a sitter, make reservations at a nice restaurant, and whisk me away for the night." She tears off a piece of bread and pops it into her mouth.

The server sets our bowls of pasta on the table. We smile and murmur thank-yous.

"This looks amazing." Blair blows on her penne then carefully takes a bite. "Mmm ..." She closes her eyes.

Again, I smile because she's beautiful and full of life. I love her smile and the way her eyes practically dance when she's excited about something. Her zest is contagious. And after we met, it wore off on me. I owe her so much, and I should spend the rest of my life showing her my gratitude.

"The wedding planner sent a computer-generated layout of the venue. How it will look with the flowers, soft yellows and white. The gold bows on the back of the chairs. The candles. It's going to be stunning. I'd show you on my phone, but it wouldn't do it justice. When we get home tomorrow, I'll bring it up on my laptop." She takes another bite and lifts her gaze to mine. "What?" she mumbles, pressing her napkin to her mouth. "What's that look? Why aren't you eating?"

"How did you do it?" I ask.

Blair narrows her eyes. "Do what?"

"When you broke off your previous engagements. How did you do it? In person? Over the phone? Text?"

She rests her napkin back on her lap, slowly swallowing. Then she takes a sip of wine. "I'm not doing that to you. You're the one, babe. Please trust me."

"I do," I say. "I just need to know."

She frowns, brow tense.

"Were you nervous? Scared? Did you have second thoughts?"

After pulling in a long breath through her nose, she holds it then releases it just as slowly. "The first time, I just showed up at his place. I ..." She shakes her head. "I was so scared. Scared of his reaction. Scared that I'd lose my nerve. And yeah, I worried about having second thoughts. But the overwhelming feeling I had was just fear of not doing it and living the rest of my life with someone I loved but just not enough." Her blue eyes find mine. "Does that make sense?"

I give her an easy nod.

"The second time was worse. I didn't want to break down into a blubbering mess before getting a single word out, like what happened the first time, so I picked a fight with him. I provoked him. And when he got angry with me, I broke it off." She glances away, blotting the corners of her eyes on a painful laugh. "I felt like such a coward. And days later, he tried to apologize, but I said it was too late."

She sniffles, and I want to disappear. Run away. I don't know, but I don't want to be here.

"If you had it to do over, what would you do?" I ask because I can't stop.

"Why?"

"Because I think it's important to learn from the past."

She takes another drink of her wine, this one a little bigger like she needs the courage. "I don't know. There's no good way to do something awful. There's no good way to give someone bad news. It's hard. It hurts. The right words are never there because they don't exist."

The tea light flickers in the center of the table like it might go out. I feel the same way.

"Do you regret saying yes when they proposed?"

She takes a smaller bite of her pasta like she's no longer hungry, and her gaze lingers on the bowl while she chews. "I don't know. Do I regret not making the right decision? I mean, sure. But I'm not perfect. Are we supposed to spend eternity regretting every mistake? Every bad decision? And maybe it wasn't a bad decision. Maybe it was right at the time, but circumstances and feelings changed. You know?"

When she looks at me, I whisper, "I do." And I'm not

sure she hears me, but then her lips part and her eyes stop blinking.

I'm not sure she's breathing.

This is the longest moment of my life. I imagine it's how Alice felt seconds before the car flipped over the side of the bridge into the water. Slow motion, one frame at a time, when in reality, it's over in a blink.

And she does. Blair blinks and the well of tears in her eyes spills down her face.

It's over.

"W-why?" She brings a shaky hand to her mouth, closing her eyes, but the tears continue to fall.

The lump in my throat swells. And despite being the deliverer of pain, my eyes sting with emotion.

There's no good way to do something awful. There's no good way to give someone bad news. It's hard. It hurts. The right words are never there because they don't exist.

I don't know what's worse, not having the right words, or stealing hers, pulling them from her one by one, leading her down a road that's a dead end for us.

Blair grabs her purse and shoves her chair back, then she runs out of the restaurant. I toss a wad of cash on the table and chase after her. When I push through the front door, I freeze. She's on the sidewalk, one hand on a light pole, the other holding her hair back, and she's bent over like she might get sick.

I swallow hard and wipe my eyes before picking up her handbag from the ground. Then I pull her into my arms. She doesn't hug me back, nor does she fight me. We hurt together and grieve the loss of our love that once was, but never again will be the same love.

"I'll take you anywhere you want to go," I say, opening the door to the car.

She stares at the seat, but she doesn't get in. "Give me the key."

I hesitate, but only for a second, before handing it to her.

"Get your bag out of the back."

Again, I give her request a second, then I pull my bag from the back.

She shuts the passenger door, posture sagging, eyes dead. "I *hate* you."

"I know."

"I'm going to Alison's. I expect you to be gone by the time I get home tomorrow."

I nod. "I'll talk to your parents."

She shakes her head, jaw clenched. "No. Don't say a word. Just get your stuff and get out. Don't let them see you. No explanation. No goodbye."

"Blair—"

"I said *no*."

"Okay," I whisper.

Chapter
FIFTY-ONE

Alice

It's never too late, until it is.

"I've fallen out of love with you."

I grin, setting the day's floral arrangement on the dining room table while Mr. Morrison frowns at his bowl of heart-healthy oatmeal with fresh berries and sweetened with local honey.

"Did you know there's a book called *Why We Are Carnivores & How Plants Try to Poison You?*"

"I did not." I laugh.

"We should start it this afternoon. I bet we can get through it before you leave me."

I refill his coffee. "My work here is about done. I'm not leaving you. I'm setting you free."

He grumbles something while I exit the room to gather the bedsheets. Blair and Murphy aren't back yet, so I strip their bed first. With them wadded in my arms, I step toward the door, but something catches my eye. It's the half-empty closet. Blair's clothes are hanging in their spot, but there's not a single item that belongs to Murphy.

I glance at the desk. His computer is gone as well as his black backpack. What's going on?

Just as I pass the stairs on my way to the laundry room, Vera appears at the top.

"Good morning," I say.

She presses her lips together and shakes her head, eyes red with tears.

"Oh, are you okay?" I set the sheets on the floor and climb the stairs.

She shakes her head a half dozen times, then presses the pads of her fingers to her eyes. I hold open my arms, and she accepts my hug.

"He left her," Vera whispers in a shaky voice. "Murphy called off the wedding." She chokes on a sob.

My head swims.

He called off the wedding. His clothes are gone.

He's gone.

Chapter
FIFTY-TWO

Alice

Go ahead and dream big.
You just never know what might happen.

Two Months Later ...

I MAKE an offer on the house in Edina, the one across the street from Cameron's, but a couple expecting their first child outbids me. I'm crushed.

The only upside is Hunter securing me a boring but well-paying job with his friend who lives in a penthouse in downtown Minneapolis. It doesn't include free residence, but that's okay. For now, I've found an apartment in Edina, so ~~stalking~~ seeing my son is easy and convenient.

I don't have Murphy's phone number, a nice dose of Karma, and I haven't figured out a way to get it from Hunter or Vera without it being a red flag. What would I say anyway? Choose me? It's a little too late for that. He chose neither Blair nor me, and I don't blame him.

Still, I miss him.

Today is the start of fall soccer season. I have no idea what field Cameron is playing on, reminiscent of the day I met Callen. Ugh, Callen ... he could be here too. A grin steals my face when I see Cameron's parents and his two younger sisters setting up their chairs near Field C. As the boys run in all directions doing their warm-up drills, I scan the cluster of blue jerseys for the dark-haired boy with freckles. Warmth spreads through my chest when I see him kick the ball toward the goal then run to the back of the line. The coach playfully ruffles Cameron's hair, drawing a grin from him.

I set up my folding chair well behind the lineup of parents. And just as I sit down, Cameron's dad stands to chat with the new coach. The two men laugh at something, then the coach removes his baseball hat to scratch the back of his head.

What the fuck?

It's Murphy. *He's* the new coach? I grip the arms of my chair, anger building deep in my belly. How could he? I was very clear about not interrupting Cameron's life. What has he done? What has he said? I push out of my chair, feeling the anger climb up my neck and settle into my cheeks. That's when Murphy's attention drifts past the sidelines and lands on me.

He grins so big that a few of the moms, including Cameron's, glance behind them to see what's caught his attention.

I want to die, but not before I kill him.

He waves me over. "Come meet the parents, honey!"

Come meet the parents? Honey?

What has he done? My stomach twists as I shuffle my feet on wobbly legs closer to the field.

"This is my wife, Alice," he says.

My eyes widen, body stiffens. *Wife? WIFE!?*

"When did you get back from Paris?" Cameron's mom asks me, tightening her short, blond ponytail.

This is the fourth wall that's never supposed to be broken. I'm so scared, yet my heart feels something new and unexpected as this pleasant woman who's been raising my child smiles at me, asking about a trip to Paris I know nothing about.

"Late last night," Murphy answers for me when the pause gets too awkward. He takes my hand and pulls me into his body. After he turns his cap backwards, he whispers, "Hi" and gives me a soft kiss.

I don't kiss him back because I can't move or speak, let alone kiss my .... husband?

"Bring your chair closer," Cameron's mom says. "We'll scoot over to make room for one more."

"I have to get back to the boys," Murphy says. "Enjoy the game." He winks and rights his hat before sauntering to the middle of the field.

"I'm Rose and this is my husband, Jonathan. Babe, grab Alice's chair for her."

"Oh, I can get—" Before I can get my brain and mouth to fully cooperate, Jonathan is halfway to my deserted chair.

"These are our two girls, Casey and Aurora."

The two blond girls don't give me a single glance. They're too busy sorting their M&Ms by color on their laps.

"Thank you," I find two more words to offer when Cameron's dad sets my chair next to Rose.

"Our son is the next one in line to kick the ball. The one with the shaggy brown hair. He needs a haircut," Rose laughs. "His name is Cameron."

"Cameron," I murmur softly.

Tears burn my eyes, so I slip on my sunglasses. This is awful. It's also wonderful. I'm freaking out, fighting back tears.

Happy tears.

Fearful tears.

What is happening?

"So Murphy told us you're an executive assistant for some wealthy businessman. Do you get to take lots of trips around the world?" Rose asks.

"Um," I clear my throat, keeping my focus on the players and their coach, "not usually. My job involves more mundane tasks at his residence. The Paris trip was a surprise."

"Do you speak French?" she asks.

"No. Not really." A nervous laugh escapes. "Not at all actually."

"Well, if you ever need help, Jonathan speaks fluent French. Right, babe?" She rests her hand on his knee.

He keeps his focus on the field. "Oui."

I feel my first genuine smile. She's the golden retriever in their relationship and he's the black cat.

"He's taught all the kids to speak French, but I'm the worst. We've been married for fifteen years, and I think I've learned less than ten words." She laughs.

A new round of tears pool in my eyes. I like her *so* much. And my son speaks French?

The game begins, and my heart can't keep up with so much emotion. I don't know what Murphy's been up to for the past two months, but somewhere along the way he decided Cameron is his son, something we will never know for sure.

I don't know if that makes him delusional or the best man who ever lived.

After the win, all the parents clap and cheer, and so do I because I have a boy on the field too. The teams line up to shake hands, fist bumps, really.

Cameron runs toward Rose and Jonathan. Thank god for my sunglasses. I wipe my tears before they slip into view. My heart might burst. Aside from the day I gave birth to him, the day I let him go, this is the closest I've been to my son.

"Good game, baby." Rose hugs him.

My heart is in my throat.

"Nice job, champ," Jonathan says when Cameron gives him a hug.

"Cam, this is Coach Paddon's wife, Alice." Rose introduces me to my son.

I can't speak, no matter how hard I try to swallow past the lump in my throat. So I smile, and I hope that says it all.

"Nice to meet you," he says, holding out his hand.

Gah!

They've raised such a polite young man. I'm grateful and proud, and a million other things that I can't articulate yet.

I shake his hand, holding it a little too long, but I can't help myself. Then I manage a quick, "You too," without completely falling apart.

He's even more beautiful, handsome, cute, just everything more than I've been able to capture from a distance. His eyes are hazel.

Mine are blue.

Chris's were blue.

I know that doesn't mean we couldn't have made a child with hazel eyes, but Murphy has hazel eyes.

"Well, I'm sure we'll see you this afternoon," Rose says.

She will?

I smile and nod.

The parents collect their chairs and children while I remain rooted in the same spot. Is this real?

Murphy and the other coach gather the soccer balls and practice cones in a mesh bag.

"See ya at practice tomorrow," the other coach says to Murphy before heading toward the parking lot with one of the players, probably his son.

"We won," Murphy says, sliding my chair into its bag. Then he sets it aside and slowly removes my sunglasses, sliding them onto my head.

I feel my puffy eyes, so I can only imagine how red and swollen they must be.

His hands cup my face, thumbs caressing my cheeks. "We won," he whispers again.

He's not talking about the game.

"I realize that's nothing new to you, but it's new to me, and it feels really fucking good." He grins before kissing me.

I wrap my arms around his neck, and we kiss until a new group of players and parents head toward the field for the next game.

Murphy ends the kiss and grins. "I want to show you something." He carries the bag of equipment and my chair in one hand while leading me to the parking lot with his other hand holding mine.

"This was risky, Murphy. I was so mad at you when I saw you on the field. You were too close. We're not his parents."

He chuckles, loading things into the back of a deep cherry-red pickup. It suits him better than a white luxury SUV.

"I know. We're something else." He closes the tailgate.

"What?"

He grabs my waist and nuzzles his face into my neck. "You'll see. Where are you parked?"

I point a few rows over.

"Okay. Follow me."

I frown which only makes his grin swell. He presses his pointer fingers to the corners of my mouth, forcing a smile.

"Stop." I turn my head.

"You stop. Stop pouting. Stop worrying. Stop feeling so unworthy. Just follow me. I've got you." He hops into his truck.

I shake my head and weave my way through the packed parking lot to my car because I'm dying to know what he has to show me. Murphy drives slowly so he doesn't lose me.

The route is familiar. Too familiar.

The tree-lined streets have been etched into my mind for years.

His brake lights illuminate just as we reach Cameron's house, but his truck crawls past it, turning into the driveway two houses past theirs. I wait for him to back out and turn around, but he doesn't. When he hops out of his truck, I park on the opposite side of the street.

"What are you doing?" I call, closing my car door behind me.

"I'm hungry. I thought you could make us some lunch. Maybe a nice steak and salad with your secret Dijon dressing recipe."

I look right before crossing the one-way street. Then I

look back at the house I wanted to buy before the current residents outbid me.

"What are you talking about?" I ask, taking hesitant steps up the driveway behind his parked truck.

"You know, a Ribeye or New York strip." He takes my hand and pulls me to the front door, then he slides a set of keys from his pocket and unlocks it.

"Murphy," I whisper.

"Don't forget the house rules: shoes off." He toes off his sneakers just inside the door of the modest, light green split-level.

I don't move, so he lowers in front of me to remove my shoes, then takes my hand and leads me up four steps to the main level with oak wood floors and white woodwork. The sun-drenched living room has a wall of windows overlooking a lush backyard. A cozy wood-burning stove sits in the corner.

I turn in a slow circle.

"I was lost," he says. "Grieving one woman while feeling unworthy of another. I hated how wanting you and being with you was wrong. My heart couldn't reconcile that. So I moved in with my mom and I told her everything she never knew." He grins. "She asked what I was doing wasting time with her. That's when I dug out the program from the *Alice in Wonderland* play and looked for a Cameron. When I discovered his last name is Beckett, it made it easier to track down his house. I knew it had to be close to the one you looked at across the street. Sadly, that house was no longer available, so I started knocking on doors, seeing who would be interested in selling their house to me."

"Murphy ..." Emotion punches me in the chest.

"The day they accepted the offer was the day I met our son."

Our son.

"His parents are really great. He's a well-spoken young man with good manners. And he was kicking a soccer ball around the yard that day, so I kicked it around with him. I asked if he played, and he said yes, but his coach was moving, so they needed a new one." Murphy shrugs. "I had the time."

I laugh, wiping my eyes.

"So what are we going to do, beautiful?" He slides his arms around my waist. "Be our son's neighbors? Coach him? Hire him to mow our lawn? Bake him cookies? Go to his plays?"

I scrape my teeth over my lip and sniffle. "Is that weird?"

He wipes my cheeks and shakes his head. "Yes. And I'm so on board. We're stalkers, but the good kind. Secret guardians."

"Just to be clear, you're asking me to live with you, correct?"

His lips twitch. "Well, since I've told everyone I have a wife, I think you living with me is a good idea."

"When were you going to find me and tell me you bought this house?"

"Never. I knew you'd show up." He grabs the back of my legs and lifts me to him.

I wrap them around his waist. "So my new role is pretending to be your wife? Your homemaker?"

"Who said anything about pretending?" He kisses my neck. "Wanna see the rest of our house?"

I tease my fingers through his hair and kiss the shell of his ear. "Yes."

"Let's start in the bedroom," he says, dragging his mouth up my neck while walking us down the hallway.

I giggle when he eases me to my feet then kicks the door shut while shrugging off his shirt.

"Choose me," I say as he pushes his shorts down his legs.

Murphy glances up, eyeing me for a moment like my words haven't registered.

"I wanted you to choose me."

He grins. "I know. I'd already chosen you. I just wanted you to say it, to feel worthy of this kind of love and happiness." He unbuttons my shorts and pulls them down my legs along with my underwear while I remove my shirt. "But you're broken, baby." He kisses a trail up my leg. "And that's okay, I'm good at fixing things."

"I'm not broken." I roll my eyes.

"You are."

I jump when his tongue teases between my legs. Then he continues up my body, removing my bra and kissing my breasts.

"It's nothing a few weeks of nonstop screwing can't fix."

I giggle harder.

He kisses along my jaw, his erection sliding between my legs. "Hi," he whispers, a breath before his lips claim mine.

Epílogue

Murphy

*Since it takes a village,
don't forget to form your village.*

Eight Years Later ...

"IF YOU TOUCH THAT, I will cut off your hand," Alice says, holding a knife when I reach my finger for the bowl of chocolate frosting.

"Don't cut off Daddy's hand," three-year-old Mia says while she and her five-year-old sister Sophie make friendship bracelets at the kitchen table.

"Then he needs to stay out of the frosting. It's for Cam's birthday cake."

"You're so sassy," I whisper in Alice's ear before sucking her earlobe between my teeth.

Her shoulder jumps. "Stop!" She laughs, cutting pineapple for the fruit kabobs Cam loves.

While we've made this our home and had two beautiful girls, Alice and I have always held our breath, praying that the Becketts don't move. Not only have we become close to Rose and Jonathan, we've formed lifelong bonds with Cameron and their girls. Our families have vacationed together. I play golf with Jonathan. And Rose and Alice are on a pickleball team at the rec center.

Jonathan sells life insurance, and Rose is a landscape architect who doesn't enjoy cooking anything that can't be thrown on the grill or tossed into a Crock-Pot. So Cameron thinks Alice is the best neighbor ever because she bakes and cooks all the time. Rose jokes that she's going to divorce Jonathan and marry Alice.

"I'll be in the garage," I say.

"Save some wood for me," Alice smirks.

Someday, our girls are going to realize their mom's idea of wood and my woodturning hobby are two totally different things.

"I always do," I say, filling a glass with sun tea before heading to the garage.

Since my art sells easily and quickly at several local galleries and shops, and I still do freelance technical writing, I make enough money to pay for a full-time homemaker who wears house dresses. However, I prefer her barefoot, traipsing through the grass yard to and from her garden.

No ponytail.

Wavy auburn hair flowing behind her.

It's the best damn life.

As I cut new pieces of wood for my next project, Cameron opens the side door and closes it behind him.

"Hey, buddy. What's up? You ready to turn sixteen tomorrow?"

His grin beams.

Neither Rose nor Jonathan have ever mentioned Cameron being adopted, so I'm not sure they'll ever tell him. But it doesn't matter. He's a spitting image of me when I was sixteen, and my mom has noticed it too. Alice and I have agreed to never mention it unless Cameron has a medical emergency and would need something like a kidney donated or a bone marrow transplant.

"What do you think about this camp?" He shows me his phone and the email about a soccer camp in Atlanta.

"Hmm, what do your parents think?" I mount my blank to the lathe.

"They said to ask you."

I laugh. "Forward it to me. I'll read through it later."

"Thanks." He slides his phone into his pocket. "What are you making?"

"Well, I think I'm going to make a chess set for Alice's dad."

"That's cool. Think sometime you could show me how to do that?"

I glance up at him. "You want to learn to turn wood?"

"Yeah." He nods. "I mean, if you think I can learn it."

My chest swells. "Of course you can. There are a lot of safety measures to learn, so I'll run it by your parents, but I'd love to teach you." I fear I sound too excited, like he might piece together my enthusiasm with my involvement in his soccer, then look in the mirror and suddenly think, "Holy crap! I think I'm Murphy Paddon's son."

It's funny how much Alice and I fear he'll find out before

Rose and Jonathan tell him. And maybe they'll never tell him he was adopted. That's fine too.

"Can you keep a secret?" Cameron asks.

"I think so."

"I want to ask this girl out, but I keep chickening out. My friends think she'll say no. And when I mentioned it to my dad, he said she'd be crazy to say no. But that feels like a fatherly response. What do you think?"

I grab my face shield and fiddle with the strap. "Well, I agree with your dad. She'd be crazy to say no. But she *could* say no. And that will suck. So you just have to decide if her saying no will suck more than never knowing if she would have said yes. When I met Alice, she warned me not to fall in love with her. But I did. So I poured my heart out to her. Nearly brought me to tears."

"She stayed?" Cameron asks.

I smile. "No. I didn't see her for eight years. But not once in those eight years did I regret a single word I said to her."

"I don't think I love this girl, yet. So ..." He scrapes his teeth along his bottom lip and shrugs.

"Well, there you have it."

"But," he wrinkles his nose, "I *really* like her."

"Then shoulders back, chin up. Brush and floss your teeth. Be confident until the last second, then give her the tiniest flash of vulnerability. Say something like, 'I'm thinking about asking you out, but I can't be the sole object of anyone's affection at the moment, so I'll let you know what I decide. And by the way, you look beautiful today.'"

A slow grin climbs up his face. "I don't think I can say that. And I was just going to text her."

I purse my lips and nod slowly. "Okay. That's cool. But I'd stick with the same line and after you type 'so I'll let you know what I decide,' end it with three dots and the sunglasses emoji."

"Did that kind of line work for you?"

"Absolutely."

Definitely not.

"I'll think about it," he says, and I know he's just being nice.

"Did you ask your mom or Alice?"

"No." He picks at the tree stump on the workbench. "My mom will just give me condoms, and Alice probably will too."

I clear my throat. "Well, condoms are a good idea if you uh, you know, think you'll need them."

Cameron lifts his gaze to me. "You know you can buy condoms before you're eighteen, right?"

I do know that. I also know Cameron is standing in my garage having this conversation with me because Alice and I did not use condoms. "I know that sometimes you think you won't need them ... until you do. And I know it's really hard to stop once you reach the point of—"

"Dude, seriously. I have condoms."

I nod a half dozen times. "Yep. Great. So uh ... this is called a lathe."

Cameron hangs out in the garage with me for over two hours, by the time I go into the house, the girls are in bed, and Alice is putting the finishing touches on Cameron's sweet sixteen birthday cake. The Everly Brothers' "All I Have to Do Is Dream" softly plays from my grandfather's turntable in the living room.

"I sent a picture of the cake to Rose. She's so in love with it, and she thinks Cam will love it too."

I rest my forearms on the counter. "Baby, are those edible soccer balls?"

"Yes. I made fondant, bigger white balls then smaller white and black ones that I stuck to the outside of the big white one to give it the soccer ball pattern, gently rolling the whole thing just to slightly flatten and connect all the little balls. Aren't they cool?"

Everything about my wife is cool, and wonderful, magnificent and awe-inspiring.

"It's perfect. Wanna know what's not perfect?"

She glances up, nose wrinkled while grinning. "What?"

I drop my head between my shoulders. "Cameron solicited my advice about asking a girl out on a date, and I fumbled the ball. I said some stupid shit then managed to segue it into a condom conversation that just got more and more awkward until I bailed."

Alice giggles. "Aw, I'm jealous that you got to have the sex conversation with him."

I jerk my head up. "Jealous? Baby, there's nothing to be jealous about. In fact, I think the best way to parent is to let someone else do it and just live next door and be more like grandparents that can spoil them, then hand them back. Really, we should see if Rose and Jonathan want to raise Mia and Sophie."

"Stop!" She laughs, wiping her hands, then carrying the finished cake to the fridge. "You know what you need?"

"Lessons on how to be cool in a sixteen-year-old's eyes?"

"Murph, you only have to be cool in my eyes." She pulls something wrapped in butcher paper from the fridge, then she slides her favorite cast iron skillet to the front burner and ignites it.

Oil.

Garlic.

Rosemary.

Salt and pepper.

Once it's heated, she tosses the steak into the pan to sear it. I can't remember the last time she made steak at nine o'clock at night.

"You need a little of this." She adjusts the heat a smidge. "And a little of this." She gives me her hand. "I have one last slot on my dance card."

I grin, sliding one hand behind my back while offering her my other on a slow bow.

When she accepts, I jerk her into my arms, making her gasp.

"I saw Hunter Morrison today," she says.

"Oh?" I lift my eyebrows as we sway to the music.

"He was at the park. Apparently, he's taken up drawing, so he was sketching a tree."

"No Vera?"

She shakes her head. "Vera's in New York watching her granddaughter while Blair opens a second gallery with her husband. That could have been you."

"Hmm ..." I twist my lips. "A stuffy life in New York or screwing my homemaker in a secluded area by the lake just after lunch every day."

Alice laughs. "Not *every* day. The girls have early out on Wednesdays." She teases the nape of my neck and stares at my mouth.

I duck my head to kiss her and she pulls away.

"I love you," I whisper.

"I love you too."

Again, I try to kiss her. Again, she pulls away.

"You have to say, 'Hi.'"

We turn our heads toward the soft voice. Sophie peeks her head around the corner. "Say it and mommy will kiss you."

"Why aren't you in bed?" Alice asks.

"Because I'm too excited for Cam's birthday party." She wedges herself between us, stepping on my toes like her mom used to do as she hugs my legs.

We make a Sophie sandwich and continue to sway to the music.

"Say it, Daddy," she whispers.

I frame Alice's face and let my lips hover over hers because I know how much our girls love seeing our affection.

"Say. It." Sophie's whisper escalates to a hiss.

Alice grins.

"Hi," I whisper, then press my lips to hers.

The End

Acknowledgments

Thank you, Beth Ann, for asking me to write a story inspired by Taylor Swift's "Fortnight." I'm sure it's not what you imagined. My interpretation of things rarely matches other people's. Still, this one was so fun!

Jyl, thanks for our girls' trip to Minnesota, where I immediately knew I'd use our location as the setting for an upcoming book. I hope we have many more of these trips in our future.

This book would not be what it is without the playlist. I used to love listening to my parents' oldies on vinyl records. They had a record player that was a large piece of furniture. I danced to "Itsy Bitsy Teenie Weenie Yellow Polka-Dot Bikini" so many times. And since then, I rarely see my dad working in his garage without hearing oldies playing in the background. So thank you, Dad.

Finally, a big thank-you to the usual suspects who help bring all of my books to you, the readers: my assistant (Jenn), my beta readers and editing team (Sarah, Monique, Leslie, Jenn, Shauna), Georgana and her amazing Team at Valentine PR, Boja Design for the stunning cover. Lyric Audio and narrators Charlotte North & Robert Hatchet. A special shout-out to Anna Shields for dreaming of her photo on one of my books. I'm so glad you tagged me. It's a gorgeous photo! Thank you.

Also By
JEWEL E. ANN

The Chain of Lakes Series

The Homemaker

Sunday Morning Series

Sunday Morning

The Apple Tree

A Good Book

Wildfire Series

From Air

From Nowhere

The Fisherman Series

The Naked Fisherman

The Lost Fisherman

Jack & Jill Series

End of Day

Middle of Knight

Dawn of Forever

One (*standalone*)

Out of Love (*standalone*)

Because of Her (*standalone*)

Holding You Series

Holding You

Releasing Me

About The
AUTHOR

Jewel E. Ann is a *Wall Street Journal* and *USA Today* bestselling author. She's written over thirty novels, including LOOK THE PART, a contemporary romance, the JACK & JILL TRILOGY, a romantic suspense series; and BEFORE US, an emotional women's fiction story. With 10 years of flossing lectures under her belt, she took early retirement from her dental hygiene career to write mind-bending love stories. She's living her best life in Iowa with her husband, three boys, and a Goldendoodle.

Receive special offers and stay informed of new releases, sales, and exclusive stories:
www.jeweleann.com

Made in the USA
Monee, IL
30 September 2025

31098201R00203